A Not So Immaculate Conception

Crystal Estell

Book design by Crystal Estell
Photo by © Fotoluminate LLC Edited by
Crystal Estell
ISBN 978-0-578-51240-2 (print)
www.estellsplace.com

To my loving family and true inspiration, James, Arin, Amari, and Lucas who endured mountains of unfolded laundry so I could follow my dreams.

To my daughter Reagan, who chauffeured her siblings around while I wrote.

To my son Jonas who awkwardly helped with the initial editing process... by force.

To my sister-in-law Danyelle who suffered through the first unedited version. She is the sister I never had, my universe twin, and way more talented than she gives herself credit for being.

And to my late Aunt Cathy, who always believed I had great things brewing inside me. If it weren't for her, I would not have the courage or confidence to pursue my passions. My only regret is that she won't be here to read it. But if she were, she'd be my biggest and maybe only fan... but hopefully not.

1

Lacey Winters had a plan. She inhaled the last few bites of an oddly craved tuna sandwich fifteen minutes ahead of schedule and then beelined her way from the deli to the corner drugstore for a pack of peppermint gum. It would leave her the precise time needed to gather her blueprints before the most important one o'clock meeting of her life.

The walking signal appeared at the final intersection, and she crossed the street along with fifty other random pedestrians, all dodging the tourist group taking selfies in their *I Love New York* sweatshirts. Lacey glanced over at the group. Despite the abundance of wide-eyes, eager smiles, and crosswalk-blocking bravery, none of them dared compete with the energetic spring she carried in her skinny legs. Not when today was poised to be a great day.

Now, the cherry on top would be sharing the wonderful news with her dad before one of his architect buddies let it slip first. Either way, though, he would be proud.

Stepping onto the curb, her stiletto heel caught in a groove, and she struggled to catch her balance. A lady with a dingy blanket draped over her shoulders helped steady her.

"Thanks," Lacey said, glimpsing the cardboard sign in the lady's arthritic hands. It read the same as all the others along the street, *Homeless*. And even though some people had become numb to the sight of them, Lacey had not. She pulled out the last twenty-dollars of cash she had on her. It wasn't enough, but it was something until she could get more from inside.

"No, honey, I'll be just fine. You keep this," the lady said, her ill-fitting dentures threatening to fall out with each word, "You need it

1

more than I do."

Lacey studied her own thin frame. Her lack of weight had nothing to do with a lack of meals. She ate all the time. For some reason, God gave her the brains and her sister the curves. "No, really, I want you to have it."

Lips and eyes disappeared behind rows of wrinkles. "Oh, don't worry over me. You keep this for the baby," she said, stuffing the money back into Lacey's hand. "I might not know much, but I know a glow when I see one."

Lacey patted her cheeks, worried the tuna had caused an allergic reaction. Or maybe the nippy breeze had chapped her face. "I'm not pregnant. I don't even have a boyfriend," she said, giving a nervous chuckle.

The lady waved a single finger in front of Lacey. "Trust me, boyfriend or not, you have the glow."

She's probably confused, Lacey told herself, shoving the twenty-dollar bill into the black bean can next to the lady. Without looking back, she scurried inside the drugstore, making a straight shot for the gum at the front counter.

Standing in line, she continued to reel over the accusation. What a ridiculous thing to say to someone? Pregnancy wasn't possible, not without sex. Had she missed her period? Yes, but because of work-deadline induced stress. Not babies, or glows. She slapped the pack of gum on the counter.

The cashier scanned it. "Is this everything?"

Lacey met her eyes. "What else do I need?"

Without a flicker of expression, she said, "How would I know? It'll be one-fifty."

There was nothing else Lacey needed. And the prophecy of some senile old lady on the street couldn't change her mind—ever. She reached for her debit card and hesitated. "Where is your feminine aisle?"

"Pads and tampons or pregnancy tests?"

"The last thing you said."

"Aisle seven." The cashier waved Lacey in the general direction. "Next."

Six minutes later, Lacey barreled into her office, still regretting being superstitiously pressured into buying an unnecessary test—which she had buried deep within her purse. It would take three minutes to end the tingling in her fingers and toes. But no need to rush, she reminded herself as she grabbed the rolled blueprints. It would be negative. She'd bet on it.

Her phone rang, and a chewing gum bubble popped in Lacey's ear before her secretary Hannah's mousy voice followed. "I didn't see the usual list for what you need me to bring to the meeting? Does that mean you don't want me to bring anything or you do? Or did you give me a list, and I lost it? Oh crap! I lost it, didn't I?" She popped another bubble.

Lacey wiggled a finger in her ear and wished someone would ban bubble-gum from America. "Stay calm, I didn't leave you one. Just take good notes in case I miss something."

Hannah gave a school-girl giggle. "You miss something? I hope I'm alive to see that day."

Lacey hung up the phone and shuddered. Her nerves refused to settle, but again, this was a crucial meeting, a meeting that would define the future of her career. A little anxiety was expected, and beneficial. She surveyed the office one last time, took inventory on her mental checklist, and then decided it was time.

Forcing her shoulders back and her chin up, she strode from her office to the conference room feeling like a freshly laid egg. Hard shell of confidence on the outside hiding insides ready to scramble if given the chance.

Before she could get both feet through the door, Mr. Caldwell, Lacey's boss with the energy and stature of a five-year-old but with less hair, greeted her. "So glad you could join us. Come, sit here." He gestured to a seat across from Margot Wallace, the head of The Sanctity of Marriage Coalition.

The architecture firm Lacey worked for had won a competitive bidding war to be the lead designer of the coalition's enormous, downtown skyscraper. And while settling on a price had come easy for all parties involved, settling on a design had not.

Lacey stared at the empty seat beside hers, the one where her secretary should have been seated.

"Oh, I sent Hannah away. We only need you." Mr. Caldwell beamed.

Lacey's bottom barely grazed the cushion before Margot fanned her thin, pointy-nailed fingers in her direction. "Yes, the lady of the hour. Might I say how overjoyed this meeting makes me? It's been way too long, but I'm sure what we discuss will be well worth the wait—and your hard work and dedication."

3

Lacey studied Margot Wallace's dark, angled-bob with a large swooping bang. It held the sheen of a well-polished boot, and the form of a well-starched uniform. No matter how much her head moved while she talked, not one strand of hair fell out of place. It was more than Lacey could say for her wild, chestnut-colored spirals—untamable on the finest of days. "And I'm thrilled to be here."

"I realize the process has been tedious, and I can only imagine your own personal stress as we honed down the design that best fits our company's needs. But the good news is we've made our final decision," Margot said, adding a quick actress chuckle, "Then again, I'm sure you figured out that part."

Lacey had, but even so, she twisted her fingers into knots in her lap. Because nothing was one-hundred percent until they confirmed it and until they broke ground. Companies could, and would change, their minds. "I assumed, but you know what they say about that."

"That you make an ass out of you and me? Not today," Mr. Caldwell interjected with an animated laugh, reminding her of Tigger ready to pounce into the air as soon as Margot gave him permission.

Margot turned her attention to Lacey. "Mr. Caldwell is correct, not today. Today, I'm offering you the lead designer position on behalf of the coalition. Your vision impressed us. It encompasses the elements needed for our company's success. Now, there's only one question left to ask. Do you accept?" She eyed Lacey with confidence.

And for good reason. Lacey had sacrificed nearly a year of her life competing for the contract. A year of sleep, vacations, and sex that had to be scratched off her calendar. And a year of fending off her super-model competition, Jocelyn, who to Lacey's advantage did not win. No way would she turn down such an opportunity.

"I'd be honored to accept. Thank you so much. You have no idea what this means to me." Warmth rushed into Lacey's face as she caught Mr. Caldwell pump his fist out of Margot's sights.

"This is a major contract, one sought after by multiple firms. So I can only assume your insides are bubbling like a glass of Dom Pérignon." Margot didn't hide her smugness. "Now, we'd have preferred a married lead designer, since we represent a company that promotes marriage. But you can't always have your petits fours and eat them too."

A twinge of uncertainty stabbed Lacey in the gut. "Is there a chance you'll change your mind?"

Margot leaned in towards Lacey. "You have nothing to worry about.

Needless to say, if you were an unwed mother, that might be a different story."

The pregnancy test flashed before Lacey's eyes. For the rest of the meeting, it consumed her. She couldn't rest until she put it to rest, which she planned to do as soon as she returned to her office.

With the remaining details ironed out, Lacey squashed the designs against her chest and marched back to her office, stretching her legs as far as the pencil skirt allowed. She whisked by Hannah without pause. "Forward my calls, please."

"Sure, no problem, did you get the lead designer position? Oh, your father—" The rest of Hannah's words disappeared behind the door Lacey closed.

Wasting no time, she dug into her purse, intent on eliminating the irrational fear she had created in her own mind. But when she heard his voice, she froze.

"There's my Ace-girl," her dad said as his strong, ebony arms stretched in her direction.

She fidgeted with the test, concealing it well. "Dad? What are you doing here?" Balanced on the tips of her toes, she welcomed his embrace.

He released her. "I came by to check on you, see how you're doing?"

She positioned her purse underneath the desk, out of his sights. "So, this visit has nothing to do with my meeting with Margot Wallace?"

In a delayed response, he jerked back. "Was that today?"

"Dan, you better not lie. God doesn't like lies, even little ones," Lacey's mom said, her voice echoing over the speakerphone.

Lacey folded her arms over her stomach. "Mom? You're in on this, too?"

Her dad lifted his cellphone, presenting a passport view of her mom. Lacey studied the composed delight held fixed behind alabaster skin and a Diane Keaton smile.

"I'm not *in* on anything. Your dad told me about it."

He twirled the phone around to himself. "Seriously, Kathleen?" The corner of his mouth twisted. "You orchestrated this entire face-time thing."

"Okay, I admit it. Lacey, it's only because I wanted to tell you how happy I am you got the job."

"Contract, Kathleen, it's called a contract," he snickered.

"Thanks Mom, even though I wanted to be the one to tell you guys,"

Lacey said, "but I guess no one can keep a secret around here."

It was true. If the daughter of the great Dan Winters took a step, she could guarantee someone would tell him before the day ended. Everyone knew her because of him, and because she was his child, everyone expected nothing less than success. In fact, it would have surprised her if they didn't tell him first.

"I may be retired, but it's still my job to know what goes on in this firm I helped build. Besides, my girl is trailblazing past my footsteps, scoring stellar contracts much earlier in her career than I ever did. People will broadcast those types of accomplishments."

"Well, I believe I own the right to broadcast it before they do," she said as a wave of queasiness struck, forcing her into her office chair.

Her dad stepped closer. "Your cheeks are flushed."

Lacey's lunch rose into her throat. "I had tuna today. I'm not sure it was fresh."

"You never eat tuna," her mom said.

"And that might be the problem." Lacey stretched her legs and knocked over her purse, exposing the pregnancy test corner. In a swift motion that left part of her bottom hanging off the chair, she stomped her foot over it.

"Be careful. You're going to fall," her dad said, dropping the phone on the desk and helping Lacey.

She white-knuckled the chair arm with one hand while facepalming him with the other. "No, I'm good. I feel less sick this way." It wasn't a complete lie.

"Someone tell me what's going on right now? Is Lacey hurt? You better not have let her fall, Dan." Her mother's anxious tone poured through the phone.

"Mom, please. Can I just lay here until I'm better?" That point being when she could safely lift her foot from the test with no risk of him spotting it.

"You sure can, honey. Dan, time to come home. You need to rest. And don't forget your blood pressure pill. It'll be due before you make it here."

Her dad's square-jaw tightened. "Yes, ma'am. Ace, do you see what I go through?"

"What you go through? I'm the one who fights tooth and nail to get you to take care of yourself. I've never met such a stubborn man. Ask him what he had for breakfast this morning. No, I'll tell you, two sausage biscuits from McDonald's. Or should I say *cholesterol bombs*?"

Lacey's muscles twitched in the new acrobatic position she struggled to support. And while she recognized her mother's badgering arose from the fear of losing her father after a widow-maker heart attack had stopped shy of stealing his life, she needed her mom to stop talking. Lacey mouthed to her dad, "Ignore her, please."

He leaned over to Lacey's ear. "You know you made your daddy proud today," he said, kissing her cheek. "Okay, Kathleen, I'm on the way home."

Her mom shouted her last goodbyes as Lacey's dad exited the office, seconds before Lacey dropped to the floor. She snatched up the pregnancy test and stormed into the bathroom, tearing into the package as she went. The instructions read simple enough. Although, it didn't stop her from reviewing them twice and following them to a tee until it was time to look.

But that was the problem. She couldn't look. Every try made the hairs on her arms stand at attention. *It's negative*, she reminded herself to no avail.

Focusing on the white marble tile lining the wall, she covered the plastic stick with a paper towel and called her best friend Doby. "It's an emergency. I need you in my office bathroom—STAT."

Lacey waited. With sweat-layered palms, she smoothed the raised arm hairs and hated that she had spent money on such a stupid thing. Her schedule allowed minimal time for sleep, much less sex, and the last time she checked, sex was a requirement for pregnancy.

The bathroom door cracked against the wall, stealing Lacey's breath. And the delayed burst of air that followed nearly blew away the paper towel. Desperate to keep it planted in place, she twisted her body in a graceless move that landed her hand on top of it just in time. She turned her sights to the doorway.

Doby stood just inside, panting and paler than usual. Her chest rose and fell hard as she sucked air through pursed lips. "I almost killed myself racing the hall in these stilettos. Again, why wouldn't you tell me what happened over the phone?"

Lacey eased her hand away from the test. "It's major. I couldn't risk someone eavesdropping."

"Does the FBI have a reason to tap the firm's phone lines? I guess I should just be glad you're still alive, since you made it sound like you were dying." Doby tapped the tips of her fingers against her cheeks. "Great, now I need to fix my make-up. Are you at least okay?"

Lacey questioned her decision to involve her overdramatic friend.

But who better to deliver it to her straight, she thought, squeezing the sides of her face. The move pushed out her already full lips and flattened the stray curls escaping her messy bun. "Do I look okay?"

Doby's pencil-thin heels echoed against the perfectly lined tiles as she studied Lacey from head to toe. "Is this a trick question? Did you get new lipstick?"

Lacey huffed, *if only it were as simple as a shade of merlot.*

Doby rushed over and patted Lacey's back. "I'm joking. For real, what's bothering you?"

Annoyed, Lacey shot a finger at the paper towel covered pregnancy test. Her hands trembled despite her best attempts to steady them.

Doby's attention followed. "Um—why is that there? Oh my god, you hooked back up with Finn and didn't tell me?" She slapped her knees and laughed. "And now you're pregnant? This is definitely something you don't say over the phone."

Finn? Lacey's break-up with him had been a bona fide disaster, memories of which she stored in the *How was I so stupid?* box, right next to a picture of his chiseled face and porcelain veneers. Memories she should destroy, not relive.

Lacey slumped forward. "I didn't sleep with Finn or anyone else in the past eleven months. Did you hear me? Eleven months."

An uncomfortable moment of silence passed as Doby circled her chin and straightened her injected lips. "Then I'm confused. Why are we worried?" She marched over to the pregnancy test. "We shouldn't be. This is ludicrous."

Doby reached for the paper towel, but Lacey jerked her arm away. "But wait, what if it's positive?"

"If it's positive then you win the *Guinness World Record* for longest pregnancy. Looking at your flat stomach, though, I don't see your name being printed anywhere except the in-patient roster at the psycho-ward if you don't get yourself together, girlfriend."

Lacey surrendered both palms. "You're right. I wish I'd never met that senile old lady."

"What lady?"

Lacey's face burned like hot asphalt as she recalled the quick walk to the drugstore, and the lady who raved about her glow.

Doby's head fell to one side. "You bought a test because a homeless woman thought you had a glow? Can't you see she wanted money?"

"That's the thing, I tried to give her some, but she refused it, said I needed it more than her." Lacey paused. "Despite your beliefs, I know old people are psychics when it comes to pregnancy. They see things."

"Like the glow?"

"Definitely the glow."

Doby took hold of Lacey's shoulders and shook her senseless. "Wake up. You are the most prepared and responsible person I know. I'll bet you even planned the drugstore trip."

Lacey wiggled free of Doby's firm grip. "Maybe? Okay I did, but only because I ate tuna for lunch."

"Ew! When did you start eating that?"

Lacey cocked her head. "Today—now—what does that matter?"

"It doesn't. Back to my point. You plan everything, and I mean everything. Why would a pregnancy be any different?"

The more Lacey considered it, the more confident she became. She was a successful woman who planned her outfits for an entire week down to the matching panty-sets and no-longer-than-lobe-length earrings. A woman who kept her calendar updated daily and was never late. And a woman, who if she wanted to get pregnant, would have planned it, or at least had sex.

"You're right. This is silly." And as one removes a bandaid, Lacey yanked away the paper towel to show—two bright pink lines.

Doby's mouth unhinged. "Shut the front door! How?"

The results jarred Lacey's world from its axis, sent it fading into dark swirling clouds filled with twinkling stars. Doby revived Lacey with cold water doused across bloodless cheeks until she perked up.

"You all but passed out." Doby yanked off a paper towel and dried Lacey's face. "Should I call for help?"

"And tell them about this?" Lacey twirled a hand in the air. "No, thanks."

"Yeah, yeah, I guess you're right," Doby said, examining the test, "It has to be defective."

Lacey straightened at the epiphany. "You're a genius. That's why they sell twin packs."

Disgusted by the same result twice, Lacey pressed the heels of her palms against her forehead.

"Don't freak out. If the tests aren't flawed, then it means there has to be a medical reason. We can figure this out, no problem." Doby's fingers scrolled through her phone's search engines. "See, I told you there's a sane explanation. It says blood or protein in the urine, medications such as tranquilizers or hypnotics, and kidney problems are possible reasons."

Lacey's right leg bounced to the point of vibration as she shook her head. None of those fit.

"Wait, here's one more—oh—never mind. It's nothing."

"Don't hold back now." Lacey snagged the phone. The only other reason glared at her in bold print—ovarian cancer.

She had cancer? But how? She'd always been healthy. She banked sick days the way Steph Curry banked free throws.

The straight lines of the bathroom waved and blurred, the walls caved. Her breath escaped her. And soon enough she realized her only hope for survival was a doctor, someone capable of providing her the best treatment options available.

Panicked, she rushed the door, twisting the knob as she rammed it, but it didn't budge. It might have even hit back. Stupid lock. She unlatched it, and using more force, pushed again. The lack of resistance sent her spinning and stumbling backward into her office. Her co-worker Zak, with his beach boy good looks hidden beneath a loose tie and rolled sleeves, caught her before she landed on the floor.

Doby was ten seconds too late.

Zak showcased his one-sided dimple as he guided Lacey back to her feet. "Hey, I'm glad I caught you."

She smoothed her shirt and glanced back at her friend now standing in the bathroom doorway. "I'm glad you did, too."

"Am I interrupting something?" he asked, glancing around Lacey.

She blocked his view, then grabbed Doby's attention. Lacey nodded at the tests. Catching the hint, Doby rushed over and mummified them with toilet paper as Lacey closed the door. She forced her face to relax. "No, the toilet stopped flushing. So I called Doby to help."

"Why don't you let me take a peek? I have a knack for those things." He proceeded towards the bathroom.

Lacey shouted, "No!"

He jumped back.

"We already fixed it," she said, lowering her tone and tucking her wild curls behind both ears. "So did you stop by for the blueprints? You finance boys don't waste time."

Zak scratched his head. "I have those, remember? You gave me a copy after I helped you fit the larger offices into the budget? It was that night we ordered from *Junior's*. The night you ate my cheesecake and yours."

Lacey laid a hand across her throat and restrained a fishy belch.

10

"Yeah, don't remind me. So then, what brings you by? Actually, whatever it is, can it wait? I was just leaving." Run away and escape better described her plans.

Zak slipped both hands in his pockets and took a fleeting glance at the floor before redirecting his attention back at Lacey. "If you could spare a second, I had something a little more personal to talk to you about. Remember the cherry Fanta I spilled in your apartment? Well, I kind of get the feeling you've been avoiding talking about what happened." A pink hue traveled up the side of his neck.

Did he fall off the crazy bus? That was weeks ago. In fact, if her test-clouded memory served her correctly, she'd spoken to him daily since, the same as she had for the past three years. Nothing had transpired during that late-night work session that needed a detailed discussion. The way she saw it, things were the same as they'd always been.

He was charming in a goofy sort of way, and her heart did an annoying flutter-thing when he came over. But she controlled those urges by keeping him confined to the *friend* box where he belonged. He computed the numbers, and she altered the blueprints, and that's as complicated as it would ever be. Besides, her work life was too busy for more.

He rocked on his heels. "I see it makes you uncomfortable, so forget I mentioned it. How about we settle the cleaning bill? The stain came out didn't it? If not, I'll replace the carpet for you. I mean, pay someone to replace the carpet. Replacing carpets aren't part of my skill set."

A carpet stain removed by a cleaning crew weeks ago was minor compared to the two positive pregnancy tests hidden in the bathroom and the words *ovarian cancer* flashing in front of her on a neon sign. The heaviness of which made her legs wobble. "We're good, Zak, no worries. You don't owe me. Now, I seriously need to go."

She grabbed her purse and left.

2

In the examination room, she dressed in an unflattering paper gown that opened in the front, leaving most of her bare skin exposed. Thankfully, the vertically challenged Dr. Hart arrived not long after wearing a lab coat that hung to her ankles. "Miss Winters, how are you?"

In no mood for small talk, Lacey answered, "Not good, I have ovarian cancer."

Dr. Hart gave a baffled expression. "You have what?"

Lacey removed the remnants of the paper sheet clinging to her moist skin and showed Dr. Hart the article on her phone. "It's the reason my pregnancy test was positive."

"Which remains positive today," Dr. Hart said without reading one word.

Lacey pointed out the facts. "Look right here. Ovarian cancer can cause false positives."

Dr. Hart tried removing the phone from Lacey's hands, but Lacey wouldn't let go. So, in a swift WWE-style move, Dr. Hart wrestled the phone from Lacey's stubborn grip and laid it on the counter. She brushed her palm against her chest. "Now, let's get on with this."

Determined, Lacey fought for the phone. "Wait, you need to read this."

With a shifted stance, Dr. Hart blocked Lacey's efforts. "The reason you took a test is that you missed your period, correct?" She spoke with the tone of a sane person trying to convince a not-so-sane person of their insanity.

But Lacey wasn't crazy, a little high-strung perhaps, but definitely not crazy. She wrapped her arms around her waist. "It's just what women do for ungodly reasons. But I can't be. I haven't had sex in almost a year. It has to be cancer."

Dr. Hart clamped a hand on Lacey's shoulder. The paper gown made a loud crinkling noise as it grated Lacey's skin. "Miss Winters, I'm sure you don't have cancer. Now, lay here so I can see how far along you are."

Why didn't she believe her? Insulted, Lacey drew her head back and considered arguing, but decided the ultrasound would be her proof.

Dr. Hart whirled the mechanic's stool around to an overbearing machine beside the exam table and pressed a few buttons. The instrument buzzed like a dryer.

With Lacey in the instructed position, Dr. Hart inserted the frigid probe. Lacey's legs jerked and nearly booted it away. But it wasn't enough to keep Dr. Hart from ramming forward. "Almost there, try to relax and slow your breathing."

Breathe? If she waited any longer to deliver the news, Lacey might suffocate.

"There it is, just as I expected," Dr. Hart said in a tone that was bubbly and unexpected.

Lacey eased her sights to the screen and saw it, a fuzzy gummy bear with a twinkling center.

A baby?

It couldn't be, not by any scientifically explainable means, but yet it was. It had to be a cruel joke, someone getting a kick out of watching her sweat. Or even a hallucination, something she had imagined. She blinked—but nothing changed.

With a bright smile, Dr. Hart said, "The measurements show you're about nine weeks and one day. That means conception happened somewhere around seven weeks ago."

Lacey pressed her balled fist to her mouth and fixated on the screen, marveling at the blob that leaped without legs long enough to do so. She had no memory of having sex seven weeks ago or even forty weeks ago. So how could she be pregnant? There was only one other way.

"An immaculate conception..." Lacey sprung forward, sending the ultrasound probe into an uncomfortable position.

At Lacey's yelp, Dr. Hart yanked out the probe with a quick snort of laughter. She removed her gloves and took Lacey's hands into hers. "I understand the news is unexpected. So give yourself time for the shock to wear off. And once it does, backtrack to around the time this happened."

Had Lacey missed something? A random night of wild sex so awesome she forgot it? Impossible! For one, she used protection always, and two, she never had sex with random strangers. She stiffened her shoulders, and said, "I didn't have sex... well... maybe in a vivid dream I did. But that doesn't count."

Dr. Hart delicately released Lacey's hands. "Um... tell me more about this *dream*."

Those were personal details Lacey would rather not share. "I don't see why you need to know about my dream. It was just that—a dream. Okay, it was the best *not real sex* of my life. There was this hot guy, and he was amazing. The way he touched me, took his time, embraced me. It was like I couldn't get enough of him. Seriously, it was so intense I woke up expecting to be spooning with him on my sofa—which is where we were in the dream. But I quickly realized I was alone... and now super embarrassed." Lacey dropped her head.

"And you are one hundred percent positive you didn't have sex any other time?"

"A thousand percent."

With a quick spin of the stool, Dr. Hart positioned herself next to the wall-mounted computer. Her fingers danced over the keys as Lacey watched. And when she stopped, Dr. Hart motioned at the screen for Lacey to follow.

"Well, although rare, transient global amnesia caused by sex is a possibility. It most often happens right after an orgasm or great sex. And given your history, it's plausible. It would explain the dream—which I argue was not a dream."

"Hold on, I thought amnesia meant you lose all memory."

"Sometimes, but in cases like these, it's more like it's shuffled, or missing chunks, or—"

Lacey interrupted. "Or blurred faces and bodies?"

Dr. Hart nodded. "Exactly."

It took a minute for Lacey to gather herself. "I'm confused. So you're saying what I thought was the best sex dream I ever had, was actually the best *sex* I ever had. But because of this amnesia thing, I can't remember with who?"

"I'd be willing to bet a year's salary on it. Now, do any features stand out, something that strikes you as someone familiar, a hint as to who it could be?"

Lacey dug deep but only came up with the same blurry images as before. "It's so vague, not enough to paint a clear picture. But I know myself. I would never let a stranger into my home—ever."

"And more than likely, especially given the chemistry you've describe, I'd say you didn't. More than likely it's someone close to you. Now, try not to stress. The upside is sex amnesia rarely happens more than once."

Only once? Should she rejoice? "Given my current condition, I don't think it matters."

"I guess you're right. But it may be helpful to know the memory can come back. If not, try seeing a neurologist or a psychiatrist to help retrieve it. Beware though, in those cases the success rates are low and might take months, even years." She signed the bottom of two pre-printed slips, one for prenatal vitamins and the other for nausea, and added, "I wish I had better news." She passed Lacey the prescriptions and left.

Lacey locked her gaze on the closed door as her mind strayed a million miles away. Without thinking, her hand fell across her stomach, now home to a baby not on her ten-year plan. She snatched it away promptly. Once dressed, she sauntered to the receptionist who took her paperwork in exchange for a return appointment.

Ready to bolt, Lacey twirled around in the exit's direction and stumbled into the man behind her. The collision knocked the wind out of her lungs.

"I'm so sorry. Did I hurt you?" the man asked, steadying Lacey.

She stared at his Bob Ross t-shirt with the slogan, *No mistakes, just happy accidents.*

Not true, she decided, lifting her sights to the man's face, noting the uncanny resemblance to Bob Ross himself. "I'll live," she said.

"I caught you staring at my shirt. It's cool, huh? And the truth," he said, hugging the bloated or possibly pregnant woman beside him. "We're on our sixth *accident*, and it's just as exciting as the first."

Lacey willed her legs to move, but they refused, much like a deer mesmerized by the high-beams of an eighteen-wheeler.

"Miss Winters, you'll want this," the receptionist said loud enough for the entire waiting room to hear. She held out a small sheet of paper in Lacey's direction.

What more could Lacey ever want? Curious, she swiped it, took a good look.

It was the picture of her fuzzy gummy bear.

* * *

Lacey burst through the office doors and took the first taxi she spotted straight to Doby's apartment. She staggered through the door with the last bit of energy left in her body and sprawled out on the bright red sofa, burying her head under one of many accent pillows.

But Doby yanked away the fluffy chenille. "I've been calling you for over an hour. What did the doctor say? Do you have cancer? You do. It's why you didn't pick up, isn't it?" Doby threw her arms around Lacey and sobbed hysterically, soaking her mint julep mask.

"Don't you worry, I'll be by your side through it all. I'll even take you to your appointments. You can stay at my place, or I can stay at yours. It doesn't matter. And don't worry about your hair, I'll buy you the best wig in town."

Lacey wiggled out of Doby's grip, wiping away the icky green tears from the side of her neck that Doby had left behind. With her non-stained hand, she pulled out the ultrasound picture and handed it to Doby.

Doby snatched the picture from Lacey. At first glance, she gasped. "Sweet mother of Jesus, it's the tumor. I searched ovarian cancer pictures after you left, and this looks like what I saw. It even has the irregular shape and those nasty little pokey thingies."

Doby pressed a balled fist to her cheek and shook her head. "I'm so angry. You shouldn't have to go through this. It's not fair that terrible diseases always strike those that don't deserve it. I mean, do serial killers and murderers get cancer? Never, but someone like you who donates to the food banks, the homeless shelters, and to whatever charity strikes your fancy, or the woman who adopts ten underprivileged kids, always. Life—"

Lacey held a finger over Doby's lips long enough to stop the never-ending eulogy. "Take another look."

Doby's facial mask cracked. "At what?"

"The picture, it's not a tumor, and as horrible as this sounds, I can't decide which is worse."

Doby twisted the paper sideways, back to normal, and back sideways again before grabbing her chest. "Oh my freaking god, it's a baby. I see the due date. But how's that possible? You didn't have sex."

Lacey stared at her open palms as she organized her scrambled thoughts. "According to Dr. Hart, I did. You remember that amazing sex dream I told you about several weeks ago, right?"

"The best sex of your life except it was a dream one? How could I forget? You talked about it for days. And I'm pretty sure at one point you said, and I quote, 'If it had been real, I'd marry that guy today.' Is that the one?"

"That's the one. Well, Dr. Hart's theory is that it was real. The problem is my brain erased the whole experience, or rather smudged it into a faded memory."

"Why would it do that?"

"I don't know. Let me ask it," Lacey said with a dollop of sarcasm.

Doby shook her head. "Sorry, dumb question. Go ahead."

Lacey recounted the remaining painful details of her visit with Dr. Hart.

"Transient global amnesia caused by sex? Is that a real thing?" Doby's face twisted.

Lacey pressed her fingers into her aching temples. "I wish it wasn't, but she showed me the proof."

Doby's head fell back against the sofa. "Does this mean…?"

The thought of what she suggested tingled Lacey's skin. "That I had unplanned sex with someone and it was so spectacular I forgot it? Something along those lines." Lacey bit the inside of her cheek. "This will kill my dad. Wait, first it's going to destroy my career, and the aftershock will kill my dad."

Doby squeezed Lacey's hand. "Don't say such things. Your dad will understand and so will Mr. Caldwell. Besides, you have a legitimate diagnosis."

Lacey recalled Margot Wallace's words. "They specifically said *no unwed mothers*, which I am. And you didn't see how proud my dad was. It was like I had just designed the next Taj Mahal. He's going to disown me."

"If he didn't disown your sister, Kate, for backpacking around Europe for two years before becoming an elementary school teacher, why would he disown you?"

"Because he realized early on Kate sucked at design. And even though he didn't force his career on me… it was understood. All the comments like, *you're just like me*, and *you will do great things*. Now everything he worked so hard to instill in me has gone to the crapper."

"It has not."

"Has to. If not, tell me—the planner—where to start because I'm stumped."

"Well, I have something to fix that." Doby pranced into the kitchen and retrieved two glasses. "First question is, do you plan to keep it?"

Lacey picked at the sofa piping. "Abortion is off the table and so is adoption. My Catholic mother might never forgive me, and I'm not sure I could carry it for nine months and walk away empty-handed."

Doby poured wine and then brought a glass to Lacey. Without thinking, Lacey came close to swigging it down. Already, pregnancy shortened her options. It was no longer about what she wanted. Basically, she had become a host of what? An alien, the Messiah, a stranger's baby?

Either way, devastating moments deserved wine, but for Lacey, there would be none. "I can't drink."

"I wasn't thinking. Let me take care of that." Doby gulped Lacey's glass of wine and then started on hers.

Lacey squeezed a handful of curls. "Dr. Hart said the memory could come back, but there's no guarantee."

Doby gave Lacey a cheesy grin. "I have an idea." She took down the last swallow of wine before turning to her phone, typing away. "You should hire a private detective. Look."

Lacey probed the list Doby produced. *A-1 Private Eyes* reminded her of a steak sauce, and *Lark Meadows PI* sounded like the name of a graveyard. She lingered at a regal name, *Henry Duke Investigative Services*. Underneath the listing, in italics, was the blurb: *Answering questions you never knew you had.*

Lacey scrolled through a few more names and then stopped. The list was daunting. And she doubted she had the strength to retell her story, or lack thereof, twice in the same week. "I appreciate your support, but I'll pass for now. I still have some time before I show. Besides, my memory might come back, and when it does who knows? It's obviously someone I liked enough to bring home. So maybe he'll be someone I like enough to marry. And then all of this fuss will be for nothing."

Doby's fingers rested against her cheeks. Her squinty eyes stretched to the max. "Oh my god, you're in denial. This guy slept with you and never contacted you again. Let's be real. I don't foresee a marriage proposal in your future."

Lacey fidgeted. "Yeah? Well, what if he's a super successful businessman who's out of the country or a philanthropist setting up fresh water in a remote village? What if he's not contacting me because he doesn't have cellphone coverage?"

"You really are in the first stage of grief. It's that stage where you pretend nothing's happening or believe what's happening isn't serious. But this is very serious. I doubt Prince Charming plans to sweep you off your feet after he completes his plumbing adventure."

Lacey's temples pulsed. "He could. But even if he's not, I just need a few days to process everything and make a plan. I can't run off all dilettante."

"I hear you. But just so you know, according to Google the next stage is anger." Doby lifted her phone in front of Lacey.

"Are you sure it's not murder? Because I'm feeling a little homicidal right now."

3

On Saturday morning, Lacey's bare feet landed on the hand-woven rug beside her bed. The strands of silk tickled the spaces between her toes, and for a moment, created a temporary comfort. A comfort soon invaded by necessary decisions about the—she hated to say it—so she wouldn't. And she wouldn't give up hope that her memory would return, just as Dr. Hart said it could. What other choice did she have? Consider the alternative? No, not when she still had options.

She headed into her color-coded closet for an outfit. There, she slipped into a turtle-neck sweater and a pair of palazzo trousers, camouflage for her scrawny legs, before spraying perfume on her inner wrists. The mist of sweet floral tones lingered in the air.

With an escaped curl tucked behind her ear, she made her way back into the bedroom with its exposed brick walls and strategically placed furniture showcasing clean lines. She stared at her four-poster bed and at the artificial greenery balancing the space. On most days, it brought her peace.

Today, it offered little solace.

She chewed on unkept cuticles while gazing at nothing in particular. Enough, she told herself; it was too soon to freak out.

She refused to dwell. Instead, she left for the *Cup and Cup* café. There was no reason to change her routine. In fact, the more normal she kept things, the more clear-headed she'd be when considering her options. And what better way to do that than over the cute foam panda she favored on top of a green tea latte?

Miranda, a college student with a septum piercing and purple lipstick, made the cutest ones, but she wasn't there. Instead, a guy with dreads filled in for her, and his artistic attempt ended up resembling

Master Splinter on drugs.

Lacey pointed at the fading art foam. "Excuse me, I asked for the panda."

He placed a silver wand in a steel container and sent up a burst of steam between them. "Yeah, I gave you a panda."

She took a second glance. "Will you look? It's a rat."

He pretended to pay attention. "It's still a green tea latte, right?"

She sniffed it. The aroma was familiar. "Yes, but that's not the problem."

He pressed a few buttons with more force. "What do you want, lady? You need me to remake a good tea because you're saying I made you a rat instead of a panda?"

Was that what she was saying? Should she punish his lack of talent on such a busy morning? "No, I'll shake it around and see what happens. Thanks."

She sipped the latte and wished she would have stood up to the barista the way she stood up to the bigwigs in her company. Then again, no one's legacy was at stake outside the office doors.

Her phone rang, and with a quick shift of her cup, she answered. It was Doby. "Are you still in denial, or has reality kicked in yet?"

"Good morning to you, too." Lacey rolled her eyes.

"Well, I was coming over for moral support, but Carson said he's taking me somewhere special today. He says it's important and to tell you he's sorry. But if you need me, I'll make him reschedule," Doby said, all without breathing.

Lacey scratched her eyebrow. "When did you say you were coming over—never mind? I'll survive. You enjoy yourself. Any idea where he's taking you?"

"He won't say, and I can't force it from him, even with the usual persuasion methods."

Lacey wanted to cover her ears. "No need to explain any further. But on a serious note, have fun today."

"Only if you're sure."

"I am."

"Well, you've made Carson's day. He broke out in a sweat when I told him I had to check with you first—but don't worry, I didn't tell him why," Doby said, reassuring Lacey.

She took a tiny sip of her latte, afraid of pushing her queasy stomach too far. "I'll be fine. I'm a big girl. I won't fall apart."

"But you shouldn't be alone. And now, I feel selfish for ditching you for my boyfriend. What am I doing? He can wait. If he doesn't understand, then we're not meant to be."

While Lacey appreciated the support, she did her best planning alone. "Carson loves you, and I'd bet whatever he has planned will be amazing."

Doby paused, "Well, promise me you'll do something you don't routinely do? Go shopping or to a movie, anything other than work."

"I still have changes to make to the Darcy House project."

"Lacey—"

"I'll consider it."

If Lacey had a boyfriend like Carson to sweep her off her feet, surprise her with a spontaneous out-of-town venture or a night of wild, passionate sex she might be more compelled. But then again her schedule didn't allow it. And would she want it to? She preferred being prepared, preferred not making costly mistakes. It was the reason she noted potential sex days in her calendar with her ex, Finn. That way they always had protection. None of those sudden, all over each other without thinking, suppressed emotion now raging, no condom nights that led to—a hijacked uterus.

Which is what she had now, despite her most meticulous planning. And the worst part was not the lack of memory, but why the lack of memory? What about the whole ordeal made her brain delete it? She held her eyes closed for a few extra seconds.

Maybe she should follow Doby's advice, go somewhere different, somewhere with fresh air, somewhere she could focus on what needed to happen—without interruptions.

She hailed a taxi. "Take me to Central Park, please."

"Which side?" the young driver asked. He pulled into traffic with one hand on the wheel.

"It doesn't matter, as long as there's a bench."

"Oh, you're trying to get some R&R. It's the perfect place for some of that."

"It certainly is," she said, agreeing it was a great place to avoid unfulfilled orders and meddling best-friends.

And if she walked away with a solid plan life would be wonderful.

When the cab stopped, she meandered over to the first bench in sight. From there, she observed kids running in circles, followed the flight paths of several balls, and saw more kissing and body groping than she had in years. As expected, her mind wandered to the what-ifs, but when it did, she checked it, reassuring herself of her ability to work through difficult problems.

She closed her eyes and captured the sweet smells of the blooming crabapple trees, the fruit-loopy fragrance of blossoming winter honeysuckle, and the occasional whiffs of stale urine. She ignored the less than desirable and absorbed the warm sunlight. This was her moment to rest and rewind—alone.

"Lacey? Is that you?"

Her eyes popped opened to him, drenched in sweat with both hands gripping his sides. "Zak? What are you doing here?"

His chest heaved as he gestured towards the paved trail in front of him. "I'm getting in a quick run. It's a surprise seeing you here. And doing something other than work?" He glanced behind her. "Hiding any blueprints back there? Remember, I'm off duty."

A bead of sweat traveled down the side of his neck, and then underneath his tight shirt, drawing her attention to his slim—but well-defined—muscles. Oh, what she'd do to follow that line of perspiration. Her fingers flew over her mouth as if she had spoken the words out loud.

Zak stretched a hand towards her. "Are you okay?"

No, she wasn't. She had become a horny teenager drooling over a hot guy, and not just any guy, her co-worker. It had to be the... she swallowed. "Something flew in my mouth. A bee?" How dumb, she'd be in pain. "Or bird poop?" Wait, that'd be gross. "Definitely not bird poop. A piece of grass or—" she fumbled for excuses, "—your sweat. That's what it was."

And why would that not be disgusting?

"How strange? The wind's not even blowing that hard."

She scrunched her face. "Yeah odd, huh? Well, it was nice running into you, but I'm actually leaving."

Zak's hand brushed her forearm. "Wait, don't run off so fast— unless you have somewhere to be."

Up under that fitted shirt sounded like an excellent starting place. Who ever imagined such sporty muscles lived beneath those dull button-downs? Shocked, she cast her gaze to the edge of grass. The libido she'd kept so carefully restrained was now a hungry tiger prepared to pounce on its prey.

Except Zak was her friend and not a cut of tenderloin.

She lugged her purse strap over her shoulder and decided nothing could keep her from reading about whatever sex-poison this was infecting her brain—tonight. She regained her composure and stood. "I should go."

He rubbed the side of his neck. "Because of me?"

Lacey jerked back. "What? No, why would you assume that?"

"You were practically napping before I came over and now you're ready to bolt."

He had a point. She would think the same thing if he'd acted like she had. And the truth was she only acted like that because crazy hormones had invaded her brain. She returned to her seat and loosened her grip on the purse.

"You're right, it's just that seeing you reminded me of work, and I always have plenty of that to do," she said.

He eased in next to her. "So the only thing that comes to mind when you see me is work?"

She dared not say what flashed through her mind today. Whatever it was, it wasn't normal, but it wasn't all abnormal. Her emotions flared around him sometimes. As expected, racking up countless hours in confined spaces had brought them closer. But only in a brother and sister kind of way, she told herself. One she might be attracted to, which was gross and the reason she kept those feelings contained like a mole, bopping it back down whenever it reared its boulder-sized head.

She glanced him. Perhaps it was the one-sided dimple or the way his tall, sporty body maneuvered more like the editor of a high-school newspaper. Or how unaware he was of his boyish good looks, flawed only by the unsubstantial crook of his nose and a higher than average forehead. The mere fact he found her jokes funny when few others did, and how he solved complicated math equations even though he couldn't write a single, error-free sentence stirred her emotions more than she cared to admit.

She would also give credit to their commonalities, the fear of frogs and the love of plain cheesecake—but not baseball. She frowned on it the same way she frowned on dating co-workers after her last experience. Not that it mattered. Her inflexible ten-year plan left limited time for extracurricular activities—Zak included.

He shifted in his seat. "Wait, now you've made me curious why you're here. Are you work-stalking me?" The corner of his mouth lifted.

She smirked. "Sure, I closed my eyes and prayed for you to disturb me. Praise God, you appeared."

He thrust both arms towards the sky. "Hallelujah, should I do the dance?"

She yanked his arms out of the air. "If you do, I'm bolting for real."

"I might give up my Derek Jeter rookie card to see something like that," he chuckled.

"Oh wow, I can't believe my humiliation is worth so much? And just when I thought we were friends."

"It's not worth much."

She angled her head. "So you're saying my humiliation is cheap?"

"No, you and your humiliation are worth a lot." He tugged at his shirt collar. "That doesn't even make sense. Sorry, how did we get here?"

"Your poor choice of analogies, but don't worry, I accept your apology." She tried to force a serious face but burst out laughing instead.

"You think it's funny watching me sweat?" he said, grinning.

Funny was not the word that came to mind when she watched him sweat, which is why she turned away. No more distractions.

"So moving on, tell me the big secret you're hiding?" he asked.

Did he know about the—he couldn't? Doby wouldn't tell him—would she? What if he figured it out after she ran out the office like a madwoman? Her body tensed. "Tell you what? There's nothing to tell."

"Are you kidding me? This is a big deal."

Her heart stopped and then jumpstarted in her chest. "Zak... I... don't know what to say."

"You're in Central Park instead of working. That never happens. So go ahead, tell me. What brought you here?"

She exhaled pure relief. "Doby told me to do something different, so I did."

"Well, lucky for me—I meant you." He wiped sweat from his forehead with the back of his hand and rubbed it onto his athletic shorts. "It's a gorgeous day." He made eye contact, capturing her attention.

Remembering the tissues in her bag, she broke the extended gaze and passed him one. "Much better than the freezing winter."

"Agreed." He dried his face. "Look at you, always prepared. What else do you store inside that thing?"

Her mind flashed to the day she hid the pregnancy test in there and half-frowned. "More than I need."

He wadded up the tissue and tried banking it into a nearby trashcan. He missed by a foot or more. "Wow, my sugar levels must have dropped."

"So that's what you're blaming it on?"

"Yes. It's past lunchtime, and I'm starving." He retrieved the tissue and dunked it into the trashcan. "Hey, why don't you join me?"

She'd had lunch with Zak hundreds of times over the years, but something about him asking outside of work made her skin feel all prickly. Even though, his intentions were obvious. To make sure, she clarified for her own peace of mind. "Lunch as friends, not like a date, right?"

He shook his head. "I'm not trying to date you," he said, pausing. "Sorry, that didn't come out right. I'd date you, but you're on a dating hiatus. But I'm not trying to date you. I mean any man would be lucky —"

"I understand. It's just lunch." She ended the discomfort for them both. And after assessing her own rumbling stomach, decided it might be in her best interest to nibble on something soon. "A friendly lunch sounds fine. What did you have in mind?"

"I guess the next food truck we see. I'm not dressed for fancier than that." He motioned to his attire, which despite her resistance, she still found sexy. "But I can change and meet you somewhere nicer… if you want?"

Somewhere nicer encroached upon the dating line, and assessing the current state of her affairs, not a boundary she'd cross anytime soon.

"Food truck sounds great."

They didn't have to travel far. A Mediterranean-themed truck packed with plenty of bland options had parked nearby. She ordered the pita chips and tzatziki dip, deciding her stomach was better left untested.

She nibbled.

"Is that all you're eating?" Zak asked before chomping his teeth into a jumbo-sized gyro with extra meat.

Did she want to eat more, enjoy a chicken pita? Absolutely, but she had a strong feeling the thing growing in her uterus had severed the connection between her brain and stomach. "I'm only a little hungry. So you run on Saturdays?"

He wiped his mouth. "I run whenever I wake up and feel like I need a run."

"You should schedule it. That way, you wouldn't have to worry about not getting in enough exercise."

Zak tilted his head. "And if I did, I'd spend the whole week dreading it and not go. Besides, my family already has one of those perfect, overachieving types who I'm sure never misses a workout. There's not room for two."

"So your theory is there can only be one successful person in a family?"

A sliver of lamb dropped to the wrapper as he pulled the gyro to his mouth and paused. "No, what I'm saying is why compete with my brother? Why turn a good relationship into a compare and contrast one? Especially when I'm content being who I am."

"Content being the self-assigned underachiever? What about the things you want? I've seen you in action. You're super talented. You could do so much more with your skill set than mid-level finance," she said, talking with her hands just as much as her mouth.

"Look, wants and needs are different. I'm doing what I need to do, and it works. What I want to do is enjoy the weekend, the designated break from schedules and routines."

Lacey dipped a pita chip in the tzatziki sauce, and touched the dill-spiced yogurt to her tongue. Okay, it might be a safe choice. "Well, suit yourself. I'm just letting you know I see potential."

"I'll take that as a compliment."

"Although, I still can't understand how you stay so calm and collected without a routine. Unexpected things happen when you're not prepared." She nearly choked on her own words.

He gulped his soda. "Yeah, like bumping into crazy-planning ladies trying to force me into a schedule. The firm has me on a tight one of those Monday through Friday. I refuse to give up my weekends."

Lacey stole one of his fries and threw one at his head. "I'll have you know, I'm not crazy." Not by any certifiable means, she thought.

"Watch out, the fun side of you might try to escape." He tossed a fry back at her, but she blocked it with her arms in a lucky move. "Speaking of fun, did I tell you the new joke?"

She took another small bite of a pita chip and grinned. "I can't wait. Is it as terrible as last time?"

He straightened. "I'll ignore that jealous attack. Why did the chicken cross the road?"

"I don't know, to visit his farm friends?"

"To show the possum it could be done." He fell over, holding his stomach in laughter. "You get it? Possums always end up as roadkill."

Lacey giggled, more at his response than the joke. "Where did you get that corny joke?"

"You're just mad my jokes are funnier."

She wiped her mouth. "Want to bet? Why did the stadium get hot?"

He stared at her as he sipped his drink.

"Because all the fans left," she said with a beaming smile on her face.

He tried not to laugh but failed. And, after several rounds of one-liners, her cheeks ached. If only for a moment, laughter carried away her troubles.

Once they both settled, she scooped out the remaining tzatziki dip with her last pita chip.

He stared at her, drew her attention. "You know, we still haven't talked about what happened that night at your apartment, when I spilled the soda on your carpet."

Was he going there again? If she had to discuss carpet stains one more time. Lacey rolled her eyes. "I swear if you bring up cherry Fanta night, I'll run away, kicking and screaming."

Zak dropped his gaze as he laid the rest of his uneaten gyro on the paper wrapper. The earlier laughter lines faded. "I didn't realize that night disturbed you so much."

"It's not that I'm disturbed, just more I don't understand why you keep wanting to discuss something so meaningless." Besides, other than the carpet cleaning, she hardly recalled the spill.

Zak balled up his uneaten gyro, then aimed his gaze at her. "Meaningless, huh?"

For the love of God, what was the obsession? Maybe she had insulted his manhood by not charging him. "How else should I describe it? If there's something I'm missing, tell me."

"There's nothing to tell. Like you said, it's meaningless. I'm overreacting." He threw a basketball three-pointer with his leftovers into the trashcan and made it.

"You are. The stain is almost gone. You made a mistake. We all do."

He stood and stretched his long legs. "You're right. It's all one big mistake. I guess the problem is I expected a different reaction."

Her heart fluttered. "To a soda spill? Please, tell me how I should have reacted."

He continued stretching, pulling each of his arms with the opposite one, and then overhead. "Telling you won't fix the way you've already reacted."

Lacey squeezed the bench and leaned towards Zak's direction. "People don't respond the same, and it's okay."

Zak stared off in to the distance. "It is. I just assumed... don't worry about it. It's my fault for having unrealistic expectations."

A heat wave consumed her. Her brain throbbed. "I'm so confused right now. What did you need me to do that I didn't? Charge you? Give you the bill when you offered to pay?"

"Now you want to charge me? Talk about adding insult to injury."

"I don't need to charge you. I'm just struggling to understand the problem."

Zak messed his hair, then shifted his eyes to hers. "Please don't struggle on my account. Don't worry, I understand. There's nothing else for us to discuss."

"Ever? Are you're breaking off our friendship over this?"

"No, but I think we should stop the late work-nights at your apartment. We're co-workers. If you need my help, you have my email and phone number." He glanced back at the paved trail, his lips in a perfect line. "I need to finish my run, burn off the fast food. I'll see you at the office—and only the office."

His remarks knifed her. "Zak, I—"

He pushed his earbuds in and took off running, leaving nothing behind other than the hard imprint of his words. Words that jumbled her into a mixed ball of emotions.

And that's how he left her.

4

With the weekend behind her, Lacey marched into work armed with the nausea medication she'd filled, a dose of caution, and a plan. She'd give her memory three weeks to return. If it didn't, then she'd hire the private investigator Doby suggested.

And she'd avoid Zak, just like he wanted.

She opened her drawer and pulled out a small can of air-freshener, spraying a few lavender and sage scented bursts into the air. The micro-droplets swirled around her and spread an invigorating aroma full of positive vibes. And she welcomed them as she zoomed through emails with no hiccups. Nothing would derail her *woman on a mission* energy, she assured herself.

Her computer dinged as an email arrived in her inbox from Mr. Caldwell. Her stomach bubbled, expecting good news about the recent meeting with Margot Wallace.

Lacey,

Everyone's buzzing about your new design, and I mean everybody who's somebody. I am so proud of you. If everything goes well with this contract, I can see a partnership offer in your near future.

Mr. Caldwell

She slapped a hand over her mouth, and muted the involuntary shrills. Partner at twenty-eight? It was a dream come true. Scratch that, it was her dream. The goal she had poured her soul into for years, invested countless hours in, and now there it was, one finished contract away. And not because of her father's friendship or any other undue influence. No, she did this by herself.

Well, Zak deserved credit for keeping her blueprint designs within budget and suggesting changes when they exceeded his predetermined finance numbers. If he hadn't been such a jerk yesterday, she'd share the good news. Too bad he killed any chance of that happening, and worse, she still didn't understand why. But at least he couldn't kill her joy, not on a day when everything flowed in her favor.

She reread Mr. Caldwell's email and marinated on the word *partner* as the corners of her mouth shot up to her ears. Unable to contain her enthusiasm, she printed a copy to show Doby, and then headed towards her office.

But halfway down the hall something went horribly wrong.

The rise of puke in her throat sent her rushing to the nearest restroom. Her stomach spewed hot vomit into a not so sanitized toilet reeking of fish and caustic cleaners. And it was the less than perfect conditions combined with bile-coated oatmeal that prompted repeated rounds of barfing.

When a break came, she dialed Doby with sweaty fingers and begged for mints. The retch in her mouth was too much to bear as was the thought of doing this for the next few months. Her whole body shook.

But when the bathroom door swung open, relief steadied her. "Thanks for being so quick—um—hold on," Lacey said, curling over the toilet while draining the last drop of liquid left in her stomach. "Morning sickness is the worst—" She put her hand to her mouth and belched. "—but bad breath is a close second."

The silence screamed at her. "Doby, is that you?"

"It's me… Hannah."

Did she confess her pregnancy to her secretary? Please God, say it wasn't so. Hannah was an excellent employee, but she was a born and bred gossiper. Now what should Lacey do? Run, ignore her, pretend to be someone else? Logistically she could do none of those things, so she did the only thing she could—lie.

"You know I'm not expecting, right? I've had a stomach bug for the past couple of days, and Doby teases me about being… that way. So I play along as a joke. But I can't be. It'd be impossible."

The silence was so strong Lacey's heartbeat pulsed in her ears. "Hannah?"

"Oh Lacey, I already knew. I take out the trash in your bathroom and office for Ms. Todd because, well, I feel sorry for her because she's so old. And she's had both hips replaced. I can't even believe she's still working—"

What Lacey couldn't believe was Hannah's ability to turn one sentence into thirty. "The point?"

"Yes, the point. Well, the bags are clear, and when I lifted one, I saw the end of a pregnancy test sticking out of some toilet paper. I couldn't see the result, and I really tried not to look. My mom always said don't be nosy, but then I started thinking I should probably know—in case I needed to brew decaf. So, I looked."

Lacey collapsed against the bathroom stall and struggled with her choice for a secretary. "You can't tell a soul."

Hannah popped her bubble gum. "You can count on me to keep a secret."

Lacey believed Hannah would no more keep her secret than she'd stop buying Bubble Yum. She peeked through the crack, spied Hannah slicking back her ponytail. A strong wave of nausea hit.

"And congratulations," Hannah added before bopping out the door.

Lacey suspected by the day's end at least half the office would know. And the fear of what Hannah would say glued Lacey to the vomit-splashed bathroom floor, where not even the possibility of contracting a horrible disease could lift her.

But Doby did, shoving a handful of Altoids in Lacey's mouth as she yanked her to her feet. They lit a five-alarm fire and triggered extinguishing sprays of saliva as the mint-laced fumes traveled into her nostrils and scorched the delicate membranes, forcing her to breathe open-mouthed. She exhaled flames and inhaled icicles as the mints dissolved into a cooling fire, burning and icing her throat and lungs.

When the temperature in Lacey's mouth regulated, she asked. "Are you trying to kill me?"

Doby wet a paper towel and wiped the drool rolling off the corner of Lacey's lips. "You smelled like you needed more than one, or is that the stuff in the toilet?" Doby heaved. "I'll flush it before *I* get sick."

Lacey leaned against the bathroom stall. "It doesn't matter, nothing does. She knows, and I'm ruined."

Doby opened the door. "Sorry, just trying to let in fresh air. Wait, who knows what?"

Lacey stiffened her body and fought the urge to collapse. "Hannah, I thought she was you, so I confessed my pregnancy. She promised not to tell, but she's the office bard."

"Bard who?"

"The person who told the townspeople's deeds in medieval times." Doby raised her penciled brows. Lacey continued. "What matters is, she's a gossiper. It's only a matter of time before she blabs."

Doby grabbed both sides of Lacey's face. "I'll keep her from running her trap. What if I tape her mouth shut before she talks? Ooh wait, I have a better idea—fire her."

Lacey stretched her eyes. "An angry employee with a big secret?"

"Yeah, point taken. I'll just *Dambe* her ass."

Doby was a pasty white child taught survival skills by the local natives in the African village where her missionary parents raised her. If anyone had the means to knock someone the hell out if the circumstances demanded, it'd be her.

"You will do nothing but help me get back to my office without having to look her in the face."

Doby steadied Lacey. "What if I accidentally elbow her in the mouth?"

Lacey didn't blink.

"Okay, I won't hurt her—as long as she doesn't tell. Wait, how did you even get in this bathroom?"

Lacey lifted the vomit-splashed email from the floor. "I wanted to show you this."

"Ew! Throw that away. You can show me on the computer."

Doby escorted Lacey down the hall towards her office. But when they reached the stretch right before Hannah's desk, they both froze. There stood Lacey's biggest competition, Jocelyn, holding a coffee mug labeled *Wake, Pray, Slay* while chatting away. But why? Lacey had mentioned on more than one occasion how Jocelyn dug into her like scabies and drove her mad.

Not only that, but she had one goal, to snag everyone's attention, and not with her talents. That wouldn't get her as far as she desired, so instead, she strutted around the office in butt-lifting elastic bandages, distracting men and alienating women. Today's color choice, fire-engine red. So bright it made Lacey's eyeballs burn—and honestly— made her a wee bit jealous.

But skimpy attire and brown-nosing employees aside, what was she to do? Jocelyn wouldn't miss a chance announcing Lacey's demise to her boss.

"Let's make a run for it before I mistakenly yank out Jocelyn's hair extensions," Doby said, tugging Lacey's arm.

"I agree." They both jetted past Hannah and Jocelyn, leaving only enough time for a quick wave.

Doby slammed the door closed. "What was that? I swear she better not say a word."

Lacey collapsed into her office chair. "I need to figure out how to explain this to Mr. Caldwell. I could tell him I'm married, but my husband's out of the country—waiting on his visa?"

"You haven't left the country in years."

Lacey pressed her palm against her forehead. "Okay, so he's in another state, trapped on a business trip. Scratch that—eventually he'd have to show his face. Because what *good* husband would desert his wife after getting her pregnant?"

And what decent person had sex with her and never bothered calling or rekindling the moment? Wow, what if it was because she sucked in bed? How embarrassing. Lacey gripped the chair for support.

Doby paced. "It's all good, just pull yourself together. This is not the time to fall apart."

It took every ounce of energy Lacey had to hold herself upright. "If Margot Wallace finds out I'm an unwed mother, my career is over."

"She can't find out."

Lacey realized that, but there was no way to stop Hannah from blabbing, not without drawing even more attention to herself. And when Jocelyn got wind of the situation, she'd end Lacey's career.

"My only other option is to call the private investigator. He can find the father. And maybe, just maybe, that person won't be a jerk." Lacey checked her phone, making sure she had the investigator's information saved. "And if I'm really lucky, we'll fall in love and get married—before I lose my job."

Doby froze in her steps. "Considering you're still in the denial phase, why don't we just settle for a name first?"

That afternoon after work, Lacey hailed a taxi to the private investigator's office, but nearly aborted the mission when she realized the only link to royalty Mr. Henry Duke had lived in his oversized belly, as he apparently ate the last King of England.

He definitely was not the splendid man she had imagined. He was a man hiding behind a tree of facial hair, a man dressed in a mustard-crusted, poop emoji t-shirt which read: *People Pay Me To Find Shit.* Her arms slumped to her sides. Why didn't she heed the red flags on the sign outside? There were only three letters of his name not faded by weather elements: *Y*, *U*, and *K*.

Inside, she surveyed the make-shift office filled with unwanted junk and countered the odor of rotting fruit and dirty laundry by inhaling through her mouth. He swiped the remaining crumbs of a hot dog from his beard, brushed his hands across his pants, and then offered it to her. "You're the one I spoke to on the phone, correct?"

Lacey nodded as she reluctantly shook his hand.

"I figured. Your face matches your voice. I knew you were a cutie." His chuckle turned into a raspy cough.

That word again, *cute*. Throughout her entire life it was the best word a man, or boy, used to compliment her looks. And Lacey knew well enough what it meant. In fact, if it weren't for padded bras and underwire, she would still resemble a pre-pubescent girl. But at her age, why couldn't they come up with a more adult*ish* word? Because children and puppies were cute—not grown women.

Mr. Duke gestured for Lacey to take a seat. She dodged a few boxes before planting herself on the flea market chair across from him. "Mr. Duke, I'm not sure if—"

"It's the belly, isn't it? It's always the belly. But don't let it fool you," he said, shaking a layer of flab. "I'm skilled at what I do. It's the reason I don't have time to work out." He shuffled through multiple pens and trashed half of them before finding one that worked. "But enough about me, how can I help you?"

"I'm not even sure you can help me. Honestly, I'm embarrassed." She fumbled with her purse strap and glared at her wedge-heeled shoes, supposing she had paid too much for them. And with a baby on the way? A rush of blood pulsed in her ears.

"No need to be." He shook his head back and forth while thumbing to a clean writing page. "This is confidential, and besides, I've heard everything under the sun. One time I had this lady who thought aliens were sneaking into her home at night and poisoning her food. When I showed her an eight-hour video of nothing but the fridge, she insisted they used invisible shields. What a nut?"

"I'm pregnant," Lacey exploded.

Mr. Duke threw both hands in the air. "Congratulations! What is it? A cheating boyfriend, jealous ex?"

She curled her upper body. "More like I can't remember who I slept with."

"Someone roofied you?" He scribbled an illegible note on the yellow ledger paper.

"No, I had a dream that wasn't a dream—never mind. The doctor says it's because of sex-related amnesia."

"Oh my, I'd call that a unique situation." He cleared his throat. "How long ago did this take place?" He pushed the pen full-speed across the page.

He didn't have to say he doubted her story. Disbelief painted his face. She tried glimpsing his notepad, sure he had written *mental case* beside her name. But regardless of if he had or not, he was still her only hope.

Struggling to contain her nerves, she fumbled around until she found her phone and then opened her calendar. "I have the conception window dates, from somewhere around seven weeks ago. Although, Dr. Hart says the dates might be off by a week in either direction."

"Who?" Mr. Duke coughed into the fold of his elbow.

"My doctor. If you pass me a pen, I can note these for you." She had a sudden burst of confidence. "The security cameras would be a good starting place since I know it happened in my apartment. Oh, and you can scratch off Zak Cooper. He's over for work sometimes, nothing more."

"Miss Winters—"

"Lacey, please," she said, laying the pen beside the page filled with a range of possibilities.

"Lacey, I can handle the investigating part." He folded up the sheet of paper and tucked it into his pocket. "Give me a few weeks, and I should have a possible baby daddy," he cackled.

She didn't share his sense of humor. More so, her stomach churned at the amount of time he suggested. Even if Hannah hadn't told Jocelyn, it wouldn't be long before she blurted the news to someone else. Lacey gripped the edge of the seat. "Will it really take that long?"

He snickered. "Of course, not. Let me just consult my Magic 8-Ball."

"You're being facetious," she said, sucking in her lips.

He leaned back, smirked. "Hey, what do you expect? Investigations take time."

She couldn't control the investigation, but she could make a plan for the near future—a plan that included making sure her pregnancy remained a secret.

5

From the moment her alarm clock sounded until the moment she stepped off the office elevator, Lacey debated confronting Hannah about what she may or may not have told Jocelyn. Ultimately, she decided she had to ask. It was the only way to find out for certain. Otherwise, she'd spend her days on the verge of panic, waiting for the world to collapse around her.

She paused at the hallway corner, inflated her chest with a deep breath, and prepared to be direct. She made the turn and headed towards Hannah, who after fumbling the phone back in place, pretended to slam her head against the desk.

Lacey crept closer as the pit of her stomach emptied. "Is everything okay? Who was that?"

Hannah looked up at Lacey. Her hand slid across her long ponytail as her jaws tightened and released, over and over. Lacey prayed she had more sense than to blow a bubble in her face.

"It was Mr. Caldwell. He said to send you to his office." Her voice barely rose above a whisper.

Despite the tone, Lacey remained optimistic. Yesterday's email suggested she had a future as a partner in the firm. No need for alarm, she thought. "Okay, give me a minute to settle my things, and I'll—"

Swift as a bolt of lightning, Hannah interrupted, "No, you don't have time. He needs you right now. His demands, not mine."

Those words zapped Lacey with electricity, inflamed her insides. Her blood boiled. "You told Jocelyn, didn't you?"

Hannah's brows rose two inches. "I did no such thing."

"Then why the urgency?"

A bubble popped across Hannah's lips as she positioned herself like a naughty puppy. "He called for you, but you weren't here. And you're usually here thirty minutes earlier than you need to be, but not today. He was like, 'oh this is late for her.' And you're never late."

Lacey's tone rolled out deep and steady. "What did you say?"

Hannah squeezed both sides of her face as she cowered even lower. "I said, 'it's the morning sickness,' and since he has a bunch of kids, he knew exactly what I meant."

Lacey slapped her forehead. "Everyone with an ounce of sense knows what morning sickness is."

"I'm so sorry. I would never tell anyone on purpose. It just slipped right out before I could stop myself. Am I fired?"

Lacey reminded herself that gossiping was a disease. Passing along secretive information to someone like Hannah and expecting it to remain confidential was the same as handing a shot of vodka to an alcoholic and trusting him not to drink. It wouldn't happen. And she wouldn't ax Hannah, not unless she favored doubling her workload. "You're not fired."

Hannah clasped her hands together. "Oh my heavens, thank you so much. I couldn't survive if I lost my job. How would I pay for my weekly manicures or my summer cruise—"

"Hannah."

Hannah zipped her fingers across her lips.

Lacey had shown Hannah mercy, a mercy she now wished for herself. In a deliberated spin, she aimed her body toward Mr. Caldwell's office and pressed forward. Once there, she lifted her hand to knock, but Mr. Caldwell swung open the door and ordered her inside before she had a chance. He didn't waste time offering her a seat, but she took one as an alternative to landing face-first on cold stone floors.

"Please tell me these rumors aren't true," he said, positioning himself across from her, his face flashing a purplish-red.

She twisted her fingers together and thought, play dumb. "What rumors, sir?"

"That you're pregnant and worse—not married." He rammed his fist into the top of the mahogany desk, and then yanked it back to his chest, supporting it with his other hand.

Her insides quivered as any possibility of an emergency plan flew out the window. "Well, sir. I..."

He invaded her personal space and words. "You landed us a contract for the Sanctity of Marriage Coalition. You can be gay, transexual, gender unassigned, or any color under the gosh darn sun—but you cannot be pregnant and unmarried. What do I do now?"

He stomped over to the wall of windows that stretched from floor to ceiling and rubbed his hand. The blemish-free glass offered breathtaking views of the city, of sunrises and sunsets that rose and fell above skyscraper roofs. Lacey appreciated it because she had spent many hours reveling in the same fantastic view from her office.

The one she may no longer have without the answer to his question.

He dropped his shoulders several inches. "I have to pull you from the project. It's the only way to salvage the contract." He massaged his face, reddened it even more. "I hate to do this, but I don't have a choice. Get with Jocelyn and bring her up to speed. She needs to take over ASAP."

Did he insist she red-ribbon deliver her sweat, blood, and tears to her arch nemesis? She white-knuckled the chair arm as her gaze darted from the floor to the wall, the wall to the door, the door to the window. She froze, catching sight of—Zak?

Zak motioned at her.

She didn't have time for his antics, not with a monsoon washing away her career and hard labor. The heavy rain pounded her heart. A rain that, between the torrential bands, reflected glimpses of her father's disappointment.

She turned from Zak, browsed pictures of Mr. Caldwell's family housed in decorative frames, scattered on the bookcase and desk. They nestled beside his awards and certificates of acknowledgment, the symbols of his importance, dedication, and success. Each showing how talented he was. What would be on Lacey's wall?

A pink slip?

Crumbling in the throes of threatened unemployment, she searched for an escape. A place where her career remained intact and her pregnancy brought celebration. A place where she was—

"Married!" She whirled around to face Mr. Caldwell. "I'm married," she repeated, with no consideration of the consequences.

Mr. Caldwell bent his neck forward. "You're what?"

"If you could give me a minute, sir." She ran to the door and met Zak. "I need your help. It's an emergency."

He dragged his feet as Lacey pulled. "Wait, what are we doing?"

She tugged harder. "Just play along, please. It's life or death."

"O… kay?" His eyes narrowed. "But you owe me."

"Whatever you want," she whispered, holding his hand until they reached Mr. Caldwell. Embracing her inner Vanna White, she gestured towards Zak. "Meet my husband, Zak Cooper."

Zak choked, stumbled backwards, and coughed out the question, "Your *what*?"

Driven by desperation, she wrapped her arm around his. "You don't have to keep pretending. I told Mr. Caldwell about our marriage. I had to, or otherwise, I'd lose my job."

Zak open and closed his mouth a few times, shuffled his feet in place. "Me and you... *married*?"

Sweat pooled in Lacey's armpits. "There's no point in us hiding it any longer. If you won't tell Mr. Caldwell that you're my husband, I'll have to give Jocelyn my contract."

Zak scratched the back of his head. "I'm confused."

Convinced he'd never catch on, Lacey's heart sank. At least before, she might have walked out with dignity and respect. Now, she would walk out with a new title, *Liar*.

Mr. Caldwell eyed Zak. "Is what she says true?"

In her peripheral, Lacey spied Zak. He resembled someone facing a firing squad, not a newlywed. Discouraged by his terrified expression, she counted the number of trips and boxes it'd take to empty her office.

Mr. Caldwell tapped his foot. "It's not a hard question, son. Are you, or are you not married?"

Zak found Lacey's eyes, plundering them longer than he should. And she milked the moment with her best attempt at fluttering lashes. Until he stuttered the words, "Y-y-yes."

And with that response, the washing machine spin-cycle in her stomach came to a sudden halt and her breakfast settled. Relieved, she pressed closer and mouthed a *thank you*.

Zak planted a constipated smile on his face and patted Lacey's arm.

Mr. Caldwell pressed his handkerchief against his chest. "So you're not an unwed mother?"

"Heavens no, I'm way more responsible than that."

"Lacey, you can't imagine how happy that makes me," Mr. Caldwell said, unwinding his tense muscles.

"Wait—you're pregnant!" Zak blurted. Red blotches coated his neck and ears.

In that instant, Lacey regretted not having a plan, a plan to prevent the calamity unfolding before her eyes, a disaster that left every hair on her body standing at attention.

Mr. Caldwell tilted his head towards Zak. "You weren't aware?"

"I—"

With Zak trapped on one syllable, Lacey had to do something, give him time to handle the news while she saved herself. "I hadn't told him yet. I planned to do so over a romantic, candlelit dinner... put a ribbon around the test, but..." Lacey lowered her head, appalled by how easily the lies flowed.

Zak lifted her chin, stared deep into her soul. "Did you plan to tell me?"

"Of course."

Mr. Caldwell stepped in between them. "I'm sorry I ruined the moment. I hope you'll accept my apologies."

"We do. Now, if you don't mind, we have a lot to discuss," Zak said, grabbing Lacey's arm and dragging her towards her office.

Lacey wanted to vanish, run for the hills, jump off a cliff. But instead, she followed him.

Once inside, he locked the door and leaned his back against it. "You're pregnant for real?"

"Is there a fake pregnant? Because I'll take it." She held up both hands. "Sorry, I don't mean to be a smart butt."

"Why didn't you tell me?"

Lacey folded her arms across her stomach. "Because it's not your problem, it's mine."

"Are you serious? You're pregnant. That makes it my problem, too." He squeezed his eyes closed, shook his head. "I can't believe you didn't stop me when I went off on you at the park. If I'd known, I would never..."

He stepped towards her, but she turned away, found comfort on the plush cushions of her office sofa. "I recognize what a surprise this is, but try not to make it a big deal, please."

"What? This is a huge deal. And if you think I'm letting you do this alone, I'm not." Zak's leg grazed Lacey's as he took a seat beside her.

She wished she had more control over the involuntary tingle it elicited. "I hope you realize I didn't plan this, and I'm sorry to bring you into it."

"Sure, I'm shocked, but I'm glad you told me. I want to be here for you and the baby, through every doctor's appointment, late night craving, the delivery. You can count on me, Lacey." He laid his hand over hers.

She pulled back. "I assumed that when you agreed to be my fake husband. Pretending to be the father kind of comes with the package."

"Wait, you want me to pretend to be the daddy?"

"I know it's overwhelming, but don't worry. I'm not asking you to adopt my baby or sign your name on a birth certificate, no obligations." She met Zak's eyes. "It's already terrible enough I dragged you into this mess."

"Don't stress, I could've said no." He leaned his back against the sofa, stared at the ceiling. "So if I'm just pretending, who's the real father?"

There it was, the question she dreaded, or more so, the question without an answer.

Pinching the bridge of her nose, she forced her eyes closed, contemplated her response, weighed the repercussions this time. Should she tell him the truth? Perhaps, but then what? She had worked so hard to be a responsible, well-put-together woman. The truth crushed that persona, opened up doors of embarrassment. She couldn't risk it before learning what happened.

So against her better judgment, she named him. "Finn."

Zak's head jerked back. "Finn? As in your ex-boyfriend Finn? How's that even possible? You guys broke up months ago."

"Why are you keeping up with my love life?"

"I'm not. It's just odd you asked me to play your fake husband when the father of your baby is on the other side of the building." Zak scowled.

She didn't expect his rebuttal or his anger, but both presented serious snags in her panty hose. What if Zak approached Finn? It would be a disaster. "He doesn't know, and I expect it stay that way."

"It's not as if you can hide this."

"No, I can't. But now that we're married, he'll think it's yours." Lacey squeezed Zak's hand, ignoring the hormonal response. She hoped to gain sympathy—even though she deserved none. "Look, I need your help more than you can imagine. Mr. Caldwell was ready to take me off the coalition contract because of this. He told me to report to Jocelyn. You of all people know it would kill me."

"I do. But this mistake could cost both of us, me more than you probably. What if you guys kiss and make up? Where does that leave me? And I won't lie, it's strange pretending to be the father of a man's baby I see daily, knowing he's clueless." Zak pulled his hand away from Lacey, rubbed the back of his head. "I mean how long can we fake a marriage?"

Everything he said made sense, except the kiss and make up with Finn part. But what choice did she have if she wanted to save her career? "At least until my part of the coalition contract is complete. After that, we divorce."

"How? We're not even married."

"We fake divorce."

He straightened. "So, I become the bum father that bailed on his child."

The decision to marry Zak had more moving parts than she'd expected. "I'll make sure that doesn't happen... no matter what."

His shoulders relaxed. "Well, I need a place to store my things. It's why I tried getting your attention before this happened. A busted pipe flooded my apartment building last night. I can stay with Mathias, but he doesn't have room for my stuff."

"No, you'll stay with me, to make it look real. We're married, remember?"

Zak eyed her cautiously. It was a wild plan, but something about her beautiful desperation made him agree.

6

By Sunday evening, Zak arrived with the rest of his stuff. Stacks of cardboard boxes, kitchen trash bags full of clothes, and mismatched hangers in every color. It was an unsorted mess, as was her mind. She focused on the plan, get him settled on his side of the apartment and then keep her distance. This was a temporary arrangement. There was no reason for them to crowd each other's space.

Lacey wheeled a box and several of Zak's unpacked coats inside her spare bedroom. "Please say this is the last trip."

He shrugged. "I told you I'd handle it, but you insisted."

She tossed one of the hooded jackets onto his mountain of belongings. "Only because I didn't want the neighbors to think I'm a crazed hoarder," she said as a colorful nickel-sized ball escaped from a pocket.

Zak rushed over and grabbed it. "Yes! I thought I'd lost it. How did it get in there?" He rolled the unidentified object between his fingers. "I remember now. I put it in there when Mathias and I went to the game against the Braves."

Lacey slid the bright-yellow dolly, with its annoyingly loose wheel from under the box. "So you took a toy to a game to do what? Play with it between innings?" She smoothed back her stray curls and surveyed the limited space left in the room.

Zak held up the red ball. "Play with a Maxus Drago Bakugan? I don't think so. He's my lucky charm. When I take him to a game, we win... well... most of the time." He placed the toy on the space-saving dresser.

"I'm sure at the same rate they'd win without Maximum Dragon Biker Gang."

44

"You just seriously butchered his name."

Lacey twisted the nut on the loose bolt, tightening the dolly's wheel. "It's not the only thing I'll butcher if you don't get this stuff organized."

She stood up too fast and had to grab the handle for balance as a ball of burning fluid threatened to spew from her mouth. But she held it back.

"You look green. Here, sit," Zak said, easing her onto an edge of the bed not buried.

"I think I need to lay flat," she said, a filmy layer of sweat forming over every inch of her skin. Zak pushed the towering mess onto the floor.

As soon as she laid her head back, the sensation passed. "That's amazing, I feel better already."

"I shouldn't have let you overdo it. Just lay here while I get the rest," he said, leaving the room.

How could he expect her to laze around when she had drifted into the world of cohabitation—without the sex? Well, at least not sex in the physical sense. There were times when she contemplated jumping his bones, and once she might have visualized him naked on top of her, from behind, and in the butter churner position she'd read up on in Women's Health magazine—only because it came with both drawn and written explanations. Nonetheless, those dirty thoughts never moved past the lust phase.

Zak appeared in the doorway, his muscle-tee drenched in sweat. "It was hard getting that last box in, but it's done."

Lacey shifted her gaze to the floor when her mind returned to Fantasy Lane.

"Is everything still okay?" he asked.

Without looking up, she said, "I'm much better. In fact, I should go to my room."

He chuckled. "Technically, this is your room."

"It's not the one I sleep in," she said, rising to her feet. Thankfully, the dizzy spell had passed. Keeping her gaze on anything but him, she headed towards the door. But her shoulder collided with his chest in a move that sent her twirling off like an unbalanced spinning top.

He laid his hands on both her shoulders, stopped her. "I didn't hurt you did I? Did you hit your stomach?"

She shook her head without looking, afraid of what thoughts—or actions—her out-of-control hormones would conjure. He dropped his arms to his sides, sending up a blended fragrance of man soap and musk. The scent tickled her nostrils, and driven by a pheromone craze, she inhaled deeper.

"I'm going now," she said walking out of the room with her back to him.

"Wait, I'm ordering Chinese, want some? Never mind, I'm sure Chinese is the last thing you'd want... being so sick and all."

No, Chinese wasn't the best choice, but she hated the thought something growing in her stomach could keep her from eating one of her favorite meals. Or that he pitied her for it. "I can eat Chinese. There's certainly no reason I can't." She headed into the living room and grabbed her laptop from off the accent table. He followed behind her. "In fact, I'll take the General Tso's chicken combination with extra sauce while I work on the Darcy House project."

"Sunday is for relaxing, not working," he said, pointing at the computer.

"Says the person who's happy hovering around the middle for the rest of his life."

"Says the person who recognizes the importance of a wind-down. Here watch TV while I grab the food," he said, edging into her personal space.

She refused to look at him. "I don't have the pleasure of relaxing. People expect me to make a name for myself, and I can't disappoint them."

"Are you serious? There are cobwebs on the remote."

She snapped her head towards his direction. "It can't be. I dust."

With his eyes aimed at hers, he grinned. "I knew that'd get your attention."

She turned away. "Don't you have Chinese to pick up?"

He powered on the TV despite her protest. "I will, as soon as I find you some entertainment." He surfed through the channels and then stopped on *Married at First Sight*. "Now, I'll be right back."

Did he expect her to watch trash TV? He might, but she didn't. And anyway, what was entertaining about watching people make crazy, life-changing decisions with a complete stranger?

A lot, she told herself, as the preview for next week's show reeled across the screen after she had watched an entire episode.

Zak walked through the door with the food at the start of a commercial. "Let's eat."

And they did. She took it down like a champ before regurgitating it back up in a fiery vengeance twenty minutes later. She buried her head in the master bathroom toilet and tried to forget the saucy, deep-fried thighs. What point was she trying to prove by ordering spicy Chinese?

Zak knocked on the door. "Can I bring you anything?"

She held her insides long enough to answer. "A drink—please."

Soon after, he arrived, passing her an ice-cold Pepsi. "Here you go." She sipped it as he folded a cool cloth across her forehead.

"Thanks," Lacey said.

"Yeah, no problem. This combo worked wonders for my sister when she was pregnant with the twins. She made sure her husband kept opened-cans stocked in the fridge. She said they only work if you let the carbonation out, but I'm hoping she's wrong. This one is still fizzing."

"It doesn't matter." Lacey bent forward for another round and strands of hair fell with her. But Zak caught them, held them back just in time. "Will you be okay? Should I call someone?"

Wow, five minutes into what threatened to be her life for the next few months, and he wanted to bail. She wiped her mouth against the cool cloth. "You're not obligated to stay with me. I can take care of myself." Determined to show her strength, she pushed herself upward, but fell back when another wave of dizziness hit.

He braced her, kept her from falling too far. "No way I'm leaving you in this condition. I meant do you have a doctor I need to call?"

Okay, she might have rushed to judgement. "No, it'll pass soon." *Or I hope so, for my sake and yours.*

"If you say so. Do you have something to keep your hair back?"

She guided him to a hair supply basket stationed on the marble-top vanity. "Be careful, please. My hair is notoriously unruly."

"No worries, I got this. How hard can it be?" He chuckled, grabbing an elastic tie. With both hands he gripped her wild mane, tugging way too strong. Her head bobbed and twisted at his yanks. "That's not good."

"What's not good? You're scaring me."

He pulled harder. "One sec… almost… there." Finished, he leaned back and eyed her from every angle. "Just stay away from mirrors."

Who cared about looks at a time like this? She was too weak to even get off the floor. "Can you pass me my pillow? I'm sleeping here for the night."

"Not on my watch." He scooped her up, and with the stride of a gentle giant, carried her to bed. He could have dropped her, left her to climb in by herself, but instead, he took his time and tucked her in proper. Then he pushed a wastebasket within her reach. "Give me a minute to grab my blankets."

Snapped back to reality, she lifted her head. "Wait, for what?"

"I won't let you stay in here alone, not after that."

But what if she snored? Passed gas in her unconscious state? "That's a little extra. Besides, I'll be asleep before you blink."

"Good, because seeing you sleep beats seeing you suffer. Be right back."

On his return, he settled in on the floor by her bed and then leaned on his elbows. She tried not to stare at the tone in his biceps, or the glint of light, a reflection of a wall nightlight, in his hazel eyes. The last thing she needed was to stir-up chemically driven emotions. "Zak, you don't have to do this. I promise, I'll be okay."

He gave her a compassionate grin as he laid his head on the navy pillow. "And I'll be here if you're not. Goodnight, Lacey."

She fell back on her own pillow as an uncomfortable intimacy swirled around her. She shielded herself from it, reminded herself of the evidence. Despite spending long hours together, they had never kissed or even brushed lips. But still, she couldn't dismiss the times when one of their legs pressed against the other's for longer than it should, or when fingers crossed reaching for the same paper. Nor could she ignore the moments when he sat close enough his breath warmed her skin.

But it meant nothing. They were two friends dedicated to work, and him sleeping on the floor changed nothing. He was a friend helping a friend. And she was a friend desperate for his help—only his help.

Lacey cracked open her eyes before the alarm clock sounded. She glimpsed Zak sprawled across his covers and knew better than to give his shirtless body her full attention. And if she was smart, she'd keep the conversation superficial, at least until the investigator could offer her answers.

She tiptoed out of bed and into the kitchen. There, she prepared the only thing she could tolerate without fail, plain toast and decaf coffee. Inhaling the dark-roast aroma, she counted her blessings it didn't make her nauseated. If anything, the warmth of the fresh brew coated her throat and awakened her senses.

Her fingertips traced the mug rim as she considered the

arrangement with Zak. It would take time to get used to having him in her apartment. And even more time to adjust to the surging hormones.

He tottered around the corner with a crusty line of drool stuck to the side of his mouth and hair that occupied several time zones. He looked crazed. But he wasn't here to impress or to seduce, and he didn't compel her to either. A brownie point for the innocence of their arrangement.

"I smell coffee," he mumbled.

See, simple requests. Lacey poured him a cup, and then guided him to the sugar, which he added in excess. He removed the stirrer and sampled his concoction. His face wrinkled, and his lips puckered.

"I should have told you I brew it strong."

He nodded as he set the cup on the counter. He pointed to the semi-burnt toast in Lacey's hand. "Queasy?"

"The story of my new life," she said, nibbling off a corner.

His gaze shifted to her lower belly. "I'm trying to wrap my head around you and Finn making a baby. I never would have guessed you guys still liked each other enough to be in the same room."

Lacey jerked backward and sent half her coffee sloshing over the cup edge. She dried off the counter, soaking up the last drop of coffee along with her regrets, the ones that involved dragging Finn into her lies. "I'd rather not go over this before work."

Zak rubbed the back of his neck. "I'm not wrong for wanting to understand how you guys went from hating each other to making a baby."

"When was liking each other a requirement for having sex? Sometimes it's just sex."

"Yeah, I guess you're right. Not too long ago I made love to someone I thought had feelings for me only to find out she thought it was meaningless. So I agree. For some people, sex is just sex."

The image of Zak and another woman tangled up together sent a burst of fire spreading into her cheeks. It shouldn't have, but it did. "Well, I don't need a visual."

"You're right. I promised I wouldn't mention it."

"Don't you mean you promise you *won't* mention it."

"If it helps you let it go, I promise I *won't*."

Her response was snippy, but justified. Who could fault her for not wanting a detailed picture of his naked, toned body thrusting against a full-bosomed beauty who only wanted one thing? Lacey shook away the cinematic-film reeling in her head and returned to the topic at hand.

"Finn and I broke up, and we won't reconnect—ever. And I refuse to tell him about this baby. Now with that established, I need you to promise me you'll stop bringing up his name."

Zak tore off a section of paper towel and dried the small puddle on the floor that Lacey had missed. "I'm sorry. It's just that—Finn is a creep."

She'd stamp her seal of approval on that fact. "All the more reason not to tell him." As Zak stood, faced her, she sought confirmation, in his sleep-crusted eyes shadowed by lengthy lashes, that he would keep her secret.

He tossed the soiled paper towel in the trash without breaking eye contact. "It's not my place to tell him."

"Thank you. So can we put this behind us? And pick up that paper towel."

"Yes, ma'am. As you wish." He disposed of the trash before attempting another sip of coffee. He made the same pained expression. "It's horrible. I thought it might be better since I knew what to expect, but it's worse. Oh, before I forget. Are we traveling to work together now that we're married?" Before she could answer, he erupted into sudden laughter.

She glanced the visible parts of her body, wondered if she had toilet paper hanging out her pants or something. "What's so funny?"

"You," he said, catching his breath in between the hysterics. "You didn't look at the side view of your hair yet, did you?"

"No, not yet..." She patted her head, noted the twisted tangles, the bird's nest. And the reflection in the bathroom mirror confirmed her suspicions. "I told you to be careful with my hair."

"I tried."

She eyed his reflection in the mirror as he shrugged behind her. Poking her fingers into the crevices, she searched for a place to start detangling. "Where's the hair tie?"

"Let me help you."

"You've helped enough."

Zak ignored her, sticking his hands into the mess. "I found it. Want me to yank it?"

"No." Lacey bordered on screaming. "It's not coming out that way. Can you grab the scissors and cut it out—carefully?"

A few clips later, the hair-tie laid in several sections in the trash with a chunk of her curls. She was grateful it wasn't worse.

"See, I fixed it," he said.

Lacey glared at the still knotted mess on her head. "You call this fixed?" She closed her eyes and remembered he didn't have her hair. "Can you get dressed so we're not late, please?"

He did. And they left the apartment only a minute later than they should have, thanks to the miracle of quality hair products and his low-maintenance routine. To make up for lost time, they sped to the A-line train and then fast-stepped the last two blocks up the street side-by-side, only separating to dodge pedestrian mobs and avoid head-on collisions with bystanders.

"Should we hold hands?" Zak asked, climbing the steps of their building.

"Let's try to keep this fake marriage as low-key as possible. I'm sure Mr. Caldwell's not expecting PDA because we're married."

7

Zak held the door for Lacey and then led the way to the elevators. Although they worked on opposite sides of the building, they had to navigate through the shared common area to get to their respective places. And the common area was a hype junction, a landing pad where people communed, caught up on gossip, and enjoyed morning pastries and afternoon fruit.

It shouldn't be a problem—if she didn't stop.

Zak loosened his tie, and Lacey repositioned a failing bobby pin as the elevator doors opened into an unexpected shower of applause from a large crowd. Surprised, Lacey shuffled backwards until she bumped the railing. She turned to Zak, who stood motionless. And with neither of them making a move to join the crowd, the elevator doors closed.

"What was that?" Lacey asked.

"I'm not sure, but maybe I should hold your hand or something."

"Totally not necessary," Lacey said, straightening her blouse collar and staying comfortably out of Zak's reach, afraid of what his touch might do.

When the doors opened again to the same cheers, she tightened her jiggly core and stepped into the waiting crowd. Smiling faces and whistling lips spiritedly welcomed her and Zak. Even Mr. John, the most introverted man in the building, had made his way from the engineering department to offer his congratulations.

And they thanked him for his good wishes, along with the others, person after person. Lacey's brain twirled inside her skull as her shaky hand brushed her forehead.

"Well, look at these two love-birds," Jocelyn said as she approached.

Her mouth twisted into a tortuous smile. And although Lacey hated to admit it, Jocelyn was gorgeous even when she tried to be ugly. It wasn't fair.

Lacey took Zak's hand into hers and pulled him close. "No, we can't."

He leaned over and whispered, "I thought you were against PDA."

She murmured, "Change of plans."

Jocelyn stared at the intertwined hands. "It would seem so, unless this is all one big act."

Lacey didn't blink.

Jocelyn waved a palm in Lacey's direction. "I'm kidding—or am I? No, really, I'm just being my usual humorous self."

What a lie, Lacey thought as her body partially relaxed. "Yeah, you're a hoot." *Straight out of Hooters*, Lacey mumbled under her breath.

"What I still don't get though is why hide something so special?" Leave it up to Jocelyn to raise doubts.

"Because it makes for juicier office gossip. And boy are you two the talk of the town," said the nameless brunette with more cleavage than brains. She came out of nowhere, stroking Zak's back in sensual circles. "And Zak, do you realize how many girls woke up broken-hearted this morning?"

Zak arched away from whoever she was. "I can only imagine."

"He doesn't care about those other girls. He's been too busy creating babies with Lacey and making me assume she had gotten pregnant out of wedlock," Hannah blurted. "And then when I told Mr. Caldwell, I felt terrible because I thought she had lost her job because of me, or worse, that I might get fired. And then how would I pay for the—"

"Hannah." Lacey stopped her, but not soon enough.

Jocelyn stretched her eyes. "Oh my, I didn't realize you're pregnant. How scandalous? Now, the secrecy confuses me even more."

"Why, it's self-explanatory? Who needed distractions with the coalition contract at stake? You see the ruckus this marriage has caused this morning alone." Lacey waved her hand around the room.

Jocelyn scanned the crowd. "Oh, they aren't here because of you and Zak. They're here to celebrate the contract. You two, and your new bundle of joy, are just a bonus."

If ever there was a time Lacey wanted to cause physical harm to someone, it was now. And while she would never have the courage to do such a thing, she found pleasure imagining herself plucking out

Jocelyn's perfect eyebrows one-by-one.

"Everyone give me your attention, please." Mr. Caldwell said from the center of the room, atop a footstool that raised him to Zak's nose. "Most of you may know, but for those who don't, our very own Lacey Winters secured the largest contract of this firm's history to date. If anyone needs translation, it means money in our pockets."

Everyone clapped and whistled. The noise bombarded Lacey's ears, making the bright red exit sign even more appealing.

"So please enjoy the chocolate croissants and lattes in the corner." Mr. Caldwell said, gesturing to a table filled with goodies.

Zak laid his hand on Lacey's upper back and made her spine tingle. "Do you want me to grab you something?"

She wiggled away. "No, burnt toast and home-brewed coffee is the most I can stomach."

He laughed. "Well, considering your coffee tasted as burnt as your toast, I'm grabbing a latte. Be right back."

Lacey watched him maneuver his way over to the table of sweet concoctions until a familiar figure standing by the same table drew her attention—Finn. Determined to avert a disaster, she raced into the mob and called Zak's name, but he couldn't hear her. She squeezed through the crowd, stepping on toes and bumping into backs, until she reached him.

She yanked him around to face her, praying he hadn't caught sight of Finn.

He grinned. "So you changed your mind?"

"Um, no. Did you notice the size of this crowd?" She peeked behind him. Finn hadn't moved. "Wasn't it nice of Mr. Caldwell to gather them here—for us, I mean for me, and the contract? Don't you agree?" She peeked over again. *Grab your snack and go,* she mumbled.

Zak scratched his head. "I thought you hated being the center of attention at gatherings like this."

Her fingers fell across her throat. "You know me, I don't mind being in the spotlight...sometimes." More like never.

Zak glanced at the food table and then crossed his arms over his chest. He turned his sights back to Lacey. "I see what you're doing. You're worried I'll say something to Finn."

Lacey jerked her head around Zak and pretended to gasp. "Finn's over there?"

"Come on, you know he is. What else would make you talk so crazy?" His face softened as he captured her attention. "Look, I told you I wouldn't confront him, and I won't. I'd never hurt you... not—"

"How is my favorite person in the whole wide world?" Doby squeezed Lacey hard from behind.

Lacey squirmed out of Doby's overzealous hold. "I'll survive. How was the vacation with Carson?" Lacey asked, running her fingers through Doby's fawn-colored silkies.

"I'll give you the trip details later. The good news is we both came back alive. And that alone speaks volumes," Doby said, scanning the room, "I hate arriving late to these things. Fill me in on the commotion. What did I miss?"

"A new marriage and baby," Jocelyn said, invading their inner circle. Lacey wished she had a vanishing spell to cast her out.

"Oh my god, you're pregnant? And just when did you get married?" Doby's mouth formed a perfect oval.

Myra, the receptionist with glasses as thick as window panes, ran over and posted herself next to Jocelyn. She drooled, eager for a crumb of information.

The whites of Jocelyn's eyes stretched. "You didn't tell your best friend? How odd."

Doby burst out laughing, maybe even sprayed a mist of saliva. "Silly you, I was the first person Lacey told. I do so enjoy sparking reactions from people."

Jocelyn's jaws tightened, and a vein pulsated on the side of her neck.

Myra pushed her glasses higher. "I'm sure Jocelyn's surprised by the suddenness of this, just as I am. I work near Zak everyday, and I've never seen you guys hold hands, or even kiss."

"Did I hear someone say kiss?" Mr. Caldwell asked, joining the group. "Lacey deserves a kiss for her hard work. Go on Zak." He patted Zak's shoulder.

Lacey interjected with her pointer finger held high. "There will be none of that. I'm sure he wants no part of my morning sickness breath. Daily vomiting leaves behind a lingering stench."

Jocelyn planted a devious grin on her face. "If he loves you so much, it shouldn't matter."

Lacey's toes and fingers went numb first. Then it spread to her arms and legs until she stood paralyzed. Zak dragged her stiff torso closer to his.

"It doesn't." He anchored his gaze onto her and stole her breath. His curled lips crept towards hers.

This couldn't be happening. He intended to kiss her with an audience of co-workers, friends, strangers, and—*frenemies* watching. Her bottom lip quivered. And as the space between them disappeared, she feared fainting. Refusing to fall apart in front of her boss, she steadied her wobbling knees, told herself, *it's just a peck.* Enough to seal the deal, make her and Zak's union believable.

Yet, it was so much more.

He didn't stop at the soft touch of closed mouths. No, he pressed firmly, searched for more. But she sealed her lips. This was Zak, her co-worker, her friend. She couldn't kiss-him, kiss-him. But he persisted, tickled the nape of her neck with his fingertips. And her betraying lips cracked against the delicate sensation.

Only a slight parting, no reason to panic. That's as far as he would get.

When his tongue grazed hers, she nudged it back. He tried again, and she shoved harder, gagging herself. It forced them apart. To anyone paying attention, Lacey was sure their kiss resembled a mama bird feeding her baby. No way was it pretty.

But it was a kiss to satisfy the crowd—except they weren't.

"No, no, no," Mr. Caldwell said, "after thirty years of marriage, my wife and I kiss with more passion than that. For gosh's sake, you're having a baby. Kiss like you love each other."

Before Lacey could prepare, Zak took tender charge of her mouth. Any efforts to hold him back failed. And with his tongue intertwined with hers, he pressed deeper. He pulled her to a place where emotion and excitement simmered. A place where the heat of passion melted her into his arms, into his kiss. Breathless, she should have craved air, but instead, she craved him. Craved every drop of the sweet kiss he commanded.

A sudden round of applause from the crowd snapped her back to reality. Her eyelids lifted to Zak millimeters away from her face. She glared.

He had taken it too far. And while her insides screamed at him, on the outside, she pulled off an Emmy-award winning smile to the mob still stuffing their faces, now full from her discomfort. She locked an arm around Zak and waved goodbye. Then, when it was safe to leave, she hauled him into her office.

"What the hell was that?" she asked in a screaming whisper while locking the door.

"It was a kiss."

Lacey tapped her foot and crossed her arms against her chest. "Oh, I know it was a kiss, just why did you kiss me like *that*?"

He narrowed his brows. "Because I didn't have a choice. The first time wasn't convincing enough. And besides, what does it matter? It's not like it's our first kiss."

"I know it's not our first kiss. We're grown-ups, and we've kissed people. I'm just worried you're taking this too far."

His head jerked back. "Me? Don't you think that's what you did when you asked me to be your fake husband?"

Lacey gritted her teeth. As much as she hated to admit it, he was right. She had dragged him into her storm, made him huddle under her umbrella. And when it collapsed on them, he'd walk away just as soaked as her. Disgusted with her poorly planned decisions, she eased into her office chair and tapped a pen against the stack of papers in front of her.

He tiptoed closer. "I didn't mean to say that. I'm wrong—"

"No, you're right. We crossed the line and things are spinning out of control because I'm not prepared." She grabbed a notepad. "What I need is a plan, a plan for every question, every possibility... every ambush. A plan for how I'll tell my parents, how we'll break up, and especially how to respond when people want to see us kiss."

"Don't you think that's a little neurotic? Sometimes it's better to wing it."

"No, planning is necessary. As soon as I don't plan, look what happens—a fake marriage and this." She pointed to her lower belly. "And who could forget the crowds of people chanting for us to kiss. But it's fixable. I can't stay a terrible person forever." She shifted her attention to her list, writing details as fast as her hand moved.

Zak stopped her. "Look at me."

She resisted.

"Lacey, please."

She lifted her head in slow motion, anchored her eyes onto his.

"You're not a terrible person, and you don't deserve this."

She dropped the pen, pressed her palm against the bridge of her nose. There, she held her wits and emotions.

"I apologize for taking the kiss too far. And I won't let it happen again if you promise to hold off planning the rest of your life in a day. It will work out. You'll see."

"Is that what you believe?"

"It's what I know." His comforting hand found rest on her shoulder.

Easier said than done, she thought, aware Zak couldn't understand her dilemma or the stakes. By tomorrow morning her dad would learn about her marriage and—the other thing—whether it was her who told him or someone else.

She slumped in her chair. The only thing left to do was polish her story for her parents.

8

That night, Lacey retreated to her rainfall shower-head before making the call to her parents. The warm water trickled across every inch of her skin, loosening tense muscles.

Through the rising steam, she recited the pre-chosen sentences and prayed she wouldn't lose it: *Zak is my person... I couldn't imagine life without him... When you know you've found the one, why wait... I should have told you, but with the contract, it wasn't a good time... You know I abhor flashy weddings... Oh, and the biggest surprise, you'll be grandparents this year.*

And those were the exact lines she used when she called them from the privacy of her bedroom, making sure Zak didn't overhear. Her mother squealed so hard Lacey feared losing an eardrum. Her dad reprimanded her, but only for not telling them sooner. And together, they insisted on a family dinner to meet her new *Hubby* on Friday night. It was the worst phone call of her life. The stab of conscience, the searing pain that shot through her with each lie and glossed over piece of truth.

When the torture ended, Lacey sprawled out on the bed and buried her head under a pillow. She cried a soul-shaking cry that soaked everything around her. A cry that left every muscle in her body weak and her throat tight. Because no matter how well she fooled those around her, she couldn't fool herself.

And that brutal truth consumed her.

Zak knocked on the door, and she ignored it, hoping he'd go away. The last thing she needed was his comfort, or false reassurance. But he persisted. "Is everything okay?"

No, it's not okay. But she refused to share her real feelings. "Yes." Her voice cracked, turned one syllable into three.

"Are you crying?"

Her denial came out a jumbled, broken mess.

"That's it, I'm coming in there."

She heard the click of the knob, felt the flash of wind. But she couldn't protest. It took what little strength she had to keep her face buried under her pillow. The mattress sank on her left side, and for a brief time, or maybe longer considering she hadn't tracked the minutes, there was no noise other than her muffled bawling.

Zak kept silent.

And when her energy reserves exhausted, she stopped. It was then, and not a second sooner, that he pulled away the pillow. She sensed the puffiness in her eyes, tasted the salted mascara in her mouth, and felt the curls matted against her cheeks. But with precision and delicacy, he peeled them from her face. "Want to talk about it?"

"Are you asking if I want to repeat the lies I told my parents? Tell you how happy they were to hear them only because they'd never dream I was being dishonest? I don't think so." She stared at the ceiling. "I'm the worst daughter in the world."

He tucked her last curl in place. "You don't believe that, do you? Your career was in jeopardy. Anyone in your position would've done the same."

"I don't think there's another person who's ever been in my position."

"Maybe not, but it's a human mistake. We all make them."

She lifted her head, eyed Zak. "That's easy for you to say, Mr. Perfect."

He pointed at himself. "Who me? I've made a mountain of poor decisions."

She waited for the wave of dizziness to pass and then propped herself up in bed. "I don't believe you. What's the worst thing you've ever done?"

He slid in beside her, folded a pillow behind his neck. "Well, there was the one time I chopped down my mom's cherry tree—or was that George Washington?"

"It's not a joking matter." She tried to hold a stern face, but cracked the slightest grin.

"No, it's not." He raked his fingers through his wild, golden spikes streaked with a hint of auburn—enough to keep it dirty. "Where do I start? I've been to jail."

Lacey jerked back and bumped her head against the wooden headboard. She rubbed the sore spot. "You're a criminal? The firm hired you with a record?"

He held up his hands. "Don't judge. When I was a teenager, a few friends and I thought it'd be cool to egg the principal's house. But during the rapid-fire session, I snatched a small rock instead and hit the window."

He chuckled. "I'm sure you can imagine the unfolding events, shattering glass, beaming floodlights, blaring house alarm, and smile— you're on candid camera. Long story short, our prank landed us at the police station."

"What did your parents do?"

"They were nice enough to get my record expunged, only after a hundred hours of soup kitchen duty."

She pulled her knees to her chest. "Well, if that's all you have, Mr. Perfect."

He twisted his fingers together, stared at the knot he created. "But worse than jail was breaking my fiancée's heart."

"Your fiancée? You were engaged?" She'd known Zak for a long time, and never had he mentioned a girlfriend, past or present. Her stomach fluttered.

"I was… to my high school sweetheart. She used to be the only person I could say I ever loved."

Lacey didn't want to assume too much, but it sounded as if he had a new love. Her chest caved. What if the reason they broke up was because she had cornered him into moving in with her? "Oh, so you're in love with someone."

"No—I mean yes." He turned his head towards Lacey, stared long enough her skin prickled. "Let's end with *it's complicated*."

Great, her problems were ruining everybody's life. "But if—"

"If nothing else, I've learned you can't force people to be with you when they're not ready." He rubbed the tip of his nose. "So can I finish?"

She struggled to let it go, knew if she dug deeper she might reach the truth. But what would that do? Open more earth to swallow her?

"I'll take your silence as a yes. She wanted to get married, so I proposed even though I wasn't ready. Back then, the girls loved me, and I loved the attention."

Lacey caught sight of the splotchy pink patches, only a shade lighter than the antiqued brick in her room, spreading across Zak's neck while she listened.

"I'd mess up, and she'd take me back. That went on until I guess she'd had enough. She left the engagement ring I gave her on the counter with a note that said, *I'm not the one, but I hope you find her.*"

"I imagine that was hard."

"Yeah, it was. I tried to forget her with more women, but it didn't work. So after a year, I drove back home with the ring, ready to prove I'd changed."

"Where's home?" And why had she never asked?

"Madison, Connecticut. It's a small coastal town about two hours away. I'll take you there one day, let you meet my family." He tugged at his t-shirt collar. "Sorry, that came out weird."

"It's not weird."

He tipped his head towards her, gave her a look of disbelief.

She caved. "Okay, a little, but only because of the arrangement. Can you finish the story?"

"There's not much left to tell. She married someone else."

"A year later?"

He shrugged. "People don't always need long engagements. Look at how fast we tied the knot." The corner of his mouth rose as if pulled by a string.

She whacked his bicep. "Stop, it's not the time for jokes." She grinned but wished she hadn't. Her circumstances were anything but humorous. "Well, for whatever it's worth, I'm sorry that happened to you."

He shifted in bed. "I'm not. It made me realize what I want in a relationship."

Lacey stroked the side of her arm. "And what do you want?"

"The same as everybody else. Someone I can be myself around, someone who makes me smile—and now here I am," he said, chuckling.

He couldn't resist jokes, and she couldn't resist reality. He was a guy any girl would be lucky to have. A girl with time to invest in a relationship, she reminded herself. Yet, here he was with her, stuck in a gridlock of lies while possibly losing out on the love of his life.

She dropped her gaze. "Yes, here you are, dead center in my pile of crap."

He lifted her chin. "Hey, don't forget the pound of sugar on top. I'm fond of sweets."

"But when everything is said and done… it's still shit."

Zak burst out laughing. And it wasn't long before Lacey followed with a few rounds of her own. Between the anthology of funny childhood stories he told and the assortment of hilarious online videos they watched, the laughter continued. In fact, it made her temporarily forget about the mess she had created.

In that moment, her mind was on something other than the replicating cells inside her uterus. And for a brief time, she didn't have to think about non-negotiable family dinners. Instead, she focused on the guy who thought cannon-balling into an ice-layered pool was smart.

And sometime between that video and the end of another showing a teen flipping off his bike into a pile of manure, Lacey fell asleep.

The next morning, she awoke to her head resting on Zak's chest, and his arm wrapped around her. It knocked the breath out of her. What if they… no, they couldn't have, could they?

She sat up straight. "Zak!"

"Um-huh," he mumbled, with his eyes still closed.

She pushed him. "Wake up, we need to talk."

He stretched and halfway opened one eye. "Did something happen?"

Lacey gripped her chest. "I don't know. You tell me. What are you doing in my bed? Did we…?"

He scratched his head. "What? No, we fell asleep."

She fisted the covers. "Are you one-hundred percent positive?"

He pulled himself up in bed. "We're both fully dressed. Besides, I'd remember if we did something. Sex is not something you forget."

Unless you have sex amnesia, she mumbled. But he had a point. They were in the same clothes from last night. Somewhat relieved, she fell back on her pillow and exhaled. She had to be more careful, exercise more caution, and beware of compromising positions, even potential ones. Life was complicated enough right now. She didn't need to add to the complication.

She pushed her curls out of her face. "I'd say it's time to put rules in place. To start, both of our bedrooms should be off limits. If we talk, hang-out, or whatever, it needs to be in the living room."

Zak narrowed his eyes. "Are you suggesting the sofa's the best place to prevent us from sleeping together?"

"I'm just saying we should stay out of each other's personal areas. We shouldn't fall sleep snuggled up together as if we're married."

"We are married."

"Not legally. Besides, you know what I mean. One minute we're cuddled innocently, and the next we're taking it places we shouldn't, doing things that friends shouldn't do, and then—"

"And then everything is awkward and someone's trying to forget it ever happened. Yeah, I know what you mean."

Lacey relaxed against the fluffy softness of her foam mattress topper. "Good, we understand each other. Now, on to the next topic— PDA. At work, it's only hand-holding or a kiss on the forehead or cheek. Lips are off limits. If someone tries to force us to do that again, one of us has to make an excuse and leave. If that's not possible, then I'll pretend to be sick, which won't be hard since I am most of the time."

Zak rubbed the back of his neck. "Wow, sounds like you've covered all bases."

"Not quite, there's one last thing. My parents insist on throwing us a reception." She took a deep breath. "The problem is they'll expect us to kiss. They're too touchy-feely for less. So an open-mouthed peck on the lips will have to do, but I swear to God if you stick your tongue in my mouth, I'll bite it off."

He jerked back. "Wow, was I that terrible of a kisser?"

He was the best kiss she'd ever had, but she'd never tell. "The quality is not the point. It's about—"

"Let me guess, not crossing the line?"

She nodded. "Exactly."

"Okay. Well, I might need an instruction manual to move forward."

"I can write it down for you."

"I was joking. But am I allowed to suggest something?" He slid closer. "What if we go with whatever feels natural? That way we won't have to stress over every detail. It'll be more realistic. Who knows, it might even be enjoyable."

She didn't expect him to understand. His parents' good name wouldn't be destroyed if he screwed up the finance budget, but if she failed, hers would. And she was sure his dad never had a heart attack because of him, but hers had. And she would never risk it happening again. With a straight face, she asked, "Can you follow the plan or not?"

"Yes, but only because I already agreed." He pinched her cheek. "Now, lighten up."

She wrapped a curl around her finger. "I will—if I live through the dinner with my parents on Friday."

Because her parents might be a lot of things, but fools they were not.

9

Lacey's eyes blurred. "I can't do this."

Zak rushed over to her side. "What are you talking about? You've been prepping for this dinner all week. You can't bail."

"There's too many moving parts. I can barely keep up with them." Her arms fell limp to her sides. "If I mess up one detail, they'll know it's a con. They're that good."

"Give me a sec," he said, reaching into his satchel and dragging out two boxes. "Which is why I purchased these. One more detail you don't have to worry about."

Curious, Lacey stared at them. "What are those?"

He passed her the tiny box. "Open it."

She fumbled the package in her hands, her fingers sliding across the frictionless outer coating.

"Let me help." He took it from her and opened it, presenting Lacey a lovely wedding band set, the full shebang complete with a princess-cut diamond engagement ring.

Her mouth fell into a perfect oval and froze. "Zak, this is—"

"Necessary, if we want people to believe our story," he said, removing a thick, yellow gold ring from the second box.

"This is too much. You could have gone simpler, and cheaper."

"It'll be fine. The jeweler assured me they'd buy them when, or if, I needed to bring them back." He tucked the empty boxes inside his satchel.

"If? Of course, you'll need to return them. I mean, not this minute, but when we divorce."

He dropped his head and slid the ring onto his finger. "Yeah... I don't know why I said *if*."

She gazed at the diamond, noted the gray and white sparkles of the stone, and found it hard to take her eyes off of it. In her detailed planning for Friday night, wedding rings had skipped her mind. But they would have been the first missing thing her parents noticed.

She turned from the glistening ring and met his soft eyes, circles of amber hugged by jade. And without saying a word, he tugged at her conscience, made her want to confess the truth that perched itself on the tip of her tongue. He was a decent person, and he deserved it. At the minimum, she owed him that much.

But what would she say?

He waved a hand in front of her face. "Ready? The driver is here."

She would say nothing, not until she had something to say. Nodding, she followed him to the waiting car.

The taxi stopped in front of Lacey's parents' Tudor-styled home in Scarsdale, NY. It was a charming half-cobblestone, half-brick, 1928 charmer that her parents had purchased and renovated a few years back to ease their way out of the noisy city. Her mother swore it was just an excuse for Lacey's dad to put his architectural skills to work on a space of his own for once.

Zak paid the driver as Lacey's nerves bounced all over the place. She prayed for a disaster-free dinner. Zak reached his hand out to hers and stared at her with understanding eyes. "Okay, Mrs. Cooper. Let's go wow them."

She intertwined her fingers with his. A necessary display of affection, she told herself. "Do you want to review the index cards?"

"Absolutely not."

She didn't push the issue. And before they could ring the doorbell, Lacey's mom and sister barreled outside to greet them. Her mom squeezed Zak. "It is so good to meet you—finally."

He returned the gesture. "You too, Kathleen."

"You'll call me, Mom. I insist." She pinched his cheek. "Aren't you so handsome?"

He glanced over at Lacey and grinned. "Thank you... Mom."

"Don't make him uncomfortable. Everyone's not as touchy-feely as you are." Kate, with her cascading ringlet curls and green-eyes, pushed her mother out of the way and eased in for her own introduction. "Hi, I'm Kate, Lacey's much younger sister."

Lacey scoffed. "Is that what you consider thirteen months? We're nearly twins."

"Can we bring the party indoor ladies—and gentleman?" Austin, Kate's ex-NFL player husband, stood by the doorway waving everyone into the house with his beefy hands.

Once inside, Lacey's father met at the door, wrapping his long, heavy arms around Lacey. "How's my girl doing?"

Her heart tangoed in her chest. "I'm doing good, Dad."

He leaned back, gripped Lacey's shoulder. "Be honest with me. I know more about what's happening than you realize."

She couldn't believe it, but somehow he had figured out she was lying to him. Her breath caught in her throat as beads of sweat rolled across her skin. He took one look at her clammy skin and then carried her to the couch. "Lay down, you look terrible."

Zak rushed to her side as Austin and Kate stood behind him.

Lacey's dad turned to her mother. "Get a cool towel and something she can throw up in. Take deep breaths, Lacey."

Panicked, she had to find out what he meant. "What do you know?"

"How sick pregnancy makes you. Kathleen had it terrible with you girls, and Kate's already vomited three times since she arrived this morning."

Wait, why was Kate vomiting? "What's wrong with Kate?"

"Well, we planned to surprise you at dinner, but she's pregnant, too," Lacey's mom squealed. "Isn't this wonderful news? I'll be a Gigi twice in one year."

Lacey steeled herself against a flash of—she hated to claim it— envy. And just what the heck was a *Gigi*? The sound of it elicited images of strip clubs and plastic surgeons. But back to Kate, who had now traveled the socially accepted path: college, career, marriage, and then a baby—by winging it. And to where had Lacey's detailed life-plan, complete with step-by-step, no-fail instructions, brought her? To unwed motherhood.

She sank into the sofa.

Zak took the wet cloth from Lacey's mom and laid it across Lacey's forehead. "Do you need your nausea medicine?"

She yanked him towards her, whispered in his ear. "Will it knock me out?"

He raised one brow, twisted the corner of his mouth. "I don't think so."

"Why not?" Pressure built up behind her eyes, threatened to bring tears.

Her dad squeezed in close. "Are you feeling better yet? Do you want something to drink?"

Only if you waterboard me with it. She knew he never would. "No, thank you. I got lightheaded, but it passed."

In slow motion, Lacey returned to a sitting position and removed the cloth.

"Hold on for a second," Lacey's dad said, "I don't want you to jump up right away. Just rest here for a while. Zak can get you what you need."

He turned and offered a hand to Zak. "So you're my new son-in-law?"

Lacey pressed her lips together. This was a stupid plan.

"I am, sir," Zak said, shaking his hand.

Her dad returned to his worn recliner. "You realize I wanted to walk my daughter down the aisle."

Zak stuttered. "Well, I—"

"Stay calm, son. I'm not upset. While I'd have loved to see her in a stunning white gown, I recognize she's a career-focused woman with little time to plan anything other than the next skyscraper. So it only makes sense why she waited to tell us. I hope you appreciate that great girl you have there."

"Yes, sir, I do." He took Lacey's hand. "I really do."

Goosebumps crept across her skin.

"I still can't believe your due date's two weeks before mine. So unfair," Kate said with a pouty face as her and Austin sat on the plush sofa across from Lacey and Zak.

"You'll survive," Lacey's mom said, bringing out a silver tray filled with crostini, olive oil flatbreads, red grapes, and mozzarella cheese cubes. She called it a pregnancy-friendly platter.

Lacey's dad stole a few cubes of cheese from the platter.

Lacey's mother snatched them back, passed him crostini instead. "Dan, you're supposed to be watching your cholesterol."

"Why not just feed me cardboard?" He frowned, tapping the hard bread.

Zak and Austin passed on the appetizers, opted for cold beers.

"So Zak, did you always know my sister was the one for you?" Kate asked, tossing her legs over Austin's lap as he chugged a big gulp of Modelo.

Lacey forced the building saliva down her throat and braced for the ad-libbed version.

"No. At first, I thought she'd be a cocky woman who stuffed

corporate's pockets, but she surprised me with her huge heart. And during our late night work sessions, I watched her battle for larger offices, bigger break rooms, and better parking, things that help the consumer, the employee. Those gestures made me fall in love with her."

He anchored his eyes onto Lacey's. "But what made me want to marry her was the night I spilled cherry Fanta on her carpet. I guess you could say I left a permanent stain on her carpet, and she left a permanent mark on my heart."

She waited for the chuckle, waited for the one-sided dimple that often came with his jokes. But his expression didn't change. And no longer able to take the strange emotions pulsing through her, Lacey broke the stare. Maybe it was annoyance at him mentioning that stupid night again, but then again, he had improvised the moment so well even she believed him.

And so did everyone else. Austin scratched his shaved head. Kate swiped tears with the arm of her sweater. Her mother's joy bubbled like a carbonated soda two shakes from an explosion. Her dad? He beamed the grandest, toothiest smile ever. And the funny thing about it—not one of them had any damn idea what happened on cherry Fanta night—not even Lacey, not really.

"Shoot, I have to check the chicken." Lacey's mother scurried into the kitchen.

"The first moment I saw Kate, I knew she was the one," Austin said.

"Are you going to force us to listen to the *it was fate we bumped into each other at that conference we almost didn't attend* story for the thousandth time?" Lacey asked.

Kate gasped.

"I'm just kidding," Lacey said, secretly hoping not to have to listen to another version of the same story. A timer sounded. *Saved by the bell,* Lacey mumbled.

"Dinner's done," Lacey's mom announced.

They followed her into the kitchen and gathered around the large rectangular table. In the center was a spread of boneless baked chicken, green beans, stewed potatoes, and rolls. It was an assortment of pregnancy-friendly food, her mom reminded them.

"Just because the girls can't eat, Kathleen, doesn't mean I have to suffer." Lacey's dad complained.

"You might not be pregnant, Dan, but your heart is a patchwork quilt. So consider this part of your cardiac-friendly diet. Now, eat more, complain less." Lacey's mother snapped the hand towel at him and giggled.

And they ate, filling their mouths with great food and their souls with good conversation. Her dad interrogated Zak on his family, interests, hobbies, career-goals, and love for Lacey—which he answered with ease. But the important thing, Lacey reminded herself, was dinner with her family was going just as she hoped.

"Well, I don't know about you guys, but I'm ready for dessert." Her mother stood, then planted a loving kiss on Lacey's dad's lips.

Lacey cringed. "Mom, in front of guests?"

"We're married adults who love each other. If you give a man a good meal and a good kiss, you'll keep him for life."

Kate giggled, grabbing both sides of Austin's cheeks. "Since I haven't been cooking, I guess I better give you an extraordinary one to make up for it." Kate kissed Austin in an overly wet display of lip-smacking.

Lacey looked to the striped table cloth and bi-color napkins, something other than the lip-locking. She knew they'd expect her and Zak to go next.

And they did.

"Okay, your turn," Kate said, pointing at Lacey.

"Family tradition," her dad added.

"Yes, and Zak is family." Her mother lifted a few dirty plates into her arms.

Zak crept towards Lacey with the stealth of a hunter coming in for the kill. She tried to be the willing prey, even puckered her quivering lips. But millimeters shy of impact, she bailed, dropping her head so fast his kiss landed in her hairline.

He coughed and extracted a curl from his mouth.

Kate scrunched her face. "What was that?"

Lacey turned to her dad, now taking a swig of his beer, and then to her mother who remained expressionless, collecting dirty plates. "How about you girls help me take care of these?"

Zak stood with his own plate in hand. "I can help."

Lacey's mom waved him back into his seat. "No, we've got this. Hang out with the men."

In the kitchen, Kate rinsed and Lacey loaded while their mother packed leftovers into glass storage containers. With the last dish tucked in the dishwasher rack, Lacey's mom turned to Kate. "Thanks, honey. Why don't you check on the guys? Lacey and I can handle the rest."

"I don't—"

Her mother all but pushed Kate into the living room. "Go ahead. We'll be right behind you."

"Whatever you say..." Kate made her way through the swinging door.

Once she was out of sight, Lacey's mom yanked off her apron. "Lacey Ann Winters, what's going on with you? And you better not lie."

A mother's intuition, Lacey thought, as she twisted the dish towel around her wrist. "What do you mean?"

"You and Zak, something's not right. He is saying the right things. He's handsome, successful, and I can tell he's madly in love with you. But it is you I question. You jump every time he touches you. Why is that?"

Great, she was being punished because Zak was the better actor. "I don't know what you mean."

"Do you love him?"

Did Zak stir her emotions, send sensations through her body she had never felt? Maybe, but it didn't matter. The question was about the feelings a married woman should have for her husband. And that answer was easy. "Yes, why else would we have a baby together?"

Her mom wiped crumbs from the counter. "Then why aren't you showing it?"

Lacey's head dropped. "I'm worried I disappointed you guys by keeping it a secret. I didn't have a big wedding like Kate."

Her mom drew closer. "You realize there's more than one way to get your panty hose over your bum, don't you? As long as you're happy, we're happy. For God's sake, we're having two grandchildren in the same year. That's a dream come true, don't you think?"

"Yes." Lacey dared not say anything different.

"Good, because you've got a loving husband out there and a beautiful baby growing inside you. Enjoy them. Life is too short for less." She untangled Lacey's arms. "Now, you have our full support to go show your husband some love."

Lacey's mom left her no choice but to be affectionate if she wanted them to believe the fairy-tale she'd created. Lacey dragged in as much air as she could and proceeded into the living room with her mom following behind.

"Just in time," her dad said, pulling Lacey's mom onto his lap.

"We're starting a movie."

On the sofa next to her parents, Austin played with Kate's perfect curls as they snuggled under a colorful afghan blanket, both of them relaxed. Unlike Zak, whose posture resembled an arthritic man. A folded quilt rested nearby on the sofa arm. Lacey glided in beside him until their legs touched. Her skin vibrated.

Time to turn on the romance. "Let's lay down?"

He studied her briefly. Then satisfied, he pressed his back against the fluffy cushions, leaving only a tiny sliver of free space for Lacey. She wedged herself into it, so close whiffs of deodorant and fabric softener filled her nostrils in an oddly sexy blend. She closed her eyes and inhaled. The incoming pheromones, the front of his body pushed into the back of hers, made her shiver with unforeseen delight.

"Are you cold?" Zak covered her with the quilt.

If anything, she was burning up, but he didn't need to know. "That's better, thanks."

From the corner of her eye, Lacey caught the smile on her mother's face. If nothing else, this was another step towards convincing them. And to persuade even the harshest of skeptics, she left Zak's arms wrapped around her throughout the entire movie, right until the cheesy ending when the star rushed into the airport and stopped the woman of his dreams from getting on a plane. As predicted, the enamored woman threw down her bags, jumped into the man's arms, and planted a passionate kiss on his lips.

And it was in that predictable but heartwarming ending that Zak's own lips grazed the nape of Lacey's neck.

She froze, despite his warm breath dancing across her skin, urging her to let loose, to give in to temptation. She rolled over to face him, reminded herself she would do this out of necessity, not want. He drew in a heavy breath, pressed his forehead against hers and closed his eyes. She admired his long, auburn lashes.

And while she had to kiss him so they'd believe her story, there was a part of her that wanted this, wanted him, wanted his hands, the ones that cradled her neck and her lower back at the same time.

His lips crept cautiously closer. It took all her willpower to resist pillaging them like they were the last basket of bread on earth and she a starving girl. Caging the feral woman inside her, she waited, held her lips in place as he brushed his lightly against hers.

Gentle at first. Delicate taps. Then stronger, deeper, and more frenzied as the brewing storm sucked them into the whirling clouds. It was a Kansas tornado, sweeping Lacey's arms around Zak's neck and twisting their mouths together with force.

It was a tempest like none other.

She couldn't remember how long they stayed trapped against one other. How long the only sound between them, the crack of lightning. But what she did know was that the wild arcs sparking around them cast their relationship into a different light—and it terrified Lacey.

"Now, that's a real kiss," her mom said, giving them a thumb's up.

Lacey swallowed hard, fearing her mom might be right. Something about that kiss felt incredibly real.

And *real* couldn't happen.

10

For the first time, Lacey skipped her normal Saturday routine and called her private investigator, Mr. Duke. He didn't answer any of her ten calls, which worried her. But then again, it was the weekend. So she would give him that. And in his defense, investigating probably required talking to people, scanning through collected data, not promptly answering every call, she reminded herself.

Either way, something had to be done. This whole shenanigan had gone too far, crossed set boundaries. And before she'd let her friendship with Zak suffer any long-term damage, she'd fix the mess she created.

She straggled into the kitchen and spotted Zak by the stove. He half-placed a lid on a boiling pot, and after wiping his hands on a dish towel, tossed it over his shoulders.

She studied him. Not that what he had on was appealing—unless a mismatched pairing of athletic shorts, t-shirt, and worn bedroom shoes qualified. And considering his wild, tousled hair matched his day-old stubble, Lacey couldn't even be sure he had showered.

Nothing about him should have been sexy, but everything about his long, toned legs standing in her compact kitchen—completely unaware of her presence—was damn sexy.

No! She yelled without words. He wasn't sexy. Or better yet, he shouldn't be sexy, not to her anyway.

"Lacey?" He lifted his head just enough she caught his eyes, the ones that stared at her so long he missed the escaping water. It sent a sizzling burst of steam into the air, snagging his attention and hers. He turned off the burner and moved the pot.

She eased over to him. The juice of chopped fruit, drops of soy milk, some unknown powdery substance, and a melting ice-cube covered the counters, along with the drying residue of whatever had boiled over the pot.

He gestured to the spread. "I've made you banana ginger oatmeal and a smoothie I'm freezing into little cubes for later."

He impressed her. "You cook?"

He chuckled. "Your mom might have given me some instructions." He held up a stack of index cards scribbled with recipes. "I see where you get your love for these things."

Lacey nodded. "Oh, so she put you up to this?"

"I asked her for some ideas… to help with the morning sickness."

She couldn't stop the heat climbing her body or the tug of her mouth upwards. "How thoughtful."

He reached for the lid and grazed the burner by accident. His finger went straight to his mouth where he blew large puffs of air at it. "Um… that was hot." He shook it.

"Ooh, let me help you." Lacey guided him to the sink and held his hand as she ran cool water over the burn. "How's that?"

He looked at her, his hand still in hers. "Much better."

She avoided staring too long. "You know I'm indebted to you for following along with this sham. When it's all said and done, I hope we don't get fired and that my parents forgive me—and you." She turned off the faucet and then patted the burn dry, examining it a last time. "Good, no blisters."

"As far as I could tell your parents loved me. I think the kiss sealed the deal." His face flashed pink, and his one-sided dimple showed.

She bet it did but feared it had been more genuine than necessary. Her stomach twisted in knots. "Yeah about that, I—"

He held up a finger. "Hold that thought." He slung some oatmeal in a bowl and passed it to her before rushing off to the TV that had been playing in the background. "You have to watch this."

She took a bite of the concoction and was pleasantly surprised. "Watch what?"

"This singing competition. Wait until you hear Lebron, he's amazing." Zak focused on the screen. "The finale comes on tonight, so I'm catching up on the last episode I missed."

He had pulled the distraction card, and it worked. She couldn't take her eyes off the TV or keep the oatmeal out of her mouth, rejoicing over being able to tolerate both. But when the show ended, with her on team Cierra and Zak on team Lebron, it was time to talk.

Zak flicked through the channels, stopping on a random action movie as she placed the empty bowl on the accent table beside her. "About the kiss…"

He kept his eyes on the television. "You don't want to repeat it."

"No, I meant yes. No… well… only in front of my parents. I just don't want to confuse our emotions."

He looked at her. "So you're saying you felt something when you kissed me?"

She jerked her head. "You kissed me."

He shrugged. "You kissed me back."

Both of Lacey's hands shot into the air. "Okay, I kissed you, too. My point is—now I can't remember what I was about to say." She huffed.

He angled his body towards her. "Let me help. You felt something when you kissed me, and that scared you. So you don't want it to happen again."

What could she argue? It was the truth. But on a positive note, at least he understood. "Let's keep it on a friend level, agreed?"

"I think living together and playing married throws the friend thing out the window. But hey, if that's what you want, I'll do my best to oblige." A commercial advertising 3-D ultrasounds flashed across the television. "Enough serious talk, have you thought about what you're having?"

More like why I'm having a stranger's baby, she said to herself. "Not really."

"Why don't we try to figure it out?"

She rolled her eyes. "It's too early."

He gave her a cheesy grin. "Come on, it'll be fun. Something other than work and lectures."

She didn't know how fun it would be, but he stirred her curiosity. "Okay, whatever."

After an extensive internet search for gender tests, Zak tied his fake wedding ring on a string and held it above Lacey's stomach. "That proves it, it's a boy."

"It says right here if it swings in a circle, it's a girl," Lacey placed her finger next to the descriptive caption underneath the picture with curved arrows showing rotation.

"It's swinging side-to-side," Zak motioned at the ring flowing in a pattern that was neither side-to-side nor circular but a mix of both.

"This isn't working. Give me another one."

Zak scanned through the vast array of articles. "I could sprinkle salt on your head while you're sleeping." He chuckled, rubbing Lacey's legs that had somehow landed across his lap.

She ignored the sensation spreading to places she would rather not think about at a time like this. "If you sprinkle salt in my hair, I'm liable to kill you."

"Noted—salt equals death. Well, it's too soon to know if you're carrying high or low, although you're showing just a little." His hand almost skimmed her belly, but she blocked him.

"What else is on the list?"

"Chinese gender calendar? Tell me the month you conceived."

Lacey's skin tingled. She had an estimated conception date, but did she really want to remind herself of how little she knew about her condition. "Skip that. What's next?"

"Okay. Got one." Zak reached in his pocket and pulled out the apartment key she had given him. He placed it on her stomach.

"Are you leaving?"

"No silly, grab it." Lacey snatched it up by the narrow end, and Zak confirmed it meant she was having a boy.

"Who came up with that craziness? Better yet, who's foolish enough to buy into any of this hocus pocus stuff?" Without thinking, she lifted her foot and poked her big toe at Zak's chest.

He pretended to chomp at it while spinning his eyes around in circles. "Be careful. I might just have a crazy foot fetish."

"You do not," Lacey said, rolling in laughter.

"Do too." Zak pulled Lacey's foot over to his mouth and acted like he would bite her toes.

"Stop! Stop!" Lacey screamed at him in a ticklish fit that left her floundering around like someone who'd been tasered. Zak let go, and she caught her breath. "I don't remember being tickled like that since I was a child."

"My dad tickled me and my brother until I left for college. It was his source of motivation. He would tell us to go get something or do something, and if we didn't move fast enough, he'd rush in for the tickle, send us to our knees."

Lacey giggled. "That sounds like torture."

"It beats the alternative. My dad always looked for creative ways to handle things, even arguments with my mom. In the middle of a heated debate, he would make the most ridiculous joke, and my mom couldn't help but laugh. It'd be just enough to forget being furious."

"It was that easy."

"Most of the time. One thing's for sure, he never held grudges. He taught us to not hold them either. 'Don't take on extra burdens. It's as simple as forgiving,' he would tell us."

Lacey's conscience surfaced. She knew telling Zak the truth was the correct thing to do and hadn't he opened the door by expressing his innate sense of forgiveness? It was in his blood. But no matter how much she believed him, wanted to just rid herself of the lie, she couldn't. It was not a risk she was willing to take, not before finding the father.

And she'd admit, having him around was growing on her. "Your dad sounds fantastic."

"My whole family is. Maybe you could meet them one day?"

"Maybe…" She turned her attention to the phone in his hand. "Anything more scientific or fact-based?"

He continued scrolling. "You can buy a gender test at the local drugstore."

"Seriously, they sell those? What are we waiting for?" Lacey darted to the coat rack, dragging Zak with her. She tied her trench coat around her waist, hoping to cover up the tattered t-shirt that had become her favorite pajama staple. "I'm praying no one recognizes us."

And no one did.

They returned from the drugstore thirty-dollars poorer. Lacey rushed into the bathroom with the baby gender test kit which required —urine. Why did everything to do with pregnancy involve urine samples? She had no clue. And who was she to complain when the gender of her baby was one science experiment away?

After transferring the sample from one vial to another, she opened the door so that Zak could witness the results firsthand. It sizzled, bubbled, and then turned a brilliant orange that, according to the color-coded label, showed a girl. "See, it's a girl," Lacey shouted, adding a few gyrations of her non-existent hips.

"Celebrate now, but—shoot! What time is it?"

Lacey pulled out her phone. "Six, why?"

Zak shot down the hall and waved for her to join him. "The finale, it's started."

He sprawled out on the compact sofa while Lacey poured herself some apple juice. It sloshed close to the edge of the glass when she caught sight of Zak, his hands behind his head and his calves dangling over the sofa edge. The white t-shirt he wore stretched across his chest, giving Lacey full view of his muscular tone. Her eyes explored every inch, every hill.

To her, Zak had perfect pecs. And it didn't even matter he had a four-pack of abs instead of six, they were perfect too.

Lacey found her way to the chair next to the couch.

"You can lay here?" He patted a sliver of space that would leave her wedged against him throughout the hour-long episode.

She considered how warm it would feel snuggled against him once again, how soothing the touch of his lips to her neck. She shut down the R-rated thoughts swiftly. "I'm good over here, thanks."

"No problem. As long as you're in the room when my boy Lebron takes down your girl Cierra."

She snickered. "If she sings like she did on the semi-final episode, I doubt Lebron will stand a chance."

"We. Shall. See."

And after a round of intense vocals highlighting Cierra's range and Lebron's beat-boxing talent, Bryan Seagull announced the winner. Lebron took home the prize, a major recording contract and a million dollars. Zak leaped off the sofa into a victory dance that looked like a fleeing chicken. "I told you," he said.

Lacey rolled around on the couch in hard laughter at his performance, which proved more entertaining than the finale itself.

He stopped. "Oh, you think I'm funny, huh?" He reached down and pulled Lacey to her feet. "Show me your moves. I call a dance-off."

Lacey used both hands to cover her face. "What? You're crazy. I'm not doing that."

He ignored her protest and put his workout playlist on full volume. "I'm not taking no for an answer. Besides, it's good exercise." He returned to his dancing attempt.

The beats had a fast tempo, and he bopped straight up and down to each of them with the rhythm of a Jack Russell Terrier. Lacey giggled with her mouth covered, still reluctant to join him. But Zak's persistent urging and his ability to make a fool out of himself allowed her to let loose.

Why not have fun? No one was here, except Zak. And it was obvious he didn't care if she embarrassed herself. So she started slow, a little shake of a leg, a gentle sway of the body. But then, as the music filled her, she grooved around the coffee table, arms and legs flinging all over, embracing the freedom of not having to impress anyone. The freedom from awkward stares and judgment. She could thrust her hips, hop on one leg, cluck like a chicken, and no one would ever be the wiser.

She let her hair down. For the first time in forever, she really let her hair down.

But when the music changed over to the slow melody of *Perfect* by Ed Sheeran, they both froze.

"Sorry, I guess it played through all the workout tracks," he said, reaching for the phone.

"It's okay." Lacey blushed, shifting from one foot to the other, steadying her breathing.

He stretched his eyes and offered a hand. "Well, may I have this dance?"

She obliged.

He placed his hand high on her hip and drew her body in as close as she would allow, which left a measurable space between them. Swaying clumsily, he dodged her feet while she resisted eye contact. But when Ed belted out the run *dancing in the dark,* Zak spun Lacey far away from him, the distance of both their arm spans.

The twirl ignited a shrill of laughter as she raveled back into his arms, this time breaking the barrier of personal space. This time they were closer than ever. His eyes locked onto hers as his hand slipped around her lower back and pressed her body against his. And when his mouth drew closer, she lost her mind.

Entranced, she shifted onto the tips of her toes and longed for the soft touch of his lips. Longed for the warmth of his breath. And waited for both. But this wasn't about what she wanted. It was about what she needed.

And kissing him didn't qualify as a need.

She flattened her feet and buried her face in his chest. "We can't." Her words came out as an exasperated plea.

He tucked her wild curls behind her ear, stroked the side of her face with a delicate touch. "Why not Lacey? We've kissed before."

She bathed in his light touch, listened to his heart pounding away with the power of a thoroughbred herd. It stoked her inner flame. But she held steady, fought the pull of passion until the intensity of battle overwhelmed her.

She yanked herself from his hold. "But if we kiss now, it's different. I—we—just can't." She rushed down the hall and into her bedroom where she collapsed in tears.

And when the cloud of emotion cleared just enough for her to catch her breath, it left a trail of mascara across Lacey's cheeks. Nothing that a make-up wipe couldn't fix.

Or better yet, a determined visit to Mr. Duke.

The next morning, she rose from bed and dressed in a casual outfit and comfortable sneakers. On the way out, she grabbed a warm jacket and locked the door behind her—while Zak slept. And even though Mr. Duke hadn't returned her calls, she planned to visit him, regardless. She would wait with the pigeons on his stoop all day if she had to because it was that important.

She hailed a cab.

Arriving at his front door, she noticed someone had repaired his sign. No longer did it only show the letters *Y*, *U*, and *K*, but his full name, *Henry Duke*. It was a good omen.

Encouraged, she buzzed the door and waited—no answer. She repeated the process—still, no answer. With a balled fist, she knocked with the same response—silence. *So much for a plan.*

Out of options, she brushed off the top step and sat. And when a nippy breeze blew past, she zipped her jacket.

Lines of vehicles trafficked the city street, mostly taxis and other paid drivers. And as she stared at each passing one, she wondered how some of them passed the emissions test. The fumes suffocated her.

She should call him again, she thought, reaching into her purse for her phone, searching around lipstick, sunglasses, her wallet. But she came up empty-handed. *Great, I left it in the bathroom.*

She stared at the early morning sky, the rays of light breaking the horizon above the surrounding skyscrapers, and regretted not being more prepared. Now she would have to go back to the apartment—without speaking to Mr. Duke. Frustrated, she jumped to her feet and marched towards the street, her hand in the air for the approaching cab.

It stopped.

And out stepped Mr. Duke wearing the same t-shirt he had when they first met, minus the mustard stain. Lacey pressed her palms together and mouthed a *thank you God*.

He waddled over. "Lacey?"

"Sorry to stop by without an appointment, but we need to talk," she said, following him to the front door.

"Yeah, yeah, no problem." He fumbled the key before finally opening the door.

She maneuvered inside to the same smells, the same clutter, and the same flea market chair. "Mr. Duke, I need answers. I'm running out of time."

He dropped his keys and picked them up, shoved them in his pocket. "I understand, and I'm working on it. It's harder than you think."

Lacey squeezed the edge of his desk. "What is so hard? I gave you my entire itinerary for the weeks in question. All you have to do is eliminate possibilities."

He stroked his beard and stared at the computer screen he had yet to power on. "And that's what I've been doing. But it is time consuming."

Her face quivered, shaking loose tears. "I don't have time. I don't even know how much longer I can keep up this charade."

He dug into the drawer beside him, came up with nothing. Went to the next drawer, nothing. He spun his chair around and shuffled through several containers before producing a half-crushed box of kleenexes. He removed the first few, all either torn or stained, and tossed them in the trash. Then he passed the box to Lacey.

Out of necessity, she took one.

"Please don't cry. I ran into a minor complication."

The room rocked. "A complication?"

He scratched his head, then blew across his fingers tips. "Nothing major, I promise. The surveillance camera on your floor malfunctioned, or got twisted in the wrong direction. The problem is it shows the hall area right before your apartment door but not the door itself. I can see the people that headed in your direction, but I can't see if they went inside."

Lacey's body sank into the chair. "What does that mean?"

"It means I have to dig deeper, since we know the event happened at your place. Now, there are five apartments after yours, so I have to cross-reference any man walking past the camera with ties to your neighbors." He shifted in his seat. "As of now, I've narrowed the list to six potentials."

"Six? I would never…"

"Don't fixate on the number. I'm still working through those." He reached for his notebook and knocked over a half-full Sprite can. The flat soda ran across his desk and dripped onto the already stained carpet.

At least it wasn't red Fanta, Lacey thought. Not that she believed he'd call the carpet cleaners to remove it, considering his method for taking care of the current spill involved piling the remaining Kleenexes on it.

And she had put her faith in this man?

Mr. Duke covered his mouth and belched. The rumbling belly quake that followed disgusted Lacey. "Excuse me. Chili and eggs didn't quite agree with me." He kept his hand there for a few more seconds while he expelled the last of his air. "Yeah, these I couldn't rule out so easily. But there was a repeat visitor... um... Zak Cooper. Do you know him?"

"Oh, he's the one I said exclude. We've been working on a major project together."

Mr. Duke cocked his head. "Are you sure it's not him?"

"One hundred percent. If it was, he would have said something— trust me."

"Well, looks like you're down to five already. While I can't guarantee they visited your apartment, I can guarantee one of them is the daddy." He tapped his pointer finger against the paper. He burped again, then held out the crinkled report. "He is on here for sure."

She paused before taking the list, her stomach pressing against her backbone, the same as it did on the upward climb of a roller coaster. With shaky hands, she took it from Mr. Duke's hand and studied it. None of the names were recognizable. They were all strangers. "This can't be right. I don't have sex with random people."

"I don't know what you do in your personal life, but I do know the father is on that list. You said you have a history with Zak, right? Maybe he's the one?"

If they would have crossed the friend zone, Zak would have said something. "Like I said, not possible."

"Well, looks like a stranger it is."

She scraped her teeth over her bottom lip. With no alternative explanation, she resigned herself to accepting the list Mr. Duke had provided her. "Please keep me updated of any new information," she said, paying him the remaining dues for his services.

"For sure, you know I will."

In the back of the cab, on a cracked leather seat, she stared at the daunting list. Her stomach churned at the notion that one of those men —each a stranger to her—was the father. And by the time she entered the apartment and hung her jacket on the coat rack, her stomach still hadn't stopped churning.

"Glad to see you're not dead," Zak said from the living room sofa.

Lacey's legs wobbled as she white-knuckled a coat hook. "Zak? You scared the bejesus out of me."

"Did I? I guess we're even then. Your breakfast is in the microwave, or maybe you ate already." He met her in the kitchen, took the last few sips of an orange juice before tossing it in the trash.

Lacey slapped her forehead with the heel of her hand. "I'm sorry. I had to run errands. If I had known you were cooking…"

He stood expressionless. "I called several times, but you didn't answer. So, I reached out to Doby, but she didn't know where you were. I almost dialed the police, convinced you were in an accident, but then it hit me, you were with Finn."

Lacey nearly choked. "Finn? Never. I ran errands and left my phone here by accident." She studied the concern on his face. "I'm sorry I worried you, but you shouldn't be. I'm an adult. You can't expect an explanation every time I leave the apartment."

His eyes drooped, and the corners of his mouth fell downward. "Yeah, I guess technically you don't owe me any explanations."

She pinched the bridge of her nose. "I didn't mean it like that. It's just living with someone is new for me. For years, I've never had to answer to anyone except myself."

"I don't remember asking you to answer to me, and I can't help it if I'm worried about you. I woke up to you being gone without so much as a note—for hours."

He drew closer, the back of his hand brushing against her lower belly. "It's not just you anymore. Having a baby is a big deal. I saw how much work it takes when my sister had her boys. The stress, sleepless nights, the doctor's visits, you name it. You can't go at it like Wonder Woman. You'll need support. So, let me be there for you."

He held her eyes hostage. And for a moment, neither of them moved nor spoke. Instead, she pondered in what form he wanted to be there for her, as friend Zak—or something more? Regardless, more could never happen. She would never allow it, never risk tainting their friendship with breakable emotions. She couldn't lose him, not when she had lost so much already—or would soon enough if she didn't figure out which one of those men was the father.

Zak broke the silence. "I think I'll chill in the room today. If you need me, you know how to reach me."

"Wait, can we at least talk about the near-kiss last night. Go over some boundaries for work tomorrow?"

He rubbed the back of his neck. "No, I'm not doing anymore rules, regulations, or plans."

If he thought she would improvise a fake marriage, then he had another thing coming. "It's the only way—"

"It is not the only way. You should just trust that in all the years we've spent together that I've learned more about you than you realize. And I don't need lists and index cards to tell me what I already know—or how to act." He walked away.

Her throat tightened as she studied him as he made his way to the spare bedroom. Sure, she should have considered his feelings, but was her insensitivity worth ditching the plan? He agreed to be here, to help her, and if nothing else, he should respect the boundaries.

She marched down the hallway towards his room, ready to demand they talk, or at least set a time to later. But the female's voice stopped her. She tiptoed closer.

"Why do you ask about my love life every time you call? It should be private."

"You can't blame your mom for wanting you to be happy, or for being nosey." The jovial tone echoed over a speakerphone.

"Since you won't stop… there might be a special person in my life."

"Serious special or casual special."

"Serious, for me anyway."

So he did have feelings for someone else. Lacey's heart dropped.

His mom squealed. "Tell me all about her. Better yet, invite her to dinner."

"Slow down, when the time's right, I will."

"Well, if I can't meet her, then details."

Lacey contemplated running off to her room, unsure of whether she could stomach his love confession another second. But the reality was it shouldn't bother her. Because she couldn't expect him to stay single for the rest of his life to follow her make-believe plan. Because he was her friend—nothing more.

"Mom?"

"Either you tell me, or I'm meeting her in person."

"Okay, you win." A few seconds of silenced passed before he started. This time, his tone was deeper, more raw.

"For starters, she's beautiful, inside and out."

Lacey shifted her eyes to her stick legs highlighted in a pair of yoga pants, and then to the tiny pudge at the bottom of her belly, hidden beneath an oversized sweater. She took a handful of her hurricane-blown curls and twisted them into a messy bun, securing it with the ponytail holder from around her wrist. A few strands escaped, and she tucked them into place on the return journey to her room with her head lowered.

Nothing good came from spying, except figuring out Zak had a new —or familiar—woman in his life, which meant she needed a new plan. She couldn't expect his leading lady to be okay with him sleeping in another woman's apartment every night, pretending to be her wife.

Tomorrow she would narrow down the potential fathers, starting with the first person listed: *Chuck Nguyen.*

11

Lacey stood outside Andrew's Coffee Shop, a place Chuck Nguyen frequented on Thursday afternoons after finishing his security-guard shift at Macy's. She reread the notes Mr. Duke collected. Chuck had never married, and other than the beagle-mix dog he adopted from the local shelter, had no other responsibilities. On paper, he didn't strike her as a person she'd date, much else have sex with.

But who knew what she did or didn't do other than God, and he wasn't talking. Staring through the tall glass windows, she surveyed the inside: yellow tabletops trimmed in dark wood accents, waitresses in white blouses, and plenty of customers to fill the seats.

Her phone beeped. She glared at the message from Doby.

Just do it. I'm watching you.

She swung her head in every direction her neck allowed. The phone buzzed again.

Across the street at Delimarie's.

Lacey squinted her eyes and spotted Doby under a dark green awning next to the deli door, half-waving. Lacey stomped the sidewalk like a small child caught in a tantrum while her fingers went to work.

I told you not to follow me.

Lacey's shoulders dropped two inches knowing Doby was nearby, although she would never admit it. Instead, she returned to the mission, scanning the seated patrons in search of anyone who resembled the provided description: dark hair and eyes, pale-skin, and a prominent nose mole. Within minutes, she spotted a man who had those traits plus a receding hairline. He also wore a too small uniform which left a large patch of exposed belly hair.

It was gross, but not as gross as watching his mouth stretch to max capacity around a burger so enormous, half its insides squished out the other side and fell to the table. Butterflies twirled in Lacey's gut at the gluttonous sight. She turned away.

There were four others on the list. Why not start with one of them? Chuck wasn't her type. In fact, any man who devoured a burger with the ferocity of a starving animal wouldn't be her type. Even in the throes of a drunken stupor and swiped of any conscious memory, she felt confident her subconscious would have firmly said *no*.

But the reality remained that Chuck was a potential regardless of how she felt about it.

With nothing left to do but tackle the crisis head-on, she proceeded inside and dove into the geometric-upholstered booth seat opposite of him. His eyes widened in surprise as he choked. And after a round of hard coughs and soda sips, he recovered—thankfully.

Because it would be horrible it he fell over dead before letting her know if they'd ever… She swallowed.

Chuck wiped away the masticated food chunks and sticky drool.

"I'm sorry I startled you," she said, twisting a napkin around her fingers.

"Uh-huh." Chuck cleared his throat a few more times. "How can I help you?"

"I guess I should introduce myself. I'm Lacey."

He gave a sarcastic grin. "Okay, Lacey, I'm Chuck. Glad we got that out the way." He took another bite of burger, a smaller one this time.

"This is odd, but what I wanted to know is…" Lacey stopped the waitress, asked for a glass of water. She couldn't talk with sandpaper for a tongue.

Unfazed, Chuck shrugged his shoulders before tossing a clump of fries in his mouth.

The server arrived with the water, and Lacey pried it from her hands, gulping half the glass before the cup touched the table.

"Somebody's thirsty." He grinned with a piece of black pepper stuck in the overlap of crowded teeth.

She pointed. "You have a—never mind." She cleared her throat.

"Have you ever met me before today?"

He chomped a fry. The inside mush dangled from his lips. "Huh?"

"Do I look familiar? Am I someone you've seen before?"

He chewed and talked at the same time. "No offense lady, but we live in New York City. I've met hundreds of people that look like you, doesn't mean they were you." Chuck inhaled the fry, swigged his soda, then burped.

Lacey's skin burned with embarrassment. "What I mean is, have we ever had—an intimate encounter?"

Chuck exploded a mouthful of Dr. Pepper across the table, distinguishable by the droplets that landed in Lacey's mouth. She had jumped back, but not soon enough.

"Sorry," he said, drying up the mess. "It's just that—" He leaned closer and lowered his voice to a whisper. "—I haven't been intimate with anyone in a long time. Not since I had to go on blood pressure medication… and gained fifty extra pounds." He reclined back to give Lacey a full view of his midsection.

"Doc blames the diabetes, too. But I'm working on it," he said before placing an order for a hot fudge sundae.

"So you can't have sex?" *There is a God.*

"Not in over a year. And don't worry, it doesn't bother me a bit." He caught the waitress' attention. "Hey, add sugar-free caramel on top of that."

Lacey's soul rejoiced, her spirits lifted, and her feet danced. "Thanks, Chuck," she added before bolting from the booth.

"Wait, what did you…"

His words faded as the door slammed shut behind her. And the sliver of sun breaking through the clouds lit Lacey's face up like the Fourth of July. She clicked open a pen and drew a solid block around his name and then colored it. "One down, and four to go."

Doby tapped Lacey's shoulder. Lacey's body shuddered. "Crap, you scared me!"

"That was short and sweet. So is he the father?"

Lacey glanced back to make sure Chuck wasn't following her. "I'll tell you after we get as far away as possible."

In the cab, Lacey shared the nauseating details through every pothole and red light. Doby couldn't contain her laughter. "I'm really not trying to be ugly, but aren't you glad he's not the one?"

Lacey pressed her fingers into her forehead. "Yes, but I can't help wonder how many more *Chucks* are on that list. What if Mr. Duke enjoys watching me suffer?"

"I can't say I buy that theory, but I do know it can only get better from here. I mean," she said, between snorted laughter, "could you imagine bringing Chuck home to your dad?"

"Talk about a disaster. I would never."

Doby settled herself. "Ooh, that reminds me. Did your parents like Zak? Are they convinced?"

"They loved him. And of course, we gave them the mother of all kisses to seal the deal," Lacey said, covering her eyes.

Doby yanked Lacey's hands away. "You kissed for real?"

"No, it just looked real to them."

Doby's penciled brows lifted. "Are you reverting back to the denial phase? Come on, I'm your best friend. You can't fool me."

"It's not what you think. Besides, I overheard Zak tell his mom he has serious feelings for someone."

"I'm sure he does—for you."

Lacey crossed her arms. "No, he called her beautiful."

"Which you are."

"It can't be me. He sees me as a friend, nothing more."

Doby leaned in close, rested her head on Lacey's shoulder. "Hey, do me a favor."

Lacey popped her lips. "What is it?"

"Can you follow your heart? I know you're used to lists and plans and organization, but sometimes those don't work so well for plotting relationships. And when you have an amazing guy living under your roof who's obsessed over you for years, you shouldn't hinder the natural flow of energy."

Lacey wrinkled her forehead and shrugged. "What does that even mean?"

"Have you never watched the Adam Sandler movie? The one where he marries his best-friend and co-worker Jennifer Aniston? *Just Go With It.*"

"I'm not going to *just go with it.*"

"I'm not telling you to… Well, actually I am… My point is it's both —the name of the movie and what you should do."

Lacey hugged her purse against her chest. "I don't have time to date, not in my condition. Besides, Zak's not into me—not in a romantic sense."

Doby gave a slow-baked grin. "Then you haven't been paying attention. Or maybe you're not as smart as I thought you were?"

The taxi stopped in front of Lacey's apartment. She exited the Lysol-scented back seat with a snicker. "I'm one of the smartest people you've ever met."

As the cab drove away, Doby shouted from the window. "Not when it comes to *Zak Cooper!*"

Lacey waved bye to Doby before heading to her apartment. In the elevator ride up, she pushed aside the notion that Zak had feelings for her. He was interested in someone else. It was obvious even if Doby refused to accept it. And although Lacey couldn't deny the near-miss moments, times when her body shivered with delight at his touch or the brush of his lips, she could reason them away with scientific explanations.

Pheromones were to blame. It was no secret that humans released them. And when people lived together, they often inhaled large amounts, enough to stir emotions. So the solution was simple. To prevent any further problems, she would open the windows and keep her distance.

Or she could hold her breath around him, she thought, opening the door. Except she wouldn't have to because he wasn't there. She hung up her purse, then went into the kitchen for apple juice. And without intention, she secretly searched for a note—a missing note.

She checked her phone and considered calling, only to ask if he planned on bringing dinner. But she stopped before dialing his number. Determined not to appear concerned or needy, she found a place on the sofa. She sipped the sweet juice and tried remembering what she did before Zak moved in with her.

Keys jingled and the doorknob clicked. And seconds after, Zak strolled inside engaged in a noisy phone conversation. "You know I wouldn't miss it... Seven, right?... I can't wait to see you either, Melanie." His smile stretched from one ear to the other.

His expression confirmed her suspicions. Zak had a love interest, and her name was Melanie. Not that Lacey cared. And by no means was she jealous, not a bit.

When the call ended, Lacey cleared her throat.

He poked his head in the living room. "You're home? From the way you made it sound earlier, I thought you'd be out most of the evening."

She twisted her fingers in her lap. "My meeting was over sooner than expected." Questions about Melanie popped in her mind, but she held them there.

He eased in beside her. "Great, you can come to the movies with me."

Go to the movies with him and Melanie? Tag along like a hangnail? She'd rather pluck nose hairs. "I haven't felt the best today. My plan is to get to bed early, get some extra rest."

"Did you take your medicine?" He rested his hand on her forearm, made her hate the involuntary tingles it created.

"I'm not nauseated, just tired. You know fatigue, one of the other pregnancy problems."

"I'll stay home with you. Just give me a minute to make a quick call." He reached for his phone.

"Go, please. Enjoy yourself. I promise you won't miss anything besides me sleeping. No need to bore yourself with that."

"Watching you is never boring." His eyes stretched wide as the color drained from his face. "I don't watch you. That would make me a creepy stalker, and I'm not. What I meant was—"

"I know what you meant." And it made her blood pulse with an embarrassing heat.

He rubbed the back of his head.

The conversation had taken an awkward turn. And she needed him to leave before it got worse. "Will you go have fun, please?" *With Melanie.*

"Yeah, I guess I'll get going."

"Great," Lacey said, hiding her shriveling insides that shouldn't be shriveling but were even though she willed them not to.

"Call me if something happens."

She forced a smile and held up her phone. "Can you believe this thing can even call 9-1-1?"

"Glad to see you're in a joking mood."

It was sarcasm, but who was she to correct him? He just needed to leave.

But instead he stood by the door with his attention fixed on her. "Are you sure you'll be okay? You'd tell me if you weren't, right?"

She fanned her fingers at him in false assurance. "Go, please. I'll be fine."

At her request, he left, leaving her with the reality of how *not fine* she actually was. And she would stay not fine until she found the father of her baby.

Well, Gene, it seems we have a date.

12

After an uncomplicated workday, Lacey headed over to the *Rizzoli Bookstore* on Broadway. She stood outside the door and prayed Gene would be a step up from Chuck, better yet—a staircase.

With her palm pressed against her chest, she completed a round of controlled breathing, then entered through the towering glass doors. Only minutes later, she found him dressed in a pair of destroyed jeans and a Givenchy t-shirt highlighting his slender muscles.

Between his flawless side-parted pompadour and butterscotch skin, she could only wonder why he had his nose stuck in a magazine instead of having his model-face printed on the cover of one. Her mouth dropped.

"Thank you, universe," she mumbled under her breath, sauntering across the psychedelic white and black marble to the section labeled MAGAZINES in exquisite gold lettering.

Noting a writing magazine in his hands, Lacey meandered over and picked up a similar one. She flipped through the pages as the space between her brows drew closer. Gene glanced over at her for a moment longer than she deemed casual, giving her a full view of his hydrangea-blue eyes.

She swallowed the drool forming in her mouth and asked, "Anything good in there?"

"Everything in here is good. It's a compiled list of award-winning short stories." His voice came out an octave higher than expected.

"Are you a fan of those?"

"Well, I write short stories myself, so this gives me a glimpse of what they're looking for in a winner." He held up the magazine. Her attention shifted from the pages to his manicured nails. "What about you? Do you write?"

"I've never been much of a writer, more design and blueprints," Lacey replaced her article upside-down.

"But you're interested in writing?" he asked, pointing at the one she restocked.

She braced herself, tried to slow her racing heart. "Not really, I'm actually here to see you."

Gene took a half-step backward and crossed his arms over his chest. "Why me?"

"I have a few questions to ask—private questions," Lacey said, gesturing to the group of college students that had now surrounded them. "Any possibility we might grab a coffee across the street?"

"Leave here with a stranger? If only you were so lucky."

Not quite the response she expected. No problem, she'd take a different direction. "Okay, but can we at least opt for a private corner?"

He nodded and escorted her to a less occupied section of the bookstore. "Now, get to it. What do you want with me? And please don't tell me you're a high-end prostitute, because you'd be wasting your time. I'm totally not interested—not if you're charging." Gene placed a hand on his hip, shifted his weight to one leg.

Lacey pointed at herself. "Me, a prostitute? That is hilarious. I have a real job. I even pay taxes." She studied his face, his flawless face, and hoped it was a joke.

"Prostitutes pay taxes. Every person who buys something pays taxes." He squinted and gave Lacey a hard smile.

She held up a finger, wanted to protest, but stuck to the purpose of her visit. "Do you remember me?"

"Should I?"

Lacey shifted her weight. "I don't know, do you?"

He jerked his head forward. "Are you trying to be a smart-ass?"

Lacey folded her fingers around her neck. "Not at all." She looked behind her and to her side, made sure no one was standing nearby. "Look, I need to know if we ever... had... sex." She gulped.

"Why would I need to tell you that? Shouldn't you remember?" He crinkled his perfect face.

"Yes, if I didn't have some sort of amnesia."

"So you don't recall that night? How could you not? I rocked your world, baby. Or at least that's what you told me before I left in the morning. In fact, I was so awesome, I'm charging for my services."

Lacey's heart leaped from her chest. "You're charging me? I should charge you for getting me pregnant."

He stumbled backward, threw up both hands. "Wait—you think—"

Lacey shushed him as a woman with blue hair and matching eyeshadow stopped right beside them. He glanced over at the woman and then yanked Lacey away to another section, a place free of listening ears.

"Before you finish, I want you to know I'm not after your money. I can raise this baby all on my own."

"Good for you. Now, sorry to pop your bubble of delusion, but there's no way I'm the father."

He was in denial. "Of course, you're shocked, but—"

He stepped inside Lacey's personal boundary and raised his voice. "You're not listening. I know I'm not the father."

She pinched the bridge of her nose. "So it's just a coincidence we had sex at the same time I got pregnant?"

"We never had sex, and even if we did, it wouldn't matter." He pressed his lips to Lacey's ear, curved his hand beside his mouth. "I was born Gina Nelson, not Gene. I changed my sex."

"Oh…"

"That makes me incapable of fathering children." Gene's fingers circled his chin.

Lacey sucked in her quivering lips at the same time an elderly man with bifocals and penny loafers moved in beside her, peeking over his glasses. With her body aimed towards the exit, she said, "I'll go now."

As Lacey sped away, Gene yelled to her. "Good luck with finding the father."

Without looking back, she hastened her steps and couldn't climb into a taxi fast enough.

Arriving at her apartment, she hung her purse on a wall hook, and then poured herself a glass of cranberry juice, pretending it was more. She needed it to be more. The journey to finding the father of her baby was not leading to the happy-ever-after she had envisioned. And now with Zak in love? The investigation had to move faster.

Until then, it might be best to give Zak space to cultivate his relationship. It wasn't fair to interfere. She took a small sip of juice and cringed. She glanced down at the bottle label. It read *Pure and Unsweetened*, words one should never associate with a cranberry, she thought, dumping a tablespoon of sugar into the glass.

A crashing bang came from Zak's room. Lacey gripped the counter, nearly losing her balance. Guess he'd made it to the apartment before her. She walked over to his door and eased her ear against it. All she heard was running water. Thinking he might have slipped in the shower, she knocked. "Are you okay?"

The bedroom door swung open. A brunette version of Barbie, spray-tanned an orangish-bronze, greeted Lacey in a blouse emphasizing her overachieving cleavage. Why couldn't she be lady-like and drape her long, glistening locks over her shoulders, hide the private things that should be covered? No, girls like her wanted them noticed. On full display, so every eye would be on chunks of breast overflowing a too small bra.

Lacey crossed her arms over her own chest and tried not to stare. "I was checking on Zak."

"Oh, Zak's in there. Want me to get him for you?" The woman pointed towards the bathroom door as if it was somewhere she would be okay going.

"I'm sorry—you are?"

"Silly me. I didn't introduce myself. I'm Melanie." Melanie pressed her palm against her chest.

Lacey sucked in her lips, inhaled, and then released. "Zak's Melanie?"

She gave Lacey a pageant smile. "The one and only. I don't mind getting him for you?"

Lacey shouldn't be upset—but she was. No decent woman would be in a married man's bedroom—alone, and no married man would do God knows what in his wife's spare bed after almost kissing her for real. No, their marriage wasn't legal, but Melanie didn't know that… or did she?

Tears welled in Lacey's eyes, one blink away from flooding her face. "No, I'll talk to him later." *Much later,* Lacey mumbled to herself as she hurried into her bedroom, locking the door.

She collapsed onto her mattress, the ceiling fan whirling above her. Why couldn't it just fall on her head, knock her the hell out, and end the pain she shouldn't be feeling? She pulled in a breath so deep her lungs nearly exploded. And she cried an ugly cry.

Zak knocked on the door. "Let me in, Lacey."

She laid on top of her striped duvet and muffled the sobbing with her pillow.

He beat on the door harder. "I know you didn't fall asleep that fast.

Open the door, please."

She refused. "Go away."

He pleaded. "It's not what you think."

Did it matter if it was what she thought it was? No, because the reality was there could be nothing between her and Zak.

The next morning she left early to the office to avoid traveling with Zak. The only problem was she still couldn't take her mind off of him or Melanie, no matter how much she tried. She stabbed holes into a stack of paper on her desk and rang Doby.

"I can't do this anymore. My life is falling apart," Lacey said, her voice trembling.

"I need you to stay calm."

"How? I've ruined Zak's life and mine. And it's all because of this baby. None of this would be happening if I wasn't pregnant." Lacey jabbed the pen so hard into the paper it broke, spraying ink everywhere.

"Don't move or do anything crazy. I'm on my way."

Lacey didn't have to, crazy things just happened. And no amount of preparation could prevent it, not her plans, not her lists, nothing would. She stood, slid her office chair out from under her, and plopped herself on the office sofa.

Doby arrived carrying a giant bag of M&Ms. "Look, I brought chocolate." Doby rushed over, and stuffed a few in Lacey's mouth.

"I—" Lacey chewed and swallowed, then grabbed a few more. "These are superb."

"See, chocolate fixes everything."

Lacey leaned forward, and rested her head on her knees. "It fixes nothing. Please remind me again why I'm having this baby."

Doby gripped Lacey's shoulders and shook her.

Lacey freed herself. "What is it with you jerking me around?"

"I'm shaking the crazy out of my friend, intervening so she doesn't say things she'll regret later."

"Regret what? Before this," Lacey said, gesturing towards her pregnant belly, "my life was on track. I was successful, driven—"

"And lonely. Don't forget that part. At least you have Zak."

"I don't have Zak. Zak has Melanie, who probably stayed the night at my apartment. And now I have to burn the sheets."

Doby tilted her head. "Do you know he's with Melanie, or you assume he is?"

"It doesn't matter. None of this is about him. He wouldn't be in this mess if I hadn't dragged him into it. And I wouldn't have dragged him into if it weren't for this pregnancy that's destroying my life."

Doby rose. "You don't mean that. You're just hurt."

Lacey jumped straight to her feet with force, ready to defend her stance, but the warm trickle of fluid running down her legs stopped her. She reached her fingers underneath the edge of her skirt and then raised her hand. Bright red blood covered it. She had wished the worst and now the worst was here.

Her stomach and chest weighed a thousand pounds. Her heart quit beating. "I need to go to the hospital."

13

In the early morning hours, after spending nearly the entire night at the hospital, Zak guided Lacey straight to her bed—per Dr. Hart's orders. The same orders that instructed Lacey to stay in the bed for the next several weeks, only allowing her up for bathroom breaks. Unless the tear in her placenta healed sooner than expected. And while Lacey detested being confined to four walls, she would do whatever it took to keep the baby safe, especially since this was all her fault. Even though Dr. Hart reassured Lacey it wasn't, she couldn't help but feel guilty.

"Give me one sec, I'll be right back," Zak said, rushing out the room after tucking her in properly.

He returned holding a computer and a stack of books and magazines.

She rubbed her eyes, then took the first book on top. *"What to Expect When Expecting?"* Then the next. *"Parenting Magazine?* How did you get these?" Amazed, she shuffled through several more.

He stood tall, gave her a mischievous grin. "Let's say I have friends in high places."

"And just who are these high-falutin friends?"

"Wouldn't you like to know?" He eased in on the edge of bed beside her as she gave him a *you better tell me* look. "Mathias owed me a favor. So I had him drop them off on his way to work."

"Shoot, work. You'll be leaving soon. Before you go, do you mind setting me up with a few snacks, drinks, breakfast maybe? It was a long night."

"Actually, I'll be here to prepare them on demand. It turns out my boss insisted I stay home and take care of my *wife*. He said I'm entitled

100

to the time. I suspect Mr. Caldwell had something to do with it." Zak leaned over Lacey and picked up one of the pregnancy books.

Whiffs of his faded cologne stirred her, and she inhaled deeper. So much for holding her breath around him, she thought, disappointed at her lack of control. "I'm sorry they're making you stay."

"I'd have stayed, regardless."

"And what would Melanie say about that?" She hated what she said, wanted to take it back. It made her look jealous, and she wasn't.

He found Lacey's eyes and stared into them. "It doesn't matter what she says because we're co-workers, nothing more. I tried to tell you, but you wouldn't let me explain."

"A co-worker who thinks it's okay to hang out in your bedroom together, or who goes into the bathroom when you're naked."

"I know that was awkward. But I didn't tell her to, or even want her to." His eyes lowered, then returned to Lacey's. "She misinterpreted our relationship, but that's not my fault. I made it very clear I'm with someone else."

Lacey fidgeted with the edge of the duvet in her lap. "Yeah, only to keep up this sham marriage. I understand you're sticking to the plan, but you're entitled to your own life."

"I wouldn't be here if I didn't care about you."

"Friends care about each other."

He scrubbed the side of his face. "Do you think I'd go along with your crazy plans if I didn't *seriously* care for you?"

She wrinkled her nose. "My plans are not crazy."

"Your plans are crazy... but is that all you heard?"

Deep inside something tugged at her, made her pay attention, and she had a good idea it was her hopscotching heart. She heard what he said and rationalized it for him. "It's normal for friends to care about each other. I care about you too."

He laid his hand on top of hers and leaned in closer, so close the lack of air between them made her dizzy. "I think it's more than that. I..."

She wanted to kiss him. Wanted him to kiss her. Maybe it was the lack of oxygen, but whatever it was she found it hard to resist.

Her phone rang.

Zak leaned back against the headboard and sighed, letting go of her hand so she could answer.

Saved by the ringtone, she thought. But it was a telemarketer. She dropped the phone on the bed, then adjusted her pillows. As she pressed her back against them, she summoned the courage to dig deeper. "What do you mean by you think it's more than that?"

Lacey watched the heavy rise and fall of his chest as he tapped his fingers against the book cover. "Why explain it? You already know. The problem is you won't accept it. Sometimes I believe you might, but then you give me a blank expression as if nothing ever happened between us... or maybe it's that you can never see me as more than a friend."

It was obvious living in the same apartment had muddled their friendship, tangled it into a mirage of something more. And Zak just couldn't see it for what it was. "Do you suppose playing married has confused our—your—emotions?"

He ran his fingers through his tousled hair, mussed it even more. "Not when my feelings started before this plan of yours. Don't worry, though, I know you don't feel the same. You've made it very clear."

The room felt hot—sauna hot. Lacey grabbed a magazine from beside her and fanned away the heat. Had she misinterpreted their relationship throughout these years? What if the only reason he answered her every beck and call was to be near her?

She dug into her memory bank files. The time when she caught the flu he brought her a different soup each night of the week until she got better, even included a comedic note to make her laugh. When she had to catch a red-eye from the airport for a business trip, he escorted her to the ticketing booth, insisting it was to protect her from the undesirables that roamed at those hours.

And when she lied and said he was her husband and father of her baby, he accepted it without complaint.

Is that why he did those things? Because he had feelings for her? Gestures such as cooking her bland meals, aware greasy or spicy stuff would end up sprayed across the bathroom tile? Or bringing her pregnancy books to read? Had she ignored the signs? Blocked her own affections? He no doubt had the power to stir her emotions, which she deliberately pushed back into place because a relationship with him wasn't workable.

Now here he was, sharing personal feelings, and what did she have to say about it? "I'm speechless."

"And it's okay. The last thing I want to do is make this awkward." He opened the pregnancy book, thumbed through the pages. "Just know I'm here for you and the baby... even if it's only as a friend."

She had destroyed the possibility of being more than friends—with her lies. He didn't know the full story. He didn't know his friend, the woman he confessed feelings for, was a person who lied to the people she cared for to save herself.

She dropped the magazine, pulled her knees to her chest and hugged them. "I'm sorry for all I've put you through."

"Forget about it. Things turn out how they're supposed to."

His overly relaxed and chilled ways annoyed her. Never stressed, never worried, when he should be furious with her. "That's easy for you to say. You have the patience of a Tibetan Monk, nothing stirs you. Unfortunately, I'm not so innately blessed." She sucked in her bottom lip, held it.

He scratched the stubble on his chin. "I guess spending my middle school years fighting cancer taught me how to worry about what matters."

She gasped. "You never told me you had cancer."

"It was a long time ago. And I'm okay now."

"But still, I feel horrible."

"Why? It served a purpose. Eventually, after a few wild years, it helped me realize I should focus on what's important in life." He shifted his gaze to Lacey. "And now that I've set my sights on what matters, I don't want to settle for less."

Guilt seeped in through Lacey's pores and attacked her soul. She wanted to go back to the day she lied and retract her words, protect him. He'd nearly lost his life to cancer, and what did she do? She rewarded him by ruining his life to save hers. "I'm the most selfish person on the planet."

"Please—you're one of the most selfless people I've met, always rooting for the underdog, even in corporate America. You wouldn't do the things you do if you were heartless."

"It doesn't feel like I have a heart. I mean, just look at what I've done to you."

The corner of his mouth lifted. "Yeah, living rent free is so torturous."

"Could you imagine me charging you for being my fake husband? Then I'd really be a monster." She drew in a long breath through her nose. "None of this is going according to plan. And now I feel terrible knowing I've probably damaged your career. After all you've been through?"

"Quit beating yourself up. I'm an adult. If I didn't want to be here, I wouldn't be." He picked up the *What to Expect When Expecting* book. "Why don't we move on to something else? Week twelve sounds like a good place to start."

It was a better place than where the discussion had taken them. She obviously couldn't solve life's problems in a single day or even a week. So she settled for listening to him read, marveled at the milestones the baby—her baby—had reached. Anything to distract her from sentimental talks. The feelings that if left unchecked would develop into commitments, and commitments into break-ups, and break-ups into heartache and never seeing each other again.

And because she didn't want to lose Zak, she agreed week twelve was the best place to start.

At week twelve, the baby was the size of a plum with a working digestive system, except he or she wouldn't pass gas or poop for a while. And all of its major organs had formed, which left one task—to grow—and it did. By week thirteen, the baby was the size of a peach and had developed vocal cords capable of crying all day. Although Lacey was still months away from dealing with any sleepless nights, unless staying up worrying about how uncomfortable Zak felt sleeping on her floor every night counted.

But he refused to have it any other way, at least until the tear healed.

Week fourteen of her pregnancy arrived on the same day as her ultrasound appointment, along with the baby's eyebrows and genitals. Although, there were no guarantees they'd appear on camera. But they did, and Dr. Hart put either a picture of its penis or vagina in a sealed envelope, at Zak's surprising suggestion to have a gender reveal party like his sister. And why not? What else did she have to do over the next couple of weeks of continued bedrest since the tear hadn't healed —other than avoid entering the more-than-friends zone with Zak?

Which was proving more difficult than she had imagined.

In the cab leaving Dr. Hart's office, Zak fiddled with the envelope Dr. Hart gave them.

"Can you believe the sex of the baby is in there?" Lacey asked.

Zak lifted the corners of his mouth enough his one-sided dimple appeared. "Yeah, it's kind of wild. Though, I'm sure it's a boy. It explains why she could see it so early."

Lacey playfully crossed her arms over her chest. "Absent male parts would be just as obvious."

He pulled a piece of gum from his pocket and removed the wrapper. "Ignore the facts, but I suggest paying ahead for a circumcision."

"Put my baby through a totally barbaric procedure? I don't think so."

He folded the gum, put it in his mouth. "I can't believe I'm pointing out the obvious here as a member of the male species, but it's necessary."

He was crazy if he thought she would torture a poor innocent baby with no choice in the matter. "You want me to say it's okay for someone to strap him to a board and slice off his foreskin. For cosmetic purposes?"

The muscles in Zak's jaw contracted when he chewed, and though she'd rather not find it sexy, it kind of was. "If you don't, it might cost him dates."

As the cab stopped at a red-light, she glanced the sidewalk full of speed-walkers. "I'd never refuse to date someone because they're not circumcised."

Zak redirected her attention back to himself with a gentle tug of her chin. "Have you slept with an uncircumcised man?"

"That's none of your business."

"You haven't because it's not common. Opt for circumcision. I had one and don't even remember it."

She returned her sights to outside the cab window, stared at the buildings and sidewalks now blurred into swirls of color to keep from imagining Zak's uncircumcised male parts. "I'll think about it... The circumcision, I meant."

"And I'll make sure I'm there so he's well represented."

They had never discussed the delivery, probably because she expected to fake divorce before that day, assuming she found the real father. Which might never happen if she stayed on bedrest. "You plan on being there for the birth?"

"I told you. I want to be there for every part." He pressed his shoulder against hers, leaned in close. "Am I invited?"

Skydiving, it was the only way to describe the adrenaline rush his question sent pumping through her veins. Because people invited their friends to join them at office Christmas parties or happy hours, not to be spectators to a bowling ball barreling its way through a vagina.

She had to ask. "Do you want to be?"

"For sure." He stared at her. "Finn's not in the picture, someone should be. Why not me?"

"But it's not your baby."

He glided his fingers in between Lacey's with no one there to expect it. "Does it have to be?"

Her breath stalled as the driver stopped in front her building. Zak gave her hand a squeeze before assisting her out of the cab and into the lobby. Inside, the doorman Raoul, an older Honduran immigrant who reminded her of a tanned Santa Claus, greeted them, distracting Lacey from Zak's question.

"Ms. Lacey, why you not tell me you having a baby?" He pointed his knobby fingers at her tiny baby bump, then turned to Zak. "I knew you two were meant to be." He tapped his temple.

She glanced at the granite floors. "You don't miss a thing, Raoul." She hated lying to him... to everyone.

Zak gestured towards the elevators, now wrapped in yellow caution tape. "What happened?"

"None of them work, not even service ones. Everybody has to use the stairs. So much complaints today, and no good for you either Ms. Lacey, you on seventh floor. Why don't you wait here? See if they fix it." The other young doorman waved Raoul outside.

Lacey turned to Zak. "I can walk it. I'll just take frequent breaks."

He jerked his head side-to-side. "No way. Besides, there's always Plan B. Lead me to the stairs."

Without warning, he scooped Lacey into his arms as she resisted. But when she realized he didn't plan to put her down, she pulled herself close to his center, hoping to lighten the load. And it was there that the mixed scents of sweat and cologne rose to her nostrils and sent a simmering heat flooding her veins.

Thankfully, the cool bed he laid her on quenched the fire. Exhausted, he collapsed next to her, throwing his arm over his head. Lacey surveyed him from head to toe, noted the beads of perspiration pooling across his forehead and watched his heart push against his chest wall.

He closed his eyes. "Don't worry, I'll get on the floor. Just give me a minute to catch my breath."

He had carried her up seven floors to protect a baby that wasn't even his. The least she could do was offer him a comfortable place to sleep, despite the raised neck hairs and tingling skin brought on by just the thought of him in her bed. "You can sleep with me. I think you've earned it."

He cracked open one eye. "Excuse me?"

She fidgeted with the DO NOT REMOVE tag on her pillow. "I

meant to say you can sleep beside me."

His mouth curved upward as both his eyes stretched wide. "Are you sure?"

Honestly, she wasn't sure, but it made sense. No need to punish his back or neck on a hard, unforgiving floor. He deserved comfort, the same comfort he brought her. "I guess I am, but with conditions. A line of pillows stays between us. You can grab the ones from your room and the sofa."

"Sure, since you insist we build a wall." He chuckled, then found his serious expression. "Hey, you know I'd never do anything you didn't want me to."

The thought of him touching her, tracing his fingers across every inch of her naked skin, flooded her mind. And sent her hands flying over her mouth. "No."

He jerked forward. "You believe I'd force myself on you?"

She dropped her hands. "No... sorry... my thoughts were somewhere else." She smoothed the blanket. "Let's just be safe."

He smirked, then moseyed out of bed. "I'm showering first, and then I'll grab the pillows."

She picked up a magazine, pretending to glance through the pages. "Okay, I'll stay here."

The soothing hum of the vibrating shower head and the calming trickle of draining water echoed into the bedroom seconds before her phone rang. She answered.

"What did the doctor say?" Her mom and sister spoke in unison over a three-way call.

Lacey thumbed through a few more pages. "The tear hasn't healed, but she said the baby looks good. We go back in two weeks."

Her mom's tone shifted to lighter, calmer. "Well, I put in a special prayer request at Bible study this week, so it's going be just fine. Ms. Rosie told me the same thing happened to her daughter, and she made it to full-term."

Lacey stopped at a photograph of a father and his infant son cuddled up shirtless, the title above them, *Skin-to-Skin with Daddy*. Her lips folded as she flipped to the next page. "I know it will. On a good note though, I found out what I'm having today, but it is sealed."

Her mother exploded with excitement while Kate protested. "How did you find out so soon?"

"I guess the baby was in the perfect position. Zak suggested we throw a gender reveal party, but I'm not sure."

Kate's pitch raised. "That is a wonderful idea. We can have ours together after my ultrasound in a couple of weeks."

Lacey's mother turned her conversation to Kate, giving her the *everyone won't find out so soon* speech. They went back and forth, Kate firing off the possibilities and her mother dousing them with reality.

Not wanting to interject, Lacey turned her attention to the cracked bathroom door, open wide enough for her to glimpse a shirtless Zak wearing only a towel. *Look away*, she told herself. It was the correct thing to do. But nothing about her inner tigress was prim, proper, or morally correct. It was wild, and the sight of bare flesh heightened its hunger.

"Hey, I'll talk to you guys later," Lacey said, no longer focused on the call. Embarrassed, she buried her head under her pillow and not long after felt more being added.

"Are these enough pillows for you?" Zak chuckled.

She escaped the tower built on top of her and took a quick glance at him, making sure he had dressed. Thankfully, he had. She picked up a pillow and playfully hit him with it. "Plenty, but they go in between us."

Zak climbed in beside her, stacked the fluffy cushions high enough to block any view of himself from her. "Is this good?"

"How funny. I didn't say build a mountain." She knocked them over, most of them landing on his head. Still laughing, she leaned over, pulled him free. When she lifted the last pillow from his face, she froze only inches above him. His eyes anchored onto hers, a transporter beam drawing her closer. Blinking didn't break the trance. No, she was on the edge of a cliff while Zak lay waiting for the fall.

She eyed his soft lips, lips she had already locked onto more than once, lips wanting nothing more than to take hers.

"I should take my shower." And she did, returning with a clean body and mind.

On her return, she divided the bed in half with a perfect line of pillows, and slid under the striped duvet on her side. Zak kept his attention on the television. "What movie do you want to watch?" He rested one arm above his head, used the other for the remote.

She tried to find a comfortable position but couldn't, fearing it might have something to do with having a man in her bed. "It doesn't matter as long as it's not spooky, depressing, action-y, gory, or too complicated."

"Hallmark it is."

Why didn't she remember to add romance to the list? Hallmark movies always included the long-anticipated sappy kiss at the end. They made lip-locking with the cute guy enticing, intriguing, like it was the thing to do, or even to try at home.

Tonight's movie was no different

When it ended, Lacey wondered how it would feel to kiss the cute guy in her bed, the one with the messy hair and a boyish grin, the same one who flexed his muscles by carrying her up way too many stairs. She faced him, traced his full lips with her eyes, paid attention to the slight part between them. If she went anywhere with him, it would be there, in the open space.

He lay relaxed, studying her studying him. He said he wouldn't touch her unless she wanted him to. If only he knew how hard she resisted the want, how hard she fought the temptation to pounce on him without warning. But what if she didn't fully engage? What if she just sampled a taste, enough to quench the pheromonal thirst? She swallowed hard, envied his control.

Just turn away, walk away, get away, she told herself.

But instead, she closed the distance, picked away the pillows as he waited, luring her with his restraint. She toyed with her impulses, gave in more than she should. Who was she to jump in front of a speeding train of emotion? Her fingers landed on the side of his neck with a delicate touch, then trailed towards his chest.

His muscles tensed. His jaws tightened. His face reddened. But he kept his hands to himself.

Driven by pure desire, she edged closer, pressed her cheek against his, nudged her nose against his, and melted under the warmth of his breath. She tried to pull back, needed to pull back, but his lips were too close, her flesh too weak. "Kiss me—please."

No longer relaxed, he cradled her face as his mouth grazed hers, once, twice, each time an explosion of pleasure inside her that left her wanting more. And he delivered, pressing his parted lips firmly against hers, drawing her into the open space between them, driving her to faraway places she had never been. Kissing was not new, kissing him was not new, but kissing him for real—was very new. She never wanted it to stop—

Wait!

Who was she, and what had she done with Lacey Winters? Better yet, what had she done with Zak? She shouldn't kiss him, not like this. She reclaimed her mouth. "I'm so sorry. I don't know what got into me." She gathered the pillows, wedged them back in place. "I seriously can't believe I kissed you."

"Technically, I kissed you."

"Only because I asked." She buried her face under the last pillow and moaned. "It doesn't matter. It shouldn't have happened."

"Maybe it shouldn't have, but I'm glad it did."

She kept her mouth crammed against the velvet cushion. "Of course, you are—ugh!"

14

The next morning, she didn't dare move until making sure she hadn't snuggled up to Zak in her sleep, as she no longer trusted her traitor*ish* body. With one eye cracked open, she spied the pillow-wall still intact and a missing Zak. Her tensed muscles relaxed.

If only she could persuade Mr. Caldwell to let her handle the coalition project from home, or have him give her something new to work on, anything to distract her from thinking about Zak. Grabbing her phone from the nightstand, she crossed her fingers and left Mr. Caldwell a detailed voicemail.

Zak entered the room holding a tray filled with avocado toast, grapes, and low-acid orange juice. It was a sweet gesture, but one that made her cringe. Men brought women breakfast in bed after a night of passionate sex, or in her case, after a passionate kiss.

"This is because of last night, isn't it? You don't have to romance me, and you shouldn't... I mean we shouldn't do that ever again."

His forehead wrinkled. "I make you food every day. How else would you eat? You're on bedrest."

"But this morning you put it on a fancy tray."

"That I stole from the living room." He placed it on her lap. "I'm using a tray to save myself a second trip." He gave her a one-sided, dimpled grim.

She covered her face. "Ignore me. From now on, question whatever I say?"

"Like *kiss me, please*?"

"Definitely those words." Her hands glided from her face to her curls, and she squeezed. "I still can't believe I said that."

He removed the pillows and rescued her hair. "Well, you did, and you can't change it. But we can move forward… if that's what you want?"

She straightened. "Awesome idea, move on to something besides… that."

"How about to these?" He produced several blueprints from his back pocket, then settled next to Lacey. "I stumbled across them on my hunt for a tray, and I'm pretty sure they're not skyscrapers."

He'd found her secret stash, her guilty pleasure. "No, they're not." She picked up the avocado toast. "Those are the small businesses I create for fun. I spend so much time on large-scale designs that when I get a free-second I experiment with less enormous ones."

She took a bite and gave him a thumbs-up.

"You enjoy doing this?" He unrolled one, a small-town grocery store equipped with curbside pickup for online ordering.

"Love it, more so than designing skyscrapers. But I'll deny it if you tell anyone." She plucked a grape from its stem and tossed it into her mouth.

"If I told on you, I'd have to tell on myself." He unrolled the second one, a vintage antique store setup to mirror the interior of a home, a bedroom for old-fashioned headboards and armoires, a kitchen for dusty beaters and bowls. "These are incredible."

"What did you mean by telling on yourself?"

He rolled the blueprints, placed them on the nightstand next to him. "I give free financial advice to people in my hometown interested in starting their own businesses. It's way more satisfying than my real job, and the fact they appreciate my work makes it worth it. I just wish I could help my mom's friend, Ms. Ethel."

Unable to find a napkin, Lacey wiped the toast crumbs from her mouth with the back of her hand. "What's the problem?"

He rubbed his head. "She's having trouble choosing a design, and without something on paper, I can't work the numbers. I've suggested several good architects, but she says none of them gets her. So until she finds… You. You're the perfect choice." He thumbed towards the blueprints. "And seeing those just confirmed it."

It wouldn't be a smart idea to take on side projects, no matter how much she secretly wanted to, not while juggling investigations, work, and preparing for a baby. "Where would I find the time?"

He patted the bed. "What else do you have to do besides lay here? I'll call my mom and let her know. Actually, you could come with me to my parents' anniversary party, meet Ms. Ethel in person—if Dr.

Hart signs off on it."

Lacey rolled a plucked grape between her fingers. "I can't go to the party, and you can't tell your mom... not about us. No more unnecessary heartbreak when this make-believe fairytale ends." She crushed the grape in her mouth.

"I won't introduce you as my wife."

Could it work? She would admit, assisting Ms. Ethel would be rewarding, but the risk was too high. "I don't have the energy to take this on right now."

Her phone dinged. It was Mr. Caldwell texting her to quit worrying about work. He had it handled. Whatever that meant. All she could do was pray Jocelyn hadn't gotten her claws on the contract, or that Margot hadn't turned it into the next *Marriage 'R' Us*.

"Who's that?"

"Mr. Caldwell telling me I can't work from home." She frowned. "And now I'm worried about what will happen to my design. For once, I showed my dad I'm capable of achieving great things just like him. Now look at me, doing nothing but keeping the bed warm."

Zak took her hand in his, guided it to the bulge at the bottom of her stomach, and held it there. "What you're doing is fighting for this baby, a baby that's fighting to be here. It takes courage to bring another life into the world. I know your dad is more proud of you for giving this baby a chance than he is about the coalition contract. And if he's not, then he is not the man I thought he was."

Zak made her think about her circumstances in a different light. It required courage to press forward with the pregnancy considering the unknowns, the risks, the complications—and to do it alone? Somewhere deep within her subconscious, she had wanted to bring this baby into the world, father or no father.

And to make sure that happened, she had to follow strict bedrest instructions.

She graduated to week sixteen of her pregnancy without one bleeding episode and without kissing Zak, no small feat considering how many times they found themselves millimeters from lip-locking.

What could she say? He made her feel comfortable. She could laugh whenever, dress however, be whoever, say whatever. He was the one person in her life who didn't make her question her self-worth or make her wonder if her actions were fitting of a career-driven woman. And that made it hard not to blur the lines of emotion between them.

But she kept their relationship platonic. She spent her time focusing on the avocado-sized baby in her belly, now large enough that her pre-pregnancy outfits no longer fit. So imagine how grateful she was when Doby stopped by for a surprise visit with three bags full of maternity clothes before flying off to Vegas with Carson.

So much so she wore one of the elastic banded trousers to her follow-up ultrasound, which the nurse insisted she fold over to make room for the goopy gel.

"Let's take a look," Dr. Hart said, skating the probe around Lacey's belly. Zak kept his gaze glued to the screen and his hand plastered to Lacey's as Dr. Hart took multiple pictures. And they waited with their breath held.

"Good news, the tear healed." Dr. Hart said.

Lacey beamed. "Seriously? I don't have to stay on bedrest?"

"I'll lift the bedrest restrictions, but I want to see how things progress with an increase in activity before I send you back to work."

It wasn't everything Lacey wanted to hear, but it was a start. The baby was safe, and now she could resume finding the father.

Zak squeezed her hand and winked. "This is good news, right?"

The part about the baby was great news. But the rest was only a reminder of how imperfect her life was. No longer being on bedrest meant she could get back to investigating the list. And when every other woman would be picking out nursery paint colors, she would traipse the city streets in search of the anonymous sperm donor who impregnated her. And so far, the only thing she knew about him was how great he was in bed. Everything else was an unfortunate blur.

Dr. Hart passed them more ultrasound pictures. "At your next appointment, you can get the AFP blood test for congenital defects. Now, I also expect you'll experience little flutter kicks before I see you again. Questions?"

Lacey couldn't think of any, not with her brain still processing the bombardment of information thrown at her. Or more so the number of potentials still left to investigate.

"I do," Zak said, grinning mischievously.

Dr. Hart held the chart against her chest. "Sure. Go ahead."

"Is it okay if we have sex?"

Lacey snatched her hand away from his and sat on it to keep from punching him.

"Good question, as long as things continue as they are, sex is safe—and healthy—during pregnancy. Just take it easy at first." She faced

Lacey. "If you see brownish or pinkish discharge after, it's okay. But if there's any bright red blood, you call me."

"Did you hear that, honey? Sex is healthy for you." Zak's face appeared strained and the color of a ripening beet, although Lacey found no humor in his question.

"I'll leave your paperwork here. And don't forget to schedule your next appointment at check out."

The door had barely shut before Lacey climbed off the table and stomped over to the dirty linens bin, tossing in the gel-covered towel. She yanked up her pants, then snatched her purse and papers from the counter.

Zak stepped in front of her, holding her shoulders. "Hey, is everything okay?"

"It was before you asked that stupid question." Lacey's tone bordered on furious.

He leaned back, shrugged. "It was a joke."

"A dumb joke."

"Well, I apologize if it offended you. But maybe it's time to ask questions, act like real parents would."

"That's the thing. You aren't the real parent." She pointed her finger at Zak. "And I'm afraid the lines are getting smudged." A searing pain shot through her chest. Unbeknownst to Zak, he had lit the fuse on her pre-assembled bomb, one full of fear and anxiety over lists and potentials. And when it blew, she knew he would get blasted.

But there was nothing she could do to stop it.

"I'm fully aware of that fact. Now tell me the real problem." He raked his hand through his hair. "Or is this your not-so-subtle way of saying back off? Because if it is, then say so."

The fuse burned into her center, turned her words explosive. "I want you to quit pretending to be the father when you don't have to. You're taking the whole fake marriage thing too far."

Every line and crease in his face folded downward. "Wow, so that's how you really feel?"

"Look Zak, I don't know what we're—I meant you're—hoping for, but it can't happen."

"Only because you won't let it." He threw his arms up. "I swear you have more crazy cycles than a washing machine. One minute you're all over me, the next you're pushing me away, then you're back all over me, and then you're telling me to get out of your life."

"You consider kissing being all over you?"

"Oh, and how'd I forget the amnesia cycle? Is that the one we're on right now? Let's pretend nothing ever happened between us."

"That is not funny."

"No, it's not, but neither is flirting with my emotions." He scrubbed both sides of his face. "You want me to back off? Fine. Consider it done." He opened the door and held it for her, staring straight ahead as she walked out.

Her words had flowed on impulse, filled the room, stole away the space and air around her until she couldn't breathe. It was a necessary suffocation, she reminded herself.

The private bubble she had shared with Zak over the past few weeks, no matter how enjoyable, would pop. It was only a matter of when. So why wait for the inevitable? Why drag out an illusion of life without lies? She forced herself to walk past him, despite the spinning in her head. And she didn't look back.

Instead, she looked ahead to the next name on her list, *Bo Jameson.*

She finished dining on French onion soup at *Bistro Les Amis* across the street from Bo Jameson's million dollar home. Impressive, she thought, assuming his ability to afford such a property suggested—at the least —a steady source of income. Not that she cared about his money. What mattered was what it implied. He was capable of commitment. And considering fatherhood demanded a lifelong one, well, she couldn't think of a better trait for him to have.

She crossed the street and stopped shy of knocking on his door. Lipstick, she needed lipstick if she expected a man like Bo to even give her a chance to speak. And it had to be bold. She dug out the closest shade to red she owned and applied as her phone dinged.

I'm leaving this evening for my parents' anniversary party. I want you to go with me. Say yes. It'll give us a chance to talk.

Why now Zak? Surely, he couldn't expect her to live on a roller coaster of emotion with him, no matter how thrilling. She pinched the bridge of her nose. A car horn blew nearby and made her body shake.

Once she steadied herself, gained her wits, she knocked, refusing to delay the inevitable a minute longer. Bo Jameson answered, and the first thing to catch her eye was his mysterious dark-blue eyes. The second thing was the shakes—as in five cups of coffee too many. Although, he didn't strike her as a heavy coffee drinker. She reached out her hand and introduced herself first.

He ignored the gesture and peeked his head outside, studying both ends of the street before tucking his head back indoors like a turtle. "Who sent you?"

What? "No one." She scanned the sidewalk around her. "Are you expecting someone? I can leave if you are."

He glared at her. "Are you selling something?"

She scrunched her face. "No, I just have a few questions for you—if you have a moment."

His jumpy eyes wandered over every inch of her body. "Fine, but ask them inside."

Lacey scanned the sidewalk one last time, fearing a surprise attack by an angry ex. When nothing happened, she shook off the unease and stepped inside his home. There, she observed a splendid art collection, one showcasing expensive tastes. Abstract paintings from artists such as Gerhard Richter hung on every wall, bringing splashes of color to white brick partitions and natural wood floors.

It screamed everything but child-friendly.

Bo went straight for the bourbon on his stocked mini-bar. "Want one?"

Lacey found a comfortable seat on the leather sofa and drew in a deep breath. "I can't drink. It's kind of why I'm here."

It didn't stop him from tossing back two shots himself. Lacey rested her thumb against her phone's side button, reminding herself she was five clicks away from emergency services.

"Are you dying or something?" He gulped a third shot.

"Not that anyone has told me."

He never acknowledged her. Instead, he stared at his phone as the color drained from his face. In a panic, he raced over to the window and peeked through oddly placed blinds. Eyesores in such an exquisite home.

Lacey studied the luxury apartment and found more oddities, bare countertops and a medium-sized safe planted beside the couch in place of an accent table. Other than the expensive wall art, the apartment lacked the most basic decorations or even signs of life. She struggled to imagine he even lived in the apartment. In fact, the more she inspected her surroundings, the more her skin crawled.

She stood and headed towards the door. "I'll just come back another time. Sorry to bother you."

He rushed over, gripping her hand with clammy fingers. "No, you can't—I mean don't go. I apologize for being a terrible host, but when someone shows up without warning, well, it makes me skittish." He gestured at his surroundings. "Everything in here costs money, so I worry about thieves."

With some wiggling and twisting, Lacey freed herself. She didn't buy his story, but did she have to? The mission focused on answers. And the sooner she got them, the sooner she could leave. "I'm not here to rob you. I just need to know if we've ever met."

He took a wide-stance, covered his chest with locked arms. "Why?"

No amount of handsome could make up for his unwarranted paranoia. Unable to deal with it a minute longer than necessary, she went straight to the point. "I'm pregnant, and I believe you might be the father."

"What?! We didn't... Wait a sec..." He pinched his prominent chin between his thumb and finger. "This is great. A baby, a fiancée."

She facepalmed him. "Hold up, you're moving way too fast."

"No, it's the perfect setup." He stared ahead with widened eyes. "If we're having a baby, we should get engaged. A man like me needs a family. It's much less—"

"Slow down, I said you *might* be the father."

"Even if I'm not, I'll claim it as my own."

"It?"

"Yeah, you know, the baby."

She hurried towards the door, but he blocked her from turning the knob. "Look, I realize we keep getting off on the wrong foot, but please give me another chance. I have so much going on, and this... this is big news, right? Here, let me get you a juice. It'll be good for the baby." He lifted her chin, drew her eyes to his, and for a minute resembled a semi-sane person. "I promise I'm a good guy."

What if she had caught him on a rough day? "Okay, I'll stay for one glass."

He guided her to the dining table, poured her a cup of red juice, and then sat across from her. She sniffed it. "So... did we?"

His thick brows touched. "Did we what?"

"The thing people do to make babies?"

He shrugged his shoulders, then took another swig of bourbon. "Oh, oh—you're talking about sex? Hell, yeah." His phone dinged, and he grabbed it. He used both thumbs, texting away as his nervous energy dissolved. "Boy will this baby change my life."

Something seemed off, like a puzzle piece that roughly fit, but didn't. She returned a finger to her phone's side button as she checked her messages and waited for him to finish. There were no messages or missed calls, not even from Zak. He was probably packing for the weekend away. And here she was with the only potential she had so far, a man who by the second sounded anything but reliable.

"I need to call Niko." But before he could dial anyone, his phone dinged again. He took one glance and scurried back to the window, peeked through the blinds.

The crazy had re-emerged, bringing with it a mountain of doubts about his story. Sure, she could wait for a DNA test but that would be months away. She needed answers now. Well, after she wet her parched mouth. She took a sip of the juice—and gagged. She enjoyed sweet more than tangy, but this tasted more like pure syrup. "What is this?"

"Cranberry?"

She waved an index finger back and forth.

"Crap, I must've poured you grenadine instead," he said, still posted by the window.

Enough. It was time to fact check him and go. "Where did we have sex?"

"Macey—"

She stood, clutching her purse and phone. "It's Lacey."

"Lace… " He stopped. In slow motion, he dropped the blind and backed away as a single bead of sweat trickled down his face. "We have to hide—now!" He sped towards Lacey at lightning speed, yanking her into a hallway with him.

She screamed. But he covered her mouth with his hand. "Shut up before you get us killed."

What the hell had she gotten herself into? He dragged her into his bedroom and dropped her onto the white-carpeted floor. "Please don't hurt me," she screamed.

He pressed a finger to her lips. "Shut up before I duct tape your mouth."

Why didn't she leave when she had a chance? Run before he locked her in his room? Her pulse slowed to a steady pounding in her chest as her stomach rolled and churned. Unable to control it, she upchucked French onion soup and grenadine syrup onto his floor. It reeked worse than death.

Bo thrust both fists by his side and grumbled, "Are you…" *indiscernible* "… kidding me?"

Lacey needed help like yesterday. And then she remembered help was right there in front of her—five clicks away. When the red SOS circle appeared, she pressed it.

A loud siren filled the room. Bo's eyes stretched out of their sockets as he tried to seize her phone, but Lacey threw it across the room before he could.

The walls vibrated as someone pulverized the front door. Bo clenched his jaws and reached underneath his mattress, pulling out a gun. "I'm not going down without a fight."

Lacey didn't have to be a rocket scientist to read between the lines. Bo Jameson was a man with troubles bigger than her and a new baby. She searched the room for somewhere to hide other than next to the attention-grabbing, silky-black sheets. But the lack of furniture left limited options. So she folded into a quivering ball and tucked her head.

From outside came more yelling, men shouting Bo's name, demanding him to open the door. Peeking, she noticed Bo slide his finger to the gun trigger.

Desperate, she pleaded with him. "What do they want? Maybe I can help you?"

He smirked. "They want the money I owe them."

The door banging continued as Lacey's underarms poured sweat. "I can help. I have savings." She would empty her bank account if it meant escaping alive.

Bo laughed. "Forgive me, but you don't strike me as a millionaire."

"You owe millions?"

"Yeah, but I'm about to flip these paintings for a profit. These bozos just don't have patience."

The pounding on the door grew louder and the voices angrier until gunfire blasts muffled them. She squeezed her eyes closed and recited the Lord's Prayer, ending with, "Please, don't me let me die." In desperation, she swore if she made it out alive, she would tell Zak the truth—the whole truth—and nothing but the truth.

So help her God.

The sound of broken glass chimed in Lacey's ears followed by a slew of commanding voices drawing near. The blood drained from Lacey's fingers and toes. She didn't want to die. She had too many reasons to live.

Footsteps marched closer. Then a deafening pop resonated through the room as hinges snapped, sending the bedroom door crashing to the floor. Bo dropped the gun and thrust his hands in the air. "I surrender."

Before Lacey could move, someone yanked her to her feet. She squealed at the top of her lungs until she recognized the uniforms. Police officers, not renegade debt collectors on a mission to kill. They saved her.

After waiting for what seemed like hours, a bushy-browed police officer arrived and took a seat across from her. "Mrs. Winters, I'm Detective Connors." He offered his hand, and she shook it. "You're lucky to be alive. Mr. Jameson and his friends have quite the track record."

Her shoulders slumped forward. "Yes, lucky me."

"If you'll bear with me a little longer, I need to review a few things before your husband gets here."

She straightened. "Wait, what do you mean my husband?"

He pulled her phone from a manilla envelope. "We called a man listed under *Hubby*."

She pressed her palm against her forehead and remembered editing his contact info in case someone doubted their story. "Zak, yes." *Boy was this going to be a fun night.*

"Don't worry, he'll be here soon. Now back to business. Mr. Jameson played nice and has turned over evidence against multiple high-profile criminals. He also confirmed you guys had met for the first time today. We already knew, but for whatever reason, he wanted to make sure we told you. Any idea why?"

A weight lifted from her body. "A case of mistaken identity... I thought he was someone else."

"Makes sense." He scratched the side of his face. "Typically, we'd want to do a thorough investigation, but considering the statement Mr. Jameson has provided us, and your obvious state," he said, gesturing towards her belly, "I side with releasing you. You're free to go. Just don't come back."

He chuckled before escorting her to the front lobby, past a shirtless giant whose entire chest had been inked with skeletons, area codes, teardrops, rosary beads, and so much more. But the best, the one that made her look twice, Penny Wise the clown wearing a life jacket with a line tatted underneath, *we all float down here.*

Her head was certainly swimming as she stepped outside the double doors. Zak stood waiting. And with only a few words exchanged between them, he assisted her into the waiting minivan. She buckled in herself. And when he turned the ignition key, she set her sights to the inside of the mystery vehicle. In the back seat, she noticed two car seats, shriveled chicken nuggets, a sippy cup, and champagne-colored luggage.

She took a second glance. "That is my suitcase. What's it doing in here?"

He turned into traffic. "I just picked you up from the county jail with no idea why you were even there. I'm taking you to my parents' house where I can protect you."

He couldn't be serious. "I can't go to your parents'."

He shook his head. "Every time you need me, I show up for you." He waved his fake ring in her face. "The way I see it, it's time for you to show up for me."

She twisted in her seat, faced him. "If you tell your parents this baby is yours and that this marriage is real, it will devastate them when we break up. Think about it, do we really want to drag more people into this *charade*?"

He kept one hand on the wheel, stroked the side of his face with the other. "I told them."

"Excuse me? What exactly did you tell them?"

He took a deep breath. "I told them I'm married and having a baby. I said we would have announced it sooner, but we wanted to make sure everything was okay... with the bleeding and all."

Her mouth dropped. Speechless, she rotated back to her normal position and stared straight ahead. At what? Blurred red and white lights, a pitch black sky, a sliver of moon? It didn't matter because she had lost her focus.

"What did you expect? I panicked—and needed a car." He gripped the steering wheel with colorless fingers.

Since he took away her choice in the matter, she would keep plenty of emotional distance to survive the weekend—from them and Zak. And she would start with silence, see how far that got her.

With nothing between them other than the hum of the van, Zak turned on the radio.

15

Zak's pajama-clad family greeted them at the turquoise door of a pale yellow colonial-styled home. The first one to make their way over to Lacey was a broad-shouldered, fuzzy wheat-headed man with a warm smile. Zak, a good six-inches taller, fist bumped him. "Lacey, my dad, Kyle."

"Nice to meet you." Lacey reached out her hand, but he pushed it away, pulled her in for a hug instead.

"You're family now. And our family doesn't do handshakes." He patted her back a few times before escorting her over to Zak's mother, a graceful woman with the face of Jane Seymour and the height of Heidi Klum. "This is my wife, Meredith."

"Call me, Mom," she said, surveying Lacey from head to toe. "You are so lovely, and Zak tells me smart, too." She draped her arms around Lacey and squeezed.

"Is no one going to introduce me?"

Lacey turned her attention to the tall, slender woman poised with both hands on her hips, her fine hair hanging just below her shoulders, her eyes clones of Zak's. Without hesitation, she embraced Lacey the same as everyone else. "I'm Zak's younger and prettier sister."

"Since I don't care if I'm pretty, I'll let you keep that title." Zak tousled Rebecca's hair. "But you'll never take away my status as the baby of the family."

"Speaking of a baby, Zak told us you guys are expecting in November." Meredith rested her steepled hands against her chin. It reminded Lacey of her own mother, who always made the same gesture whenever she was excited.

If only Lacey had waited to investigate Bo, she would be enjoying a warm bath in her apartment instead of creating false hope in a group of people that embraced her, called her family. She lowered her eyes.

Zak slipped his arm around her lower back and drew her close. She wanted to push him away, fault him for bringing his family into the lie, but she couldn't blame him for the pile of crap she laid. If she wished out of her current position, then she would confess, follow through on the promise made at the brink of death, stop this before they grew attached to a baby that by no blood relation could be part of the family.

It was now or never. She pushed back her shoulders. "I need to tell you all something. This baby is—"

Zak spun around and faced her, pressed his forehead against hers. "So blessed to be surrounded by so much love." He leaned back and pleaded without words.

Lacey turned her attention to his family, Rebecca's shuffling feet, Kyle's widening grin, and Meredith's glossy eyes. And back to Zak, who just held her. How could she crush their spirits? Embarrass him? She couldn't. "I was about to say the same thing."

"How sweet," Meredith said, her folded hands now held firmly against her chest. "Well, come inside. It's late, and I'm sure you guys, and our new grandbaby, need rest."

Kyle led them into a home filled with colorful walls, floral patterns, wainscoting, and heavy drapes. The traditional things that made a person feel at home.

Meredith guided them along the hall and then into a cozy but masculine room. "Here you are."

Lacey surveyed the space. Taped to the closest door was an aging *Sports Illustrated* poster and lining the shelves were several high school trophies. Baseball hats hung on the corners of the dresser mirror and the headboard of a small bed.

"This was Zak's old room. We haven't upgraded the double yet, but I believe you two should fit comfortably enough."

Zak rolled Lacey's suitcase over by the closet. "Mom, do you have any extra pillows? Lacey needs them." He smirked.

Meredith tapped her finger to her cheek. "Um… probably not too many because I gave most of them to Rebecca and Roy for the twins." She turned to Lacey. "Roy is Rebecca's husband, and they have two of the cutest identical boys you'll ever meet."

"Aren't all toddlers cute?" Zak asked, slipping out of his shoes.

Lacey would say *no* silently to herself. "It's okay Meredith—I meant

Mom," she said, gesturing towards the bed. "Those are plenty enough."

"But what about the wall, honey?" Zak's face reddened, and his cheeks puffed as he enjoyed himself at Lacey's expense.

"Oh, we can move the bed away from the wall. Here, help me Zak," Meredith said, gripping the footboard.

"You don't have to do that. Zak is just being silly."

"The same as his father I see." Meredith hugged Zak and Lacey and then danced her eyes between the both of them. "I'm so excited for you guys." She wiped a happy tear with the edge of her robe. "Look at me. I better go before I try to stay the night in here. See you two in the morning." Her housecoat swayed back and forth in perfect rhythm as she strolled away.

Lacey squeezed the back of her neck.

"Don't worry. I have a plan." He picked up a pillow from the bed. "I'll take the basement couch."

She noticed the bags under his eyes. He was tired, and it was her fault. For weeks she had been dragging him around by the gonads for her own selfish purposes. The least she could do was make sure he got a good night's sleep. "If anyone deserves to be on the couch, it should be me."

"That won't happen, not in your condition."

"I knew you would say that. So you can take the left," Lacey said, unzipping her suitcase and pulling out her pajamas, the tattered tee and joggers. The fact he remembered her favorite pair brought a rising warmth to her cheeks as she held them up for him to see. "Thanks."

He stared too long. "You're welcome."

"Well, I'll shower, unless you want to go first."

"Ladies first," he said, waving his hand towards the attached bathroom.

She bathed under the narrow stream of water in a fiberglass tub-shower combo with a baseball stamped plastic curtain and then returned to bed as Zak took his turn soaping his hot, naked body. She palmed her forehead. Control it, she told herself. The space was too small for raging hormones stirred by a near-death experience. Even on her back with both arms and legs tucked next to her body, she wondered how he'd fit.

And when he slid in beside her, she had the answer. He didn't, not without parts of his body pressed against hers. "Are you going to survive without a pillow-wall?" He chuckled.

She rolled on her side, faced him. "You're getting a kick out of this, aren't you?"

"Maybe a little." He shifted, tried to give her more room. "I'm just relieved you're safe. Want to talk about what happened?"

She twiddled her fingers beneath the plaid comforter. "There's nothing to say other than I was in the wrong place at the wrong time. Thankfully, the police recognized that, and thankfully, you rescued me. Although, I wish you hadn't brought your parents into this."

He folded the pillow under his head. "My parents seem thrilled to be a part of this."

"Only because they think the baby is yours, but it's not."

"It can be."

She stretched her eyes, absorbed his words. "What do you mean?"

"I mean I want to stay together, be there for you and the baby."

For a while, she kept her lips slightly parted, unable to speak. She gazed at the soft lines on his face, the relaxed posture, and knew he meant every single word. And more than anything, she wanted to agree. Locating the father had become a disaster. And considering the potentials she had encountered so far, she was afraid to continue the search.

But at some point she'd have to, and where would that leave her and Zak?

He found her hands and held them. "Don't answer yet. Just promise me you'll think about it."

"I promise," she said, finding her body drawn to his by invisible forces.

And while she wanted to resist the pull, bury the urge, it was impossible. Her crazy hormone-driven libido had awakened. So with a steady stream of raw, unadulterated emotion, she leaned forward to kiss him.

But Zak bypassed her attempt and pressed his lips against her cheek instead. Then he pushed her back, held her at a distance. "Wait, if we kiss and you regret it, do you plan to send me to the basement couch?"

His lips were such a short distance from hers. And they were all she wanted. "I won't regret it this time."

"I hope not," he said, easing his lips onto hers, taking his time exploring. If her mouth was a forest, then his was the spark that ignited the raging fire inside her. His arms slipped around her, and her body melted against his. And together they burned, a combustion of oxygenated passion and want, until his lips, his tongue, his kiss consumed her.

When they rose for air amid the smoldering ashes, Zak anchored his eyes onto hers and—wrinkled his face? Shocked, she had to ask, "Was it that horrible?"

"What? No, it was amazing. I thought you might kick me or something." He held a safe distance. "Well, are you?"

Kick him? If anything, she wanted to kiss him all over again. "No, I think you're safe."

"In that case, I might press my luck." With a delicate touch, he ushered her face closer to his. "Do you realize how beautiful you are?"

She cocked her head to one side. "Now you're trying to score points."

"No, I'm not. You're gorgeous. High cheekbones..." He stroked a finger across each, one at a time. "And skin like creamed coffee... your freckles, the coffee grounds floating on top."

Lacey burst into a fit of laughter. "Where do you come up with this stuff? Coffee grounds, really?"

"Don't interrupt me," he demanded, his expression much like a professor studying his work. "On to your lips, they're—um—not overly plump and not too wide, just perfect. And super soft, which is why I enjoy kissing them."

He leaned in and took her mouth, tender at first and then fervent before stopping abruptly. He turned away for a second, blew out a heavy breath. "You're trying to distract me, but I won't let you. On to those enchanting eyes, the perfect shade of reddish-brown, like mahogany."

"The color of Mr. Caldwell's desk? Your compliments are spiraling downhill."

"Well, while I'm on that path, I should add that your nose is a little pointy."

"You went from flattery to insults? You realize I'm dealing with fragile hormones don't you?" She ran her finger down his nose. "I guess if we're being honest, your nose is slightly crooked."

"Ooh, someone's upset. No need to be. Everything about you, your personality, your face, your curls... and your sexy body... makes you irresistible." He took a deep breath. "Just more reasons why I don't want to break up or fake divorce. I want to be with you."

If only she knew who the father was, knew what to expect, then she could make a solid plan for the future. One that might include Zak. But with so many unknowns, she needed time to think. Even though she wanted desperately to concede. "I'll consider it."

He raked his hands through his hair. "I hope so... because I'm in love with you. I have been for a long time."

Those words should have angered her. At a complicated time in her life, the selfish mention of such a thing should have made her blood boil. But it didn't. It didn't because underneath the stacks of lists and plans, laid buried the same feeling. And whether or not that feeling surfaced into words, she couldn't deny it existed.

"You don't have to say anything. I just wanted you to know."

Her heart stopped and restarted. Before, raging hormones had driven the insatiable hunger for him, for every inch of his body, but in that moment, love led the way. A slow-simmer of delight boiled over and flooded her veins with a burning need. And the growing heat building inside her fueled her eagerness to touch, drove her hands to his chest where they landed on the soft cotton t-shirt he wore.

His muscles tensed as his lips released a low moan. And it was there in that place she found the words. They flew from her mouth, a surprise even to herself. "Make love to me."

He hesitated, forcing some distance between them. "Is that what you want?"

Fisting his shirt, she tugged at him, drew him closer. "Take me—before I overthink it."

He pried her fingers from the cotton material now wrinkled from her grip and slowed her down. "If you're sure, then why rush it? We have all night."

He meant it, taking his time with each softhearted kiss, gingerly set in places that triggered the most exaggerated reactions, the kind that arched what should be straight.

This was happening.

He raised himself into a sitting position. And with one smooth and swift motion, positioned her onto his lap. Face-to-face with the man who said he loved her, the man who wanted to be the father of her baby whether he was on paper on not. With trembling hands, he fought with the clasp on her strapless bra—and won.

Her tattered tee fell cool against her bare chest, but not for long. His hands slipped underneath and lifted it. Suddenly, she couldn't remember the last time she'd shaved her armpits. But he didn't care, dragging her shirt over her head and dropping it to the bed.

But she did, about armpit hair and milk-filled breasts. She crossed her arms over her chest, ignoring the flames in his eyes. "Can you turn off the light?"

His one-sided dimple appeared. "No…"

No? "Okay, I'll do it."

He shook his head. "No…"

"You can't stop me." With one arm still covering her breast, she used the other to reach for the lamp.

He pulled her back. "You're acting like this is the first time I've seen them."

She wondered if he had ever peeked when she dressed, and now she knew. "That was different."

He lured her closer, walked both hands up her back, leaving a trail of tingling goosebumps. For a moment, she nearly lost her grip. But he didn't stop. "No, it's not. You're beautiful pregnant, too beautiful to hide in the dark. Let go—please."

She could sense the ache in his voice. But still, she couldn't find the courage.

Deliberately enticing, he removed his shirt, one arm, the other, and then over his head and onto the floor. She studied the toned hills, mapped every mole, scar, and tan line. Watched the heightened rise and fall of his chest.

All before he pressed his naked skin against the only wall keeping them apart, her arm. "Let me make love to you."

There they were, those words that turned her into a woman without self-control, a wild animal operating on pure instinct. Her arm fell to her side. Free to explore, he did just that, his hands setting fire to open fields that his lips then cooled, sending shivering chills down her spine. No longer reserved, she dug her fingertips into rippled muscles, planted her lips on the nape of his neck, and pressed her body as close to his as her belly would allow.

She couldn't get enough of his tender touch, or his manly scent, or the taste of his mouth, which she delighted in more than once.

With the care of fragile glass, he rolled her onto her back, tucked the pillow beneath her head. Towering above her, his eyes took in her fully exposed body from head to toe. She resisted the urge to hide under covers and allowed him the pleasure. Satisfied, he hooked his fingers underneath the elastic band of her pajamas and slid them off. His fingers grazed her thighs, spreading warmth in their path.

If ever her insides ached for a man, it was then.

But he left her wanting as he jumped off the bed and kicked out of all his clothes, except his knee-high socks. Thankfully, he wasted no time finding his way back to her, rolling her onto the side, curling his body around her from behind.

From there, he kissed the tops of her shoulders and then the nape of her neck. He tickled her with his breath. "You still have time to stop me."

She blocked the racing thoughts of whether she would be good enough, or if she even remembered what she was doing after a year without sex. But she had come this far, given this much. Why stop now? She closed her eyes, absorbed every sensation, every rhythmic vibration and melodic titillation of flesh craving to be united.

"Never." And she meant it.

There were no more words to be spoken, only actions to be taken. And her body talked, rocking in motion against his, arms and legs tangled in an ensemble of passion. Tongues locked together in perfect harmony.

Sweat dripped from his brow as he delved deeper. And beads of perspiration scaled down to meet hers, then rolled away in a gentle chord across naked flesh. "Am I hurting you?"

To show him he wasn't, she pushed her back against his chest and gripped his arms, the ones locked tight around her. "The exact opposite."

The easy motions intensified, becoming a crescendo of sensuality that sent the headboard banging against the wall. She pressed a hand against it, held it quiet, and caught the quick catch of his breath, like the fermata on a sheet of music.

"Lacey..." Her name left his lips in a wild pitch as urgent hands found her hips, steadied them as he thrust into her, drove harder, tuning her sweet spot. She couldn't think, couldn't breathe. She was far too invested. He had driven her to the pinnacle of pleasure and then pushed her over the edge.

She gasped, frantically clawing and pinching at the stiff, shuddering muscles wrapped around her. Suddenly, he wasn't deep enough, and she wasn't close enough. Her wild legs locked against the wall. And using what might she had left, she propelled herself against him, taking everything he offered, meeting every motion with equal drive.

And when he had emptied all he had, his strong, rigid body collapsed.

She gave one last push against weak muscles and sent him careening to the ground in a resounding thump that shook the quiet house. She jumped up, turned her gaze to his sexy body sprawled across the floor wearing nothing but a pair of white socks. "I'm so sorry."

He gave an exhausted grin. "I couldn't think of a better ending."

A loud knock on the door startled them. Lacey heaved the covers over her naked body.

"Is everything okay in there? We heard a crash." *Shoot, Zak's parents.*

Zak muffled a chuckle as the doorknob shook. "They're persistent," he whispered to Lacey.

"Say something before they barge in here."

He tousled his wild mane. "We're—"

"The baby kicked," Lacey squealed, dropping the covers to study her baby bump with intensity.

"Are you sure? How did it feel?" Zak asked, moving himself into a kneeling position.

Her cheeks lifted. "Like someone's tickling me from the inside."

"Look at that strong little man—or woman," Zak said, leaning over and kissing Lacey's belly.

The door swung open and both of Zak's parents charged in the room. Lacey barely got the covers pulled over herself in time. There was no hope for Zak.

Meredith shrieked as she reflexively slapped her hand over Kyle's eyes. It didn't hide his gaping mouth. In a quick motion, Meredith spun Kyle around and then herself. "Looks like you guys... um... are okay."

"Better than okay," Kyle added.

Meredith whacked him on the back of the head. "Kyle."

"I'm trying to make it less awkward."

Zak pressed his fingers into his forehead. "You guys leaving would make it less awkward."

"Yes, let's do that. See you in the morning," Meredith said, locking her arms around Kyle and guiding him out.

Lacey crashed on her pillow. "I can never face your parents again."

"Don't worry about it. They'll be too embarrassed to mention it *ever*. And I bet they'll never barrel themselves into my room again." She slid over to her side of the bed as he climbed in beside her. "Enough about them, though. That was amazing."

It certainly was. Never in all her years had she felt this, never even knew such a thing existed. Well, maybe in the sex dream, but she wasn't sure that even counted. And before then, sex had always been just that—sex. But with Zak, it was different. They connected. Although, she couldn't rule out the reason being pregnancy hormones —or maybe a lack of recent experience. She hugged the pillow beside her, pressed it against her chest. "I hope I wasn't too rusty."

"It wouldn't have mattered. But if you must know, it was better than the first time for sure."

Did he pity her? Was that the nice way of saying it wasn't remarkable? "It doesn't take much to exceed a first time."

"I don't know, the first time was pretty great."

He obviously didn't have the same disastrous first experience with sex she had. He rolled her over to face her, his sweaty and flushed skin catching her attention. "Maybe I didn't make myself clear. If we're having sex like that for the rest of our lives—I'm never letting you go. I just hope it wasn't too rough for the baby."

She dropped her gaze, ashamed of the replay reeling through her mind. "No,… everything's great." She giggled. "Except the part where your parents got involved."

He lifted her chin and savored her mouth with his. "They won't be back." He removed the pillow from between them.

And this time, she made sure not to knock him off the bed.

16

When the rays of morning light beamed through the blinds, she opened her eyes to her head laying on Zak's chest and his arm draping across her back. And before she could move, the exhilarating—and terrifying—memories of the past night's events flooded her brain. So much for her plan to not cross the line with him. Not only did they cross it, they annihilated any evidence of its existence, leaving her in uncharted waters so to speak.

"You're finally awake," he said, rubbing his heavy-lidded eyes.

"How do you know I didn't wake up first?"

"Because I've been watching you sleep. I figured you needed the rest." He gave her a lopsided grin.

She kept her position, listened to the steady thump in his chest, a sharp contrast to the desperate pounding she'd heard at the height of passion. "After last night, I would say that's a correct assumption."

He kissed her forehead. "But everything's still okay, right? I didn't hurt you?"

She ran her hands over his bare skin. "Zak, stop worrying about me so much. I'll let you know if something's wrong."

"I can't help it," he said, twisting her curls around his fingers. "Yesterday I drove a hundred miles per hour to the county jail to get you. And the only thing that raced through my mind was if something happened to you I'd never forgive myself for not staying behind, for not protecting you."

"Even if staying with me meant missing your parents' anniversary?"

"To keep you safe, I would."

It was that selfless commitment to her well-being that drew

attention to her own shattered moral compass. She should have never lied to him. Because the resulting guilt from not telling him weighed on her like a concrete block—as it should. Zak deserved the truth. He always deserved the truth. And while in the beginning she worried about losing the contract, now she couldn't help but worry about losing him. Enough so, she kept silent on the matter.

Zak's chest lifted as the smell of bacon surrounded them. "That's our cue. Probably best if we get ready for breakfast before they beat down the door."

She slapped her hands over her face. "Don't remind me. Can I eat in here?"

He slipped his arms under hers and pulled her close, in the perfect position for a kiss, which he gave—and she accepted—with pleasure. "Trust me, they'll act like nothing ever happened."

He was right. When they arrived at the dining table, Meredith and Kyle greeted them as if they hadn't seen their son buck naked on his bedroom floor post-sex with his *wife*.

"Glad you guys made it," Rebecca said, "One more second and Dad would have rammed the door. He loves his bacon." Rebecca pointed at the piece he held millimeters from his mouth.

If only she knew, Lacey thought.

"He shouldn't even be eating bacon. It raises his blood pressure," Meredith said, giving him a stern facial warning as she snatched the other two pieces from his plate.

"If you didn't cook it, I couldn't eat it." He shoved the only piece she had left him in his mouth.

"Kyle, shut it, or you'll get a bowl of oats every day."

Kyle zipped his fingers across his lips and winked.

Zak pulled out a traditional dining chair with a weaved basket bottom for Lacey. She took her seat at the same time Meredith took one across from her. "So, how long did you and Zak date before you got married?"

The question caught Lacey off-guard and left her speechless.

"Sorry, I didn't mean to come off rude. We're thrilled to have you join the family. It's just that while Zak has mentioned you lots of times, he said nothing about you two dating, much less being married with a baby on the way."

Lacey wished she had consulted with Zak before stepping into the morning ambush. It was hard to answer when she didn't have a clue what he had or hadn't told them. "We've been friends for years, and at some point the friendship turned into something more. So it's hard to narrow down the exact time when we started officially dating."

Zak swallowed the bite of pancake in his mouth. "I'd say about seven weeks of official dating. The baby was a quick surprise—just like Meghan and Harry's."

"Well, aren't you the comedian?" Meredith took a sip of coffee and then set the cup on the table. "But Lacey getting pregnant is a wonderful sign."

Zak added more syrup to the rest of his pancakes. "Yes, it is. It means the plumbing works."

His plumbing worked just fine, Lacey mumbled to herself. But probably not in the way his parents had considered.

"I'm not surprised he waited to tell us. Other than those few wild years he had, he's kept his love life private. He was waiting for *the one,*" Kyle said before shoving a forkful of egg whites into his mouth.

"Well, I'm glad he found her. He deserves it," Rebecca said with a beaming smile aimed at Lacey. "Besides, I'm tired of what's her name asking if he's available every time I enter her check-out line at the grocery store. You remember her, Zak? *The one* who always slipped the perfumed notes in the mailbox?" Rebecca poured herself more juice.

Zak nodded. "The ones that attracted the swarm of bees that stung our mailman? How could I forget?"

Rebecca rested her hand on Lacey's forearm. "The mailman swore we planted them there on purpose and even threatened to sue my parents."

Meredith giggled. "Thankfully, the little girl confessed before we had to hire a lawyer."

Zak wiped his hands on a napkin. "Okay, enough about secret admirers. I've found the one, and that's what matters." He squeezed Lacey's thigh, sent a jolt of electricity down her leg.

"You certainly did." Kyle said, using a remaining piece of pancake to swipe his plate clean before tossing it in his mouth.

"The twins will be so excited to have a cousin. I wanted you to meet them this morning, but Roy had to run errands for the party. Of course, they wanted to go with Daddy." Rebecca glanced at the clock. "Which reminds me, we need to hurry and get to the florist."

Meredith stood from the table, along with Kyle. "We sure do. I don't want to be late. You guys relax and enjoy yourselves while we're gone. I promise we'll be back soon."

Zak stood. "If there's something you want us to do, we can."

"Zak, you get out the chairs from the garage and place them by the tables Roy set up—while Lacey props her feet up. She needs to take it easy. Now Lacey, if he's not taking good care of you, call me and I'll set him straight," Meredith said, kissing Zak's and Lacey's cheeks.

And within no time, they rushed out the door, leaving Zak and Lacey alone.

"What do we do now?" Lacey asked, pushing aside the rush of R-rated imagery flashing before her eyes.

Zak scooped her into his arms. "You heard my mom? I have to take care of you."

"Put me down," Lacey said, laughing out her commands.

He carried her to the sofa and laid her down gently, hovering only inches above her as his fingertips danced under her shirt, then under her bra. She pushed him away, blocked him with her own hands.

"Stop doing that. Stop hiding yourself." He removed her hands and replaced them with his own. He took hold of her breast in a grip firm enough it left her center tingling. "Now are you comfortable?"

Suddenly, it didn't matter they were on his parent's sofa or that at any second someone might return and catch them. The yearning to have him on top of her blocked any sane thought she had. Her hands wandered his chest as his lips brushed hers, delicate at first, then plunging deeper, faster, a wild current driving her into an abyss of pure passion.

And if she drowned on his kiss, at least she'd die happy.

Lucky for her, he ended the kiss before it went that far. "I'm going to put those chairs out—before I forget. Prop your feet up and rest for when I get back."

She swallowed hard. "I'll try."

He gave her one last quick kiss before heading out the door, leaving her alone with nothing but her thoughts.

What did she think she was doing? And where did she think this relationship would go without a map, a sense of direction? She couldn't just keep having sex without considering the repercussions. Eventually, she would find the father, and once she did, would Zak be okay with the *sorry I lied to you* story? Or would it destroy his trust in her? She dragged her hands down the sides of her face.

Why had she let it get this far? Why let him confess his love for her? Never mind, it was a stupid question. She knew why. Because she loved him as much as he loved her and love made people act foolish.

And so did carrying on without a plan.

In need of guidance, she called Doby, explaining her new found position before even saying hello.

"Oh my god, you finally had sex with him. Was it all you imagined?"

Lacey clenched and unclenched her jaw. "I didn't imagine it—well, maybe I did—but that's not the point. I'm calling because I need help."

Doby snickered. "It sounds like you're doing fine without me."

"You know what I mean. Should I tell him I lied? Tell him about the list?... Stop sleeping with him?"

"What do you want to do?"

"It doesn't matter what I want, it's about what is best. I still have two potentials left to investigate."

"Exactly, two potentials who don't have a clue you're pregnant. Hell, they might not even remember who you are. So why give up your bird in the hand for those two bats in the bush?"

Lacey pinched the bridge of her nose. "Can you be serious right now?"

"I'm being very serious. Zak loves you and wants to stay with you. He's choosing to help you raise this baby. What more could you ask for? Is he making demands for the truth?"

Lacey squeezed her eyes closed. "No, but only because he thinks it's Finn's baby."

"Even better. Did he demand you tell Finn?" Doby paused. "No, he didn't because it doesn't bother him. He doesn't care about the extra details. And you shouldn't either. It's time for you to do what makes you happy, not for your father, not for your job, but for you. Do you love Zak?"

She wished she didn't, but she did. "Yes, I do."

"Then you already know what to do."

Doby was right. What harm could come from taking a short break from the list to enjoy a few nights of well-deserved adult pleasure? It wasn't like she had to make any immediate major decisions, or any changes for that matter. Zak had already moved in with her, and they had already announced their relationship to everyone. Well, minus the part about it being one big sham.

But that wasn't the point. The point was Zak had asked her to postpone the fake divorce, not make a lifelong commitment. And considering how natural being with him felt, why not oblige, relish the moment while it lasted?

Starting with the anniversary party she had fancied up for in a maternity-friendly, black satin cocktail dress, courtesy of Zak's packing skills.

She stood by one of the photo props, waiting for Zak to finish his baseball talk with his buddies. And as her mind drifted to the ways Zak made her insides quiver, she half-watched Meredith greet guests at the side gate. Until a person, and not just any random person, stepped into her line of sight, stopping even her breath.

Brent Walker, the co-founder of the Sanctity of Marriage Coalition, strolled in holding a present adorned with a big silver bow. From a distance, Lacey watched Meredith take the gift—and Brent—into her arms.

How did Meredith know him? Was he such a close family friend he would leave the hustle and bustle of New York for a backyard shindig in Connecticut? Lacey certainly needed to find out before someone told him who she was. Because even though he wouldn't physically recognize her, as they had never met in person, a man like Brent Walker would recognize the name of the person designing his new building. And if he was friends with the Cooper family, then a messy divorce, even a fake one, could hurt her career more than losing the contract.

Because there was not one person in corporate America who didn't know who Brent Walker was.

She had to find Zak, get the scoop on the relationship, and make a quick plan. And she found him mingled in with a group of men his age, each holding a beer while arguing sports statistics.

Lacey grabbed him by the biceps. "Excuse me, I'm stealing him."

They lifted their beers, and in unison said, "Sure."

Zak held up a finger to the guy wearing a baseball cap and a tie. "Hold that thought," Zak said, following Lacey to a private space beside the vinyl fence.

She shook his arms. "Brent Walker is at your party, *the* Brent Walker. Please tell me he's not a close family friend," she begged, suppressing the urge to vomit.

He gave her a smug grin. "Don't worry, he's not a family friend."

She could finally let go of the breath she'd been holding onto forever. "Oh, thank god."

"He's my brother."

Her mouth dropped as she yanked both Zak's arms, tried to rip them from his body. "Why would you say that? That's a cruel joke. You don't even have the same last name."

Zak pried her pincher claws from his arms and restrained them with his. "Because he took his husband's last name."

The yard spun. Her legs lost balance. Zak caught her and seated her on a nearby dead tree stump. She buried her face in her hands. "Why would you hide the fact that Brent Walker is your brother? Don't you think that's something I should know"

"Maybe, but he's big on keeping family ties separate from business. He doesn't want people to claim he makes decisions based on favoritism."

"You mean *nepotism*?"

"They're the same. But despite that, I'd rather not have everyone comparing me to him or reminding me of how much he's accomplished. Because my work is important, too."

Of course, Zak's work was important, but couldn't he see this had nothing to do with his work and everything to do with the contract right now? Brent wouldn't destroy his own flesh and blood's career, but the horrid ex-wife?—With a snap of a finger. She wanted to squeeze her curls, but she had trapped them in an elegant bun. So she opted for yanking at the strays. "This can't be happening."

Zak crouched until he met her at eye-level. "It's okay. You don't have to stress. He'll love you just like my parents love you."

"Are you kidding? When he finds out about the lie, and how I forced you into all of this, and how the baby's not yours—"

"He will still support us. He's not a monster, and he would never hurt me or the people I love. Besides, he only finds out if you end it."

She leaned forward, hugged herself. "But that's the plan, it's been the plan since the beginning."

He stroked the sides of her arms. "Plans can change, Lacey. You said you'd consider it, so please do. Until then, see the good side of this. You have access to someone Margot respects and will listen to, so... if anything goes wrong with the project while you're out on leave, we can call Brent. As long as you don't play the *disgruntled employee* card, of course."

Her cheeks rose high on their own. "Zak Cooper, did I hear you make a plan?"

He chuckled, revealing the dimple she found herself so fond of. "You're wearing off on me. Now, can we get back to the party?" He pulled her to her feet, and then hand-in-hand they joined the rest of the crowd, the seventy-five plus people that had gathered to celebrate his parents' thirtieth anniversary. She relaxed her shoulders, inhaled the aroma of spicy meatballs and the sweet cinnamon spice of apple-pie martinis, Meredith's favorite. Although, they forced Lacey to drink the child's version.

The only thing missing from it was the buzz, but she didn't need it. She had plenty to be buzzed about, starting with one very handsome Zak Cooper.

"There they are," Meredith said, guiding Brent towards Lacey and Zak, past the lights twinkling in rhythm to '70s music.

Zak slipped his arm around Lacey as his mother and brother approached.

"Brent, this is Zak's wife, Lacey."

Lacey offered a trembling hand to him, but he ignored it and hugged her. "My new sister-in-law, huh? Nice to meet you." He leaned back, held her out at arm's length. "I can't believe my brother married the lead designer on one of my biggest projects. What a small world?"

"Yeah... a tiny world," Lacey said, noticing how much Brent favored his father. He had a stocky build, a face that showed age easier than his siblings, fuzzy orange hair, and freckles. The only similarity he and Zak shared were the eyes.

Brent hugged Zak. "And a baby? So everything works after all? This is great news. I can't wait to be an uncle again. I hope it's a girl. We need more estrogen in the family."

What was the obsession with a man's plumbing in this family?

Zak kissed Lacey's cheek. "We do, but I'm sure it's a boy. Wait, where's Vance? Did you bring him?"

Brent shook his head. "Oh, he couldn't make it. He had an ad shoot. I barely made it myself."

"Well, I'm glad you did. I don't think I would have forgiven you if you didn't." Meredith poked a finger at Brent's chest.

"Now Mom, you know that's not true." He closed the space between his bushy brows.

Something caught Meredith's attention and made her smile. "Ooh, it's Chad and his wife." She grabbed Brent's arm. "Go introduce yourself. He's the one I told you about who's trying to start up the domestic abuse shelter downtown."

"Okay, sure." Brent turned to Lacey one last time. "So nice to meet you. We must have dinner one day so you can meet Vance."

It may be sooner rather than later if Margot allows Jocelyn to change my design, Lacey mumbled to herself. "That would be great."

As he and Meredith scurried away, she noticed Zak scanning the crowd. "I wanted you to meet Roy and the twins, but I don't see them. The boys must have fallen asleep." He looked around one last time and then laughed. "See this." He pointed to a tall, slender woman with a sharp nose and chin. Her thin lips turned inward. "That's Mrs. Krump, our cantankerous neighbor, and just in case you're wondering, that is her happy face."

She reminded Lacey of a tyrannical headmistress. "Poor Mr. Krump —if she's married."

"She is, to a man half her height and with fewer balls." Zak chuckled. "Come on, let me introduce you to some people."

He did, to the entire room. And not one time did he have to say anything about the baby. Meredith and Kyle beat him to it. Although the story they had shared with everyone was a far cry from the truth. But Lacey secretly pretended it was the truth. Because it felt good to be pampered, to be congratulated for being pregnant. As it should be under normal circumstances. To taste what could be, to relish in the comfort and support of family... was beyond magical.

And if only for a night, she was Cinderella and Zak her prince—at least until the stroke of midnight.

So when the glasses of champagne and cocktails raised high in the night sky after Brent's toast, Lacey lifted her glass of sparkling grape juice with them. From then on, she embraced the moment, embraced belonging, no matter how time constrained. And after everyone lowered their drinks, and with Journey's *Faithfully* blasting through the speakers, she accepted Zak's dance request.

He guided her to the paved patio where she clung to his body and danced. With each sway, she set flight to the burdens, the stress, the future, and the what ifs. And with each tap of her heel against concrete, she danced away the anxiety over potential fathers. Then, in a carefree twirl of freedom, she reached her arms to the stars until Zak spun her back to his earth, back to the strong hold that made her feel safe.

But most importantly, back to the man that made her feel loved.

He stopped mid-rhythm and tilted her chin with the gentle touch of his hand. With a sparkle in his eye, he explored her face, studied every freckle, every mole. She waited for the kiss, waited for his lips to take hers. It was the next predictable step. But he didn't.

Instead, he held his blink longer than he should—breathed in all the air his lungs could take—and then found her once again. "I love you... I've always loved you. You don't know how long I was afraid to say those words, afraid of how you'd react. But now, despite my fear, I can't *not* say those words."

Her hands cupped the sides of his face. And without overthinking, without analyzing each breath and step of her life, giving no consideration to the nagging list, she responded. "Then don't stop. I love you, too."

The corners of his mouth rose to his ears. "Then marry me—for real."

In that moment, they were the only two people on earth. The noise, the crowd, the lights, everything else disappeared. But love remained. It drove her senses, assured her that her marriage was more than a fairytale. Marriage could be a reality. And why not? He made her laugh when she wanted to cry, took care of her when she was sick, turned her half into a whole. She couldn't picture life without him.

And weren't they nearly married, anyway?

She pursed her lips, ready to respond, but stopped. "What if you realize it's too much for you? What if raising another man's baby isn't what you expected?"

He stroked the side of her face with the back of his hand. "I won't walk away from you no matter what. In fact, I have a plan if you say yes. All we have to do is ask Finn to sign away his parental rights. I'm sure he would. Then I could adopt the baby and make all of this real, us, our marriage... our baby." He cupped his hands over her belly.

If only Finn were the father, but he wasn't. And marrying Zak, having him adopt her baby, forever would be another unfulfilled dream. She glanced the room, the loud noises, the bright lights, the boisterous crowd, all now a suffocating mix. Her arms slumped to her sides as the sudden pops and sizzles of fireworks illuminated the night sky in a colorful explosion.

It didn't last long—the same as everything else in life. The lights burned, faded, and plummeted back to earth as nothing more than black ash. She looked to Zak.

His face beamed brighter than the surrounding radiance. "What do you say? Want to marry me?"

She ran a finger under both eyes, hoped her mascara hadn't smeared from the falling tears. "I need to think about it."

He tried to pull her close, but she held stiff, grounded. "I don't feel well. I'm going to lay down. Will you let your parents know I said congratulations once again?"

He tugged at her again. "Lacey—"

"Please Zak, just give me some time."

17

The dream world, full of antique lace gowns and rose pink peonies, faded into reality as Zak's words floated into her ears. They arrived as nothing more than an irritating buzz. "Wake up, we need to get dressed."

Was it morning already? "Can't I sleep in a little longer?"

"You can take a nap later," he said, kissing her cheek.

Since it was him, or rather what he had proposed, that had kept her up half the night, the least he could do was allow her decent rest. She stretched her arms and legs, "I need sleep."

"I understand. But remember my mom's friend I told you about, Ms. Ethel?"

Lacey forced open her heavy eyelids. "The one who needed someone to design her shop? You scheduled a meeting with her without consulting me?"

"No, but after my mom mentioned that I married a super talented New York architect, Ms. Ethel invited herself. By the way, she's convinced you're *the one*."

"Yeah, well, I'm thinking being *the one* isn't worth the hype." Lacey jerked the covers over her face, held them, and then yanked them back in place. "I'm not in the mindset to sketch designs today."

He stepped into the bathroom and grabbed his toothbrush before peeking his head out the door. "She doesn't expect a design today. She only wants to show you her ideas... in thorough detail," he added as he disappeared behind the bathroom walls.

Lacey squeezed her curls, no longer constricted by the pins and hair ties. "It was a long night. Even if I listen to her spout off her wish list, I won't remember it. Trust me, my brain feels like jello."

He returned to the bed and sat beside her, smelling of minty toothpaste. "And who's fault is that?"

"Yours, *Mr. Marry Me.*"

He tapped her on the nose. "And yours, *Miss I'll Think About It.*"

She studied his real face, the one hidden behind a plastered grin, and noted the droopy lines and dull eyes. Her lack of acceptance hurt him. And she could see it. "I meant it when I said I love you, though."

"Yeah, then why won't you marry me?"

Because you added telling Finn as a requirement. "Because I don't want to give you—or myself—false hope." She laid a hand on her belly. "My life's complicated right now. I can't imagine getting married before figuring out my new normal. And all factors considered—I'm not sure when, or if, that will ever happen."

"But it could if you stopped trying to plan your entire future. Look, you said you love me and that you'll think about it. Until then, all I can do is hope."

Hope that the baby becomes Finn's? Impossible. "Did you miss the part where I said I don't want to give you false hope."

"*Hope* means wanting something to happen or be the case. There's nothing false about me wanting us to be together forever."

Unrealistic, that's the word she should have used… *unrealistic*.

The door bell rang, and based on the chatter that came shortly after, Lacey assumed Ms. Ethel had arrived.

"Time to throw on your clothes," he said as a slow, sexy grin formed, "Even though I prefer you clothes-less." He slipped a hand under her shirt.

Lacey whacked it away. "And I'll prefer you toothless if you don't let me get dressed."

Zak surrendered both hands as Lacey threw on the most professional*ish* looking outfit in her suitcase, a maternity sundress and cardigan. Afterwards, she slapped on deodorant and a spritz of perfume before speeding down the hall.

The portrait Lacey had painted in her mind of who awaited her included a silver, curly perm and a tennis-ball driven walker. But the actual diva standing before her smashed that picture.

Ms. Ethel, a violet-haired, magenta-lipped tigress with a bag full of ideas for her new business, greeted Lacey. "Well, hello dear. I hear you are just the woman I need to meet, a woman who can do great things, things no one else who came before you can." She gave Lacey a hard, raspy laugh. "No pressure, huh?" She nudged Lacey with a sharp elbow and laughed again.

It was a tall order, and one Lacey wasn't sure she had the time, or energy, to fulfill. "I can't make any promises... but I'll try."

With a single thumb, Ms. Ethel gestured to Meredith. "If she says you're *the one*, you're *the one*."

Lacey glanced at Zak, who stood out of the spotlight chuckling under his breath, then returned her attention to Ms. Ethel. "Okay, then. Well, let's hope I can live up to your expectations." *And kill Zak later.*

Ms. Ethel made herself comfortable on the sofa as Lacey took a seat on the chair across from her. "What type of shop are you looking to open?"

"That's an easy question—a wig shop. And I don't mean a run-of-the-mill hair supply store, the kind with multiple aisles filled with varying shades and styles of synthetic-blends hideously balanced on the head of blank-faced mannequins. I want a grand, full-service wig shop where my people will create customized hairpieces to fit each person who steps through the door. I want to make wig-buying an experience, not a *hide my face until I get home and doctor this bush* experience."

Meredith passed Ms. Ethel a cup of hot tea, and she took a sip. "Excellent, Meredith, you make the best peppermint tea." She took another sip, then placed the cup on the table beside her. "Now Lacey, I don't imagine you've stepped foot in a wig shop, but if you ever do, you'll understand the problem I'm trying to fix. You strut in and choose whatever monstrosity you want from the display, and then straight from the packaged box those workers will pin that baby to the last sprigs of hair you have left."

Ms. Ethel patted her own pixie-styled wig and gave a disgusted look. "Then, as if that's not awful enough, they let you walk out looking as if Davey Crockett just sewed his latest kill on top of your head. It's an injustice, and one I intend to remedy." With her tiny fist balled, Ms. Ethel flexed her insubstantial muscle like *Rosie the Riveter*.

Lacey fought the urge to giggle—and the urge to add another project to her plate at a time like this. Her mind was a discombobulated mess. But to be honest, the project had piqued her interest. And Ms. Ethel's passion pushed her. "From what you're telling me, it is a definite injustice."

"I knew you'd understand, so I brought over everything you need to get started." Ms. Ethel lifted the oversized leather briefcase with a slight moan.

Zak rushed over and took it from her. "I'll help you with that."

"Thank you, Zak. You are too kind." She eased back into the chair. "And I know you'll help Lacey with all the numbers. Because we have to do something. Those other wig businesses are turning a profit only because women with limited funds have limited options. So they force those poor women into buying rat-nested Chinese plastic. And the sad part is, I have porcelain dolls with better hair than those wigs."

Which China also made, Lacey thought, but dared not mention.

Zak plopped the briefcase on the table by Lacey. "Well, Lacey's the boss. I'm only here for the ride. If she's onboard, so am I."

Great, Zak left the decision up to her. And from the looks of it, Ms. Ethel did not strike Lacey as a woman who enjoyed disappointment— or even a woman who took *no* for an answer.

Lacey reached into the briefcase and removed a folder containing magazines clippings, sketches, and material samples of design elements Ms. Ethel refused to live without.

Lacey ran her fingers across a purple leather swatch designated for the salon chairs in the wig-styling section as tons of structural ideas, everything from wall partitions to square footage, flowed through Lacey's brain. No doubt this would be a fun project. And if she was being honest—a project more in line with what she preferred to design. But she would never say it out loud, especially not to her father.

Lacey replaced the folder and material samples. "I'll do it."

Ms. Ethel clapped as Meredith steepled her hands against a big smile. Zak rushed over and planted a closed-mouth kiss on Lacey. "If anyone can make this happen, you can."

Ms. Ethel nodded in approval. "And just so you know, there's plenty of business in store for you when, not if, you finish this one. Enough you two might have to quit those big city jobs and move back here, start up your own architecture firm."

Meredith bounced from one foot to the other. "Wouldn't that be wonderful?"

Zak draped his arms over Lacey's shoulders from behind, let them fall across her chest. "If I can persuade her to keep me, we might just consider it. It would be a great place to raise a family, fresh air, big backyards, less-crowded beaches. And we wouldn't have to take the baby to Central Park just to see a tree or to play in grass."

Ms. Ethel picked up her teacup, held it with both hands. "Well, I'll give you both my two cents, not that you have a reason to care about it, but because it's based on seventy-five years of real-life experience.

Life is a journey. Now, you can take that journey on a speeding train aimed at a single destination, or you can get off at the station and change it up. Walk a little, ride a little, bicycle a little—just open yourself up to new places and ideas."

After taking the last sip of tea, Ms. Ethel set her cup on the table. "And while I'm on my soapbox, ignore anyone who tells you do what makes you happy. How the hell do you know what makes you happy if you never try new things?"

Lacey guessed Ms. Ethel had a point. For most of her life, Lacey's train had been speeding to one place only until the pregnancy forced her off track and into a new experience. An experience she was beginning to favor over the boring, work-heavy life she had made for herself.

And sure, backyard picnics, child-friendly tree houses, starry nights on outdoor swings, and Zak teaching her child baseball were as close to Heaven as she may ever get. But those images would remain a dream. Because those things came with the stipulation of getting Finn to sign away parental rights not his to sign away.

Zak leaned over, whispered in Lacey's ear. "Ms. Ethel's right. Why not give us a try? It might make you happy."

Not might, it would. But it wasn't an option. "Let's get through this project first."

Lacey's mom called twice before Lacey could unlock her apartment door.

"Why didn't you pick up your phone?" Lacey's mom asked in a semi-frantic tone. "I thought something happened to you."

Lacey wedged the phone between her shoulder and ear as she rolled her suitcase with one hand and carried her keys and her purse with the other. Zak trailed behind her with his own belongings and Ms. Ethel's oversized leather briefcase. "Because my hands are full." Lacey found a place for her baggage. "What's the emergency?"

"No emergency, your sister and I wanted to run something by you. She's on the call, too."

"Guess what? I found out what I'm having, too." Kate's tone rose to pre-squeal pitch.

"Only after three ultrasounds in three days. I'm surprised they didn't ban her from the office."

Lacey laughed as she took a seat on the sofa. "I'm sure they made a nice *pain in the butt* patient note in her chart."

Kate gasped. "You're wrong for that, but I'll forgive you because we're sisters—and because we're having our babies at the same time."

"Technically, two weeks apart," Lacey corrected her.

"Anything can happen," Kate added.

"Listen here you two, back to the purpose of this call. Now, I want to host a double gender reveal party here at the house, if it's okay with you and Zak. And if it is, I need his family's phone number so I can invite them."

Lacey stretched out her legs and propped up her feet on the armrest of the sofa as Zak made himself a glass of ice water. "But what if I prefer not to know?"

"You already said you wanted to know."

"Maybe, but can't I change my mind?"

"Seriously? How many times will we be pregnant at the same time? This is like a one-in-a-million event," Kate blurted.

You can say that again, Lacey thought, praying she'd never be so unlucky again.

She pondered her options. If she found out, it would end the ongoing gender debate with Zak and allow her to better prepare for the baby's arrival. So why not give her mother the pleasure of hosting the reveal? "Hold on for a minute."

Ignoring the groans of her sister and mother, she motioned Zak to come closer. He did, easing himself onto the edge of sofa next to her. "What's up?"

"My mom insists on throwing a gender reveal party for... us... and Kate at the same time. And she wants to invite your family."

He beamed. "I think that's a great idea. And thanks for asking." He leaned forward, planting his lips on her forehead as his fingertips danced across her cheeks. A burning heat rose into her ears, then faded as he walked away.

"You can plan it—but only on one condition."

The excitement bubbled in her mother's voice. "You name it, it's yours."

"I don't want a huge party, just close family and friends."

Kate jumped in to add her opinion. "Remember, this is a party for both of us. We have to agree."

"Neither of you have a say, I'm hosting—" Lacey almost interrupted, but her mother stopped her. "—But I'll do my best to keep it to a tight-knit group. Now, I'm trusting you to text me the numbers I need. The party is in less than two weeks, so I have to get the invitations sent today."

Lacey ended the call with the typical *I love you* and *goodbye*, and then crossed her fingers, hopeful that her mother would follow her guest-limiting stipulations.

18

"It's locked." Austin pointed his sausage-sized finger at the door as Zak and Lacey approached.

Not only did Lacey's mother schedule the gender reveal party on a day her father was out of town, but she made them wait outside in the heat. Lacey didn't have time for the dramatics. All she wanted was to find out what she was having and go home—in one emotional piece.

"Unbelievable," Kate mumbled, "they locked us out of our own party."

A muffled voice yelled out from inside. "One more minute."

Kate wiped a bead of sweat from her forehead. "This is crazy. We've been waiting twenty minutes. If you don't let us in, we're—"

The door swung open to a cheering crowd of fifty or more people, more people than Lacey considered a quaint gathering of friends and family. And while it should have overwhelmed her, would have overwhelmed her, it didn't. Because the striking decorations, chairs trimmed with cream tulle and satin bows, tables topped with sparkly glitter and pastel-colored flowers, distracted her. She glanced at the ceiling plastered with shiny gold stars and twinkly lights before turning her attention to the scattered balloon bouquets in gold, mint, and blush pink. She blinked away the tears of joy.

To her left, rustic cupcake and cake pop stands trimmed in antiqued lace displayed their pom-pom and glitter topped desserts. She tasted the sweet frosting by sight alone. And with each breath, she inhaled the fragrant scent of live flowers, perfectly placed throughout the entire room.

Her mother hooked her arms through Kate's and Lacey's and guided them to the centerpiece before they greeted those around them. "I can't wait for you to see this. Kyle, turn off the lights."

The artificial lighting may have faded, but there was nothing dark about the room. It glowed bright and enchanting under numerous strands of string lighting. And covering the back wall was the best display of all, a large chalkboard sign decorated with flashing lights, gold stars, and pillow-stuffing clouds. The message painted on it, *Twinkle, Twinkle, Little Stars... How We Wonder What You BOTH Are?*

"Are you freaking kidding me, this is amazing." Kate squeezed both her cheeks.

Despite the room being filled with people, it was quiet enough Lacey could hear herself breathe. And with each draw of air, she soaked it in, every intricate detail.

"Wait, you still haven't seen everything." Lacey's mother directed them to yet another table where a pair of matching, two-tiered cakes sat, both frosted with a swirled mint-colored layer on the bottom and a swirled blush-pink layer on top. Tucked in along the line where the two tiers met were edible pastel flowers. "Now, before you give me the sole credit, I had lots of help. Kyle, Meredith, come over here."

They both obliged, meeting Lacey and Zak in the center of the room and greeting them their usual affectionate hugs.

"Meredith—mom—" Kate said, scanning everything within her line of sight, "you guys have outdone yourselves."

Lacey's heart danced in her chest. "I don't know what to say. This is... I can't even find the words."

Zak leaned closed to Lacey, whispered in her ear. "I hope it's everything you dreamed it would be."

Lacey anchored her eyes onto his. "It's so much more."

He brushed his hand across her ever expanding belly and touched his lips to her forehead.

Doby wrapped her arms around Lacey from behind. "How's the mommy-to-be?"

"My stomach sticks out farther than my butt. How do you think that makes me feel?" Lacey giggled.

"You're just noticing? That happened two months ago. I mean, it's not like it took much." Doby laughed.

"I should slap you. If I wasn't too busy admiring everyone's hard work. I can't believe they went through so much trouble for us?" Lacey waved her hand around the room. "I'm in awe."

Doby slid closer into whisper position and glanced over at Zak and her boyfriend, Carson, now engaged in what looked to be a humorous conversation. "See what happens when you go with the flow? That man is so in love with you, it's ridiculous. Now, when Carson starts looking at me like that, I might have to marry him."

Lacey noticed Carson's gaze bouncing between Zak and Doby. "Are you crazy? He already does."

"Maybe. And maybe one day I'll marry him." She blew Carson a kiss as he pretended to catch it. "And you can marry—Zak."

"I'm sure he'd love it if I said yes to marrying him."

"You two obviously—wait, what? Did he ask you?" Doby worked to keep her voice low.

"He did," Lacey said as the blood drained from her cheeks. "Right before he asked me to have Finn sign away his rights."

"Well, damn."

"Yeah, my sentiments exactly."

Doby angled her head. "I have an idea. Why not tell him the truth? He's so in love with you he won't care, trust me. He'll just be happy to have you and this baby to himself, and then you can forget about the list."

"I—"

"There's my little Lacey." Aunt Ruthie appeared from nowhere and smothered Lacey with her fur coat, the one that weighed even more than her. And the same one Aunt Ruthie wore to every event, during every season, and possibly even slept in. Or at least it smelled like she did.

Lacey pushed her away before she suffocated in the mothball-scented, matted-hair coat. "Aunt Ruthie? Wow, I wasn't expecting you to be here."

"What are you saying? You didn't invite me?"

Lacey swallowed hard. "I wasn't in charge of that department, Mom was. But I would have invited you."

"I'm just surprised to see you at your own party—knowing how busy you always are."

"You're right, I have to work," Lacey said, her patience for passive aggressiveness running thin.

Aunt Ruthie propped both hands on her hip and grinned. Lacey couldn't help but stare at the dentures mounted with teeth twice the size as her originals, or at the rusty-orange splotches left over from cheap tanning lotions. And while Aunt Ruthie and Lacey's mother shared DNA, they didn't share personalities, the exact opposite, actually.

But Aunt Ruthie was family, and out of obligation they always invited her, even though they regretted it as soon as she dragged herself and her dead animal through the door.

"So what's this I hear about you and Kate planning to get knocked up at the same time." She gave a grated and distasteful cackle, the result of forty years of chain-smoking. The breath that followed was even less pleasant.

Doby tapped Lacey on the shoulder. "I'll leave you to handle this, but I expect to finish this conversation later." Doby disappeared into the crowd.

Lacey returned to her Aunt and reminded herself of the reason for her attacks. She always had been jealous of Lacey's mom, of her family and marriage. No doubt, she would swear it was the other way around. But Lacey sensed the regret Aunt Ruthie had in chasing dreams. Instead of settling into a satisfying life, she had squandered her years searching for the next big break in her modeling/acting career—which included infomercials, Walmart ads, and a Valtrex commercial.

Lacey dug deep, reminded herself it wasn't personal. "Now Aunt Ruthie, you don't really believe that, do you?"

"Who knows what to believe about you young people anymore? Just so you know, I bought both of you a pack of diapers. You won't have time for all that other fancy-schmancy stuff with a screaming newborn stealing your sleep and good looks. And don't get too fat. No matter how much your husband tells you he doesn't care, he's lying. Now, tell me where I can find decent food before I pass out."

Lacey happily pointed her in the food table direction. Kate, holding a plateful of various appetizers, crossed paths with Aunt Ruthie as she made her way over to Lacey. She rolled her eyes. "Doesn't she make your blood boil?"

Lacey stole a chocolate-dipped strawberry and bit into it.

"I know you aren't talking about me." It was Uncle Teddy, who was in reality either their third or fourth cousin on their Dad's side through adoption—or marriage? No one could quite explain the particulars, but regardless, he was family. More than that, he was always perky, full of good advice, and as fluffy as a teddy bear—thus the nickname.

"Never you, we love you, Uncle Teddy." Kate stood on her tippy toes and gave him a big hug.

"I love you girls, too." He pulled two twenty-dollar bills from his pocket. "Take this and buy those babies something nice."

"You know we're not kids anymore, right?" Lacey asked.

Kate snatched both bills. "Let's pretend I'm still sixteen. And I'm taking Lacey's share because she makes more money than me."

"I'll let you girls work that out." He kissed them both on the cheek before heading off to mingle with the next group of people.

Austin swooped in on Kate, planting a kiss on her lips. "How's my lovely, pregnant wife?"

Seeing Austin's affections for Kate made Lacey miss Zak, so she glanced around the crowd in search of him.

"Boo."

Lacey startled before an arm reached around her and held her shaky body still.

"It's me, calm down." Zak passed her a plate of food.

"Not funny," she said, wasting no time taking the food. She bit into a sweet and tangy meatball. "This is so good. You want some?"

"No, I can't eat. My stomach feels off." Zak placed a hand over his sexy abs—not that she could see them. But her mind had a vivid picture imprinted in its memory bank.

"Are you getting sick?"

"I think it's nerves."

"I know. My mom always invites more people than necessary."

He scratched the back of his head. "It's not the people."

"Then what is it?" She cut a second meatball in half and tossed it in her mouth.

He lowered his voice. "We're about to find out the sex of this baby—our baby—and that means something, like a rite of passage. The thought of growing closer to you and this baby, being there for ultrasounds, gender reveals, the birth, only to leave with nothing? It would kill me."

She swallowed quick to keep from choking. "What are you saying?"

"That I can't continue being a part of something so special knowing that one day it'll be ripped away from me."

Her heart dropped to her knees. "Are you ending this, us, right now?"

"No." He pressed his body closer. "I'm telling you I never want this to end. I don't know what I'd do if it did."

She couldn't break him, couldn't tear him apart, and she damn sure couldn't afford to lose him. Taking his hand, she dragged him over to a table, laid her plate on it, and grabbed his other hand in hers. She had wasted too much time with the list, with the lies. If he loved her, then he would forgive her. And perhaps this wasn't perfect timing, or even the most proper timing, given the fact he might bolt out the door as soon as she told him. But she couldn't wait. The truth clawed at her insides, begging for its release. "Zak... I need to tell you something. I —"

"If I can get everyone's attention for a minute." Lacey's mother clanged a spoon against the side of her glass.

"Everyone gather round," Meredith added. "And where are our new mommies?"

Lacey sensed eyes landing on her from multiple directions, but hers remained on Zak.

He squeezed her hands. "Tell me. What is it?"

"There they go. Come on over girls." Lacey's mom motioned for both her and Kate to join them.

There wasn't time to confess. And besides, too many people were gawking. Lacey rose on the tips of her toes, pressed her mouth against his, parted his lips, and took what made her the happiest. When she let go, she left him with the only thing she had time to say. "I love you."

Lacey rushed over to her mom's side, and Kate joined them. Her mom grinned from ear to ear. "We want to first thank you all for coming to celebrate with us today. This is a very special moment in our lives, the moment we can finally reveal the gender of our newest family members." Everyone cheered and clapped.

"How this works is: each of them has their own cake, baked the color of the gender they are carrying. Mint-green is a boy, and blush-pink is a girl. Now, they didn't make these babies alone, so we're not letting them cut cakes alone either. Come on over, boys."

Zak and Austin followed directions and took a place beside their wives. Kate examined the cake in front of her. "I hope you guys were careful not to mix this up because I don't see my name anywhere."

Lacey's mom shook her head and pointed to a corner of the gold plate where a place card held Kate's name. Lacey's cake had one, too.

Kate giggled. "Okay, we're good."

Meredith stood in between the two tables. "Before they slice into them, I want you in the audience to hold up the sign that matches what you presume each of them is having."

An abundance of mint-green and blush-pink signs fanned the air in almost equal amounts, though for Lacey, the girl signs outnumbered the boy ones. She caught Zak's attention, pointed out her observations.

He passed her the cake-cutter. "Soon enough, the cake will reveal the truth."

She gripped the fancy handle with unsteady hands and shifted her eyes to Kate, who appeared more than prepared for cake butchering. Zak slipped a hand around Lacey's lower back as the countdown began. "Ten, nine, eight..."

She slowed her breathing, tried not to ruminate on the obvious, the fact that with one slice, one tiny crumb, she would know the sex of her baby. Everyone would.

Zak laid his hand on hers, steadied the cutter. "It doesn't matter what we're having. We'll love him or her either way." "... seven, six..."

Lacey and Zak had made nothing together. However, she and a random stranger did. And that person was someone clueless about the gender reveal party, someone who hadn't met her family, or the other thoughtful people she had lied to over the past few months. So if she longed for something in that moment, then it was freedom from created burdens. And for the first time, she had the strength to stop the charade and spill her dark secrets amongst the twinkling lights and gold stars. Warm tears coated her cheeks as her lips vibrated.

"... five, four, three..."

Zak increased the pressure on her hand, but kept it delicate enough. His soft, but manly touch eased her panic. No, he wasn't the Dad by blood, but he absolutely was the Dad by heart. And at the shout of cut, she and Zak plunged the cake-cutter through the fluffy frosting, slicing into a—white cake?

She whirled her head around and noted dark chocolate chunks flying into the air as Kate murdered hers. "The bakery made a mistake. Call them."

"You didn't think we'd make this easy, did you?" A mischievous grin painted Lacey's mother's face, as the crowd murmured.

Great, games and more waiting, Lacey thought. Her nerves couldn't take much more.

"Now, I'm really worried you guys mixed up our results with the extra steps." Kate slung cake crumbs from her hands.

"We were extremely careful, I promise." Lacey's mom answered.

From the other room, Kyle and Uncle Teddy carried in two large boxes, both labeled with Kate's and Lacey's names. Lacey tried to rip into hers, but the overzealous tape job mandated assistance. Before Zak could help Lacey, Kate had already stabbed hers open with the cake-cutter and released a bouquet of solid gold balloons. "Don't worry about opening yours. I'm sure it's the same," she informed Lacey.

The crowd laughed, but Lacey had lost her humor.

Kate tossed her hair over her both shoulders and groaned. "I swear, the anticipation is killing me."

"You're almost there," Meredith announced. "Look behind you."

Lacey eddied around to see—her Dad standing behind her. He held a bright smile and two rectangular-shaped packages, both wrapped in cream-colored paper with gold polka dots and a mix of mint-green and blush pink ribbon. Lacey bypassed the presents in his hand and went straight for a hug. "Mom said you couldn't make it."

He kissed her forehead. "I couldn't miss my girls' big day, so I booked an earlier flight."

"Happy to see you made it home safe, Dad." Kate jumped up, kissed his cheek, and then yanked away the package with her name on it. She ripped into it at once. "It's a girl! I can't believe it. We're having a baby girl!" She slapped her lips on Austin's so hard he nearly tumbled over.

"Open yours, Lacey." Uncle Teddy yelled.

Lacey neatly removed the wrapping paper to uncover a framed ultrasound picture, the one Dr. Hart had sealed for them weeks ago. Her stomach fluttered as her eyes roamed to the corner of the black-and-white photo where the gender had been printed in a brilliant baby —*blue*. "It's a boy!" They both said in unison, Zak shouting and her barely able to push out the words between the sobs.

For the first time, she could see the baby, *really* see him. See the tiny baby features that melted her heart. And she felt him—*really* felt him. He was her son, and if nothing else around her was real—he was.

"I told you," Zak said, his voice low, his warm words tickling her ear.

Lacey didn't remember much of the party after that moment. She only vaguely recalled people vomiting chunks of child-rearing wisdom on her, most of it about the differences between raising boys and girls. Because her thoughts had traveled to a world where a ringlet-headed baby with chestnut brown eyes existed. To a world full of slobbery kisses and sweet baby smells.

A world she was reluctant to leave, even on the ride back to the apartment. It was then she imagined his first words, his first steps, his first day of school, his first girlfriend—and his first heartbreak, all as

Zak slept beside her.

Without a doubt, she could comfort her son, raise him, educate him, but what could she teach him about being a man? Boys needed male guidance, role models, somebody else with a penis that could understand the effects of testosterone. That was a fact now made vivid by the bold blue letters on the picture—B-O-Y.

But more than anything, her baby boy deserved a father.

As the driver stopped in front of her building, she stared at Zak, so handsome, peaceful. She wanted him to be the father, wanted him to raise the baby with her. And she wanted to marry him. Only one thing stood in the way, a confession—but not for long. Regardless of the repercussions, she was ready to share her story.

And if he forgave her, she would most certainly marry him.

19

Back at the apartment, Zak laid down on the sofa, his head resting on one end and half his legs dangling over the other. "Why am I so tired?"

"It's understandable after a long night."

"And an exciting one... a boy," he said, mussing his hair as Lacey hung her purse on the wall hook.

She stepped into the kitchen and grabbed a bottled water from the fridge. Zak was still floating along on cloud nine. Which might make this the time to confess, she told herself. But first, she needed to gather her strength. Hope for the best but prepare for the worse. If he bailed, ran out on her, how would she handle it? Call it an early breakup? An early divorce?

If she labeled it a mutual departure, her career and contract could remain intact, as Zak would tell no one about the scam, no matter how much it hurt him. But what would it do for the broken heart she would be left carrying? Nothing. And that was the bigger problem, a problem not easily fixed.

Her phone dinged, and she made no hurried effort to check it, certain it was her mother making sure they arrived home safe.

"Hey, before I forget," Zak said, grabbing her attention, "I looked at the blueprint sketches for Ms. Ethel, and you're way over budget. I'll tell you by how much after I run the numbers tomorrow."

"I'm not over budget. Why do you always assume I'm over budget?" Lacey grabbed a bag of mini-pretzels and left the kitchen to join Zak in the living room, taking a seat in the chair across from him.

"Because in all the years I've worked with you, there's never been a time when you weren't over budget on the first draft. And never a time when you didn't use those puppy dog eyes as a bargaining chip."

"Somebody has to stand up for the necessities in a design. You finance people have no heart." She opened the bag of pretzels and crunched a few.

Her phone dinged three more times in a row. Boy was her mom persistent.

"Who's that?"

"My mom, I'm sure," Lacey said, retrieving the phone from her purse.

She glanced at the screen, and her mouth dropped. It was multiple texts from Mr. Duke demanding a callback—STAT. Her head spun in circles as she considered the best way to call without Zak eavesdropping. The bathroom—yes—he wouldn't follow her in there. "Ooh, my stomach's upset. Be right back."

"Do you need your medicine?"

"Nope, it's the other end, the result of too many appetizers," she said as she sprinted down the hall and into the master bath, locking the door behind her. Taking a seat on the tile floor, she dialed Mr. Duke with trembling fingers.

"Miss Winters, I have good news for you."

She hesitated joining Mr. Duke in celebration, as he held an unreliable track record. "Good news?"

"Yes, I've ruled out most of the names on your list." Papers shuffled in the background. "You can mark off Liam Fitzgerald, Chuck Nguyen, and Oliver Callum."

What was good about having zero leads? "That leaves me with no one."

"Huh? You eliminated Bo and Gene?"

Eliminated in more ways than she cared to discuss. "Yes…"

"Excellent, then we have the father."

Her shoulders curled around her caving chest. "How? You wiped out the entire list."

He gave a raspy cough into the receiver. "Yeah, about that. My assistant transcribes my scribbled notes into neatly typed lists, but somehow she split the data. So on this other sheet I have the name Zak Cooper, who you already ruled out, and the last man standing, who is most definitely the father. Good thing I take the time to review every document before I file them away."

Lacey braced herself. This was the moment of truth. And once she found out, there was no going back to normal. She would confess, tell

Zak, but this time with answers. "Just spit it out, please."

"Looks like his name is Finn Huckabee. Know him?"

Did she know him? Of course, she did. And for the first time, hearing his name excited her. "He's my ex-boyfriend."

"Then it makes perfect sense. Oh, I've gotta go, there's a call on the other line, but you have my number if you need me."

She didn't buy the perfect sense theory, but it made better sense than sleeping with a random stranger, and maybe even explained the amnesia. Who wouldn't want to forget jumping back in the sack with a jerk ex-boyfriend, especially one she swore to avoid forever? But as disappointed as she was with her choice to reconnect with him—without protection—she couldn't be happier it was him. Even though she still couldn't imagine why her brain turned an encounter with him into her best sex dream ever. He was never that great.

But it didn't matter because him being the father meant she hadn't lied to Zak. Well, technically she had, but did he have to know? Sure, she could do the honorable thing and tell him, but what would that accomplish? Destroy his trust for her? Destroy a moment of celebration? That's exactly what it would do at a time when she wanted nothing more than to accept his proposal. And she could now, knowing Finn would sign away his rights, especially if she committed to not seeking child support—or telling anyone.

And she was sure he wouldn't tell a soul either. Never. He was way too vain and womanizing to want anyone to discover he had a child outside of the good, old-fashioned wedlock way.

Energized, she jumped to her feet, texted Doby the good news. Not only the news about Finn but also her plan to accept Zak's proposal and legally become his wife. She couldn't wait to tell Zak, practically tripping over her own feet as she rushed out of the bathroom and back down the hall.

"Where are you going?" He yelled out from the bedroom.

Lacey returned, slightly embarrassed. "I thought you were still on the sofa."

"Yeah, the sofa's not too comfortable, so I came in here. Join me," he said, his strong arms open only for her. "Wait, did you clear out the system?" He snickered.

"Not completely, I saved some for you." She winked.

"In that case, maybe I should rescind my offer."

"Too late," she said, climbing into her bed, their bed, and snuggling in beside him.

He intertwined one hand with hers, kept the other behind his head. "What a spectacular night?"

He had no idea. "The greatest ever."

"Yeah... something about finding out it's a boy made it seem... never mind."

She knew exactly what he was trying to say without him saying it. "I understand. Before, I always envisioned two possibilities—both images a blur of what might be. But now it's like I can see him."

"That's exactly what I was trying to say." He let go of her hand, then rolled onto his side, fixing his gaze on her. He pushed back her stray spirals.

"I've been thinking a lot about what I asked you to do with Finn. I realize he's done nothing except cause you serious heartache. And him knowing wouldn't make him any less of an asshole. But he needs to know... because he doesn't deserve this baby." Zak trailed his fingers down the side of Lacey's face, along the side of her neck, and over her full breast, stopping only when he reached her growing belly. "I do."

If there was ever a time to tell him, to share the good news, it was now. And she would, in just a minute, after she readied herself. Because this was big. No—committing to one person for the rest of her life was more than big. It was major. She nervously plucked at a loose string around one of the duvet buttons as her heart drummed against her chest wall.

Until a tiny kick snapped her attention. She had experienced flutters, those gas-bubbling sensations, but never a solid kick. Ecstatic, she took Zak's hand, laid it across the place where it happened and held it there. Another kick. "Did you feel that?"

A smile rosed his already flushed face. "Yeah, barely, like a tiny tap."

She studied the joy in his expression. "I think he likes you."

Zak brushed his lips against hers and whispered, "And what about his mom? Does she like me?"

If only she had the proper words. If only those words existed. But they didn't. Until then, she'd do the best she could to explain an ache so deep it could never be soothed. A love so great it hurt like hell. "I'm pretty sure she knows you're the best thing that ever happened to her... And she's madly in love with you... And... she wants to marry you."

His mouth parted. "Wait, does that mean—?"

163

"It means if your question still stands, then my answer is yes. I'll marry you. And I'll have a lawyer draw up the papers for Finn. Because you're right. You deserve this baby, and this baby deserves you."

Zak leaned over her, cupped the sides of her face as his lips lingered dangerously close to hers. "So we're doing this? We're getting married?"

Marrying Zak wasn't part of the original plan, but it was definitely part of her new plan—the best part. Lacey ran her hands through Zak's thick hair and nodded.

"Well, I'd say that makes me the luckiest man in the world," he said, finding her lips and plundering them like a newly discovered world.

A world she opened to him. Him, her soon-to-be husband. The future father of her baby. The man whose hands now gripped the back of her neck as he plunged deeper, taking her with him. But there was nothing he took that she didn't give, no place his lips landed that she didn't welcome. Everything she had—she gave.

Because she was his.

And when he had his fill of her, he released her, pressing his slightly crooked nose against her slightly pointed one. "You, me, this baby—it's forever. None of us are going anywhere." He planted a sweet closing kiss on her lips. "There's only one problem."

She wrinkled her forehead. "What's that?"

He rolled onto his back and rested a hand across her bulging belly. "He needs a name. Any ideas yet?"

Truthfully, she hadn't given it much thought, but a few had caught her attention. "I like Jaxon and Lukah. Oh, and at the doctor's office, I met a baby named Ridley. I thought it was unique."

"Sure, if you want him to be some crazy psycho-killer. It reminds me of Jack the Ripper."

She punched his arm. "And you have a better suggestion?"

He gave an exaggerated winced, rubbing a place four inches from where her fist landed. "Actually I do. Jude."

"Jude?" Lacey repeated.

"Not just Jude. Jude Cooper."

He met Lacey's eyes and robbed the air from her lungs. To hear him offer his last name for her son, a son she had feared would never have the love of a real father, brought happy tears she quickly brushed away with the back of her hand. "And where did that name come from?"

"It was my grandfather's. And just so you know, you have him to thank for this." Zak waved his hand over himself.

She shoved away the images of the naked body beneath his button-up shirt and slacks, afraid she might give into carnal desires. "For your good looks?"

He laughed. "Great-Grandpa Jude was about five and a half feet tall and just as wide with a quarter-inch gap between his front teeth. And did I forget to mention the wiry red hair surrounding the big bald patch in the back of his head?"

"Oh, wow."

"I know, true love can be blind. It might explain why he and my grandmother stayed married for over fifty years."

"I guess you overlook the less than desirable features if you truly love someone," Lacey said, glancing down at her skinny legs.

"True, my grandpa always said a good relationship had little to do with looks and everything to do with the fit, like the foot and the shoe."

Lacey shook her head. "What a crazy analogy?"

"Why don't I tell you the story? And then see how crazy you think it is." Zak readjusted in the bed, closed what little distance existed between him and Lacey. "He said when you shop for a shoe, you find the one that fits the best, but it's never perfect. The toe area's too tight, or the arch is too high. But if you stick with the shoe, then over time it fits better. The problem is by then it's lost its shine, worn down its edges. And for some people, that's an issue because they only care about the outside."

She snuggled into the curl of his shoulder, rested her head on his chest. He draped his arm over her and kissed the top of her head. She concentrated on the thumping of his heart, joyed in the rise and fall of his pecs.

"Now since some people only care about looks, they throw out the old shoe and get an upgraded version, one that fits good enough. What they don't realize is that the old shoe has weathered storms, protected, and carried. It has been there without fail, and through the wear and tear, it has become the perfect fit. Because it takes time to learn the curves, creases, and mold to each other. When the foot stretches and sinks, the shoe widens and rises in all the right places. There will never be another new shoe that will ever fit like that old one."

"The foot and shoe, according to Grandpa Jude, have a relationship," Zak said, chuckling, "He called it—*sole* mates."

Lacey joined him in laughter. "Well, I can see where you get your corny sense of humor from now."

Zak painted a big grin on his face. "And as corny as this sounds, you're my shoe, Lacey. I'll never need another pair." He rolled her on top of him, slipped his hands under her shirt, under her bra, and let out a deep moan.

She loved the way his hands felt against her skin. And sure, what he said might seem corny to some, but to her it was deep, deep enough she opened herself to him—to the possibility of forever.

And he seized what she gave.

"See how good we fit," he said, giving her every inch he had.

She'd have to be crazy not to see it, and even crazier not to feel it. He was right, they were the perfect fit. And he showed her how perfect... all... night... long.

20

The courier delivered the parental termination and adoption paperwork into Lacey's hands, exactly fifteen weeks from the day she had stepped into a lawyer's office to file them. What a relief! It had only taken forever. Although in all fairness, the lawyers had hit several unexpected bumps. Who knew Finn would take a job overseas right after Mr. Duke announced that he was the father of her baby? And to a third-world country at that.

But enough of that, they were here now, and that's what mattered. Because Jude was no longer a yawning sweet-potato. At only six weeks from his arrival, he was a vernix-coated pineapple according to *What to Expect When Expecting*. Lacey scanned the papers and let out a sigh of relief. Her greatest fear throughout the entire ordeal had been that she would go into labor before Zak could adopt the baby, but with these, it was no longer a concern. And even though Zak had made it clear that regardless of any legalities Jude was his son, she still preferred it locked in on paper.

Now, the only thing left to do was to meet with Finn and present the papers—after filling him in on the whole *you're the father* thing. Sure, she had wanted to tell him sooner, but he didn't make it easy by rushing off to a place with limited means of contact. And forgive her for not wanting to tell him over an informal letter or poor phone reception.

No, this was information shared only in person. So it was great news to hear he had booked a return flight home for a short visit.

When the doorknob clicked, she clutched the papers against her chest and hurried over. Barely able to contain her excitement, she shifted from one foot to the other as if someone had infused her blood with coffee. She knew Zak would be just as elated as she was to be only one Finn Huckabee-signature away from adopting Jude after the nail-biting lawyer sessions and court filings. How could he not?

Impatient, she swung open the door and awkwardly leaped into Zak's arms, knocking him and his satchel on the ground. Most of his spreadsheets flew into the air and now laid scattered across the public hallway. He reached to gather them.

Regaining her balance, Lacey waved the document high in the air. "The papers are here."

He stopped. Slow and controlled, he returned to an upright position, rested his hands on her shoulders. "*The* papers?"

With her lips stretched thin and her cheeks pushed into her eyes, she nodded. He took the documents from her, scanned over each one. "This is great news." His lips pressed against hers, and as one would welcome an expected guest, she opened her mouth to his.

A draft of air blew past at the same time someone's throat cleared. Breaking apart, they noticed one of the neighbor's speeding past with her head down and gaze fixed on the floor. Embarrassed, Lacey covered her mouth with both hands as Zak scooped up the remaining mess from the floor.

Once back inside the apartment, whiffs of charred food reminded her of the garlic bread she had left unattended in the oven.

"Is something burning?" Zak asked.

With a striped potholder, she rescued the sheet pan from the oven, examining the crisp toast with blackened edges and bottoms. "Yeah, the garlic bread. Hopefully, I can save it."

Remembering the boiling spaghetti sauce, she quickly reduced the heat, removed the lid, and stirred. At least it had survived her inattention.

Zak hovered above the pot. "Now that smells delicious. Did you make it?" He scanned the counters.

She replaced the lid, crossed her arms over her chest. "I know you're looking for the pasta sauce jar, but I'll have you know I made this from scratch. My mother shared her recipe."

His soft lips pecked her cheeks before swiping a beer from the fridge. "I'll call and thank her later—after I taste it."

She tossed an uncooked noodle at his head and missed. "I figured I better learn how to cook with a baby on the way. Besides, what else do I have to do with all this free time. Ms. Ethel's designs are just waiting for your final budget approval. The coalition's ground-breaking ceremony is on indefinite hold—permit issues Mr. Caldwell said. Which I find odd considering we had those worked out before I left." She added a splash of olive oil and a dash of salt to a pot of boiling water. "What bothers me is why it's taking so long. If I could go back to work, I'd investigate, find out what the problem is."

"I wish I could help you, but on a budget level, it had passed. But now, for whatever reason, they've brought it back through but assigned it to someone else. I guess they don't like me as much as you do."

She grinned. "Who told you I like you? I love you." She scooped out a small sample of sauce and blew over it before placing it in Zak's delicious mouth. "If I was there, I'd make it my business to know what was going on."

His eyes widened. "This is amazing." He wiped his mouth. "Now back to the coalition project. Mr. Caldwell is sending you the updates, right?"

Her mind raced. "He does. But something's just off about the whole thing. I swear if something awful happens, I'm faulting Dr. Hart for keeping me on this ridiculous half-time, work-from-home schedule. The only projects Mr. Caldwell sends me are the ones I could do in my sleep."

Zak slipped his arm around Lacey's lower back. "Dr. Hart's looking out for you and the baby. You have a high-stress job. Sure, you sit down and design but after that you're all over the place. And the long hours? It's not good for the pregnancy, considering what happened in the beginning."

Lacey slipped out of his grip and broke the noodles in half, dropped them into the water. "Oh, the irony. I made up this whole story to save my job and then spent over half my pregnancy out of work. I still don't understand the problem. I haven't had anymore bleeding."

"Which is a good sign considering the fun we've been having." He thrust his hips against hers, sending bolts of electricity shooting through her core.

She wiggled away, not ready to be distracted by his charms. "No dessert for you until after dinner."

"After dinner?" He made his way to the documents, drummed his fingers across the papers. "I think these deserve a proper celebration right now."

She watched him, his eyes scanning over every word, the tense muscles in his jaw relaxing. She sensed the relief, the heavy burden lifted. Although, she reminded herself it wasn't over until Finn signed. "It does, but only after I get Finn's official ink stamp."

Zak took a gulp of his beer, a big one. "Have you called him yet?"

Using a butter knife, Lacey scraped the burnt areas on the toast. "Not yet, the papers showed up by courier less than an hour before you did. I figure I'll call him when he's scheduled back at work, which according to Hannah is tomorrow. I'll try to set a time to meet then. Is he still dating the girl from finance?"

"I'm not sure." Zak pointed to the least burnt piece of bread. "I'll take that one. Should I worry?"

Lacey plated the spaghetti and his specially requested toast. "About what? Can you take these to the table?"

Setting his beer on the counter, he carried them for her. "About why you're interested in Finn's love-life."

Lacey poured herself a glass of green tea, grabbed his beer, and took both to the table. "I'm asking because I know him. If he's dating, then he'll be eager to get this over with as quick as possible. If not, he has the propensity to make others suffer."

"Maybe I should go with you." Zak twirled the pasta around his fork and slid it into his mouth. "Yum."

Lacey tried to take a bite, but something in her stomach wouldn't settle. "Actually, I need to be the one to handle it."

Zak wiped his mouth. "I get it. It's his baby, and he has to be the one to say he wants to sever the relationship forever. I'm sure it's difficult, even for a man like that." Zak bit into the toast with a loud crunch.

Lacey toyed with her pasta as she considered what Zak said. What if she had over-estimated Finn's ability to let go? What if Finn wanted to be a part of the baby's life? Where would that leave her and Zak? She hoped Zak would be okay with whatever did or didn't happen. And she hoped he realized that while signing away rights for Finn might not be easy, neither was raising another man's child.

"I need to know you're okay with this, too. That you won't get cold feet. It's one thing to be entangled in the honeymoon of a blooming relationship, but this is a baby we're talking about. A crying, pooping, snotty-nose, baby. Sleepless nights, vomit-covered clothes, spit-up in the eyeball—and that's just the early years. Someone told me the teenage years are much worse."

"You can't scare me away. I know what I'm signing up for. I'm not naïve enough to believe there'll never be bad days. There will be." Zak laid his fork down and intertwined his hands with hers. "But my love for you, for this baby, it's a commitment I don't take lightly. I wouldn't ask you to be my wife, or to adopt Jude if I thought there was even a slim chance I couldn't handle it. So try not to expect the worst."

Her free hand fiddled with the napkin in her lap. "I know I shouldn't. It's just so hard not to. For every awesome thing that happened in my life, something terrible always followed. Did you know my first kiss almost killed me?"

"Are you being dramatic?" He returned to his meal. "This is so good."

"You don't believe me? Brandon McAllister, he ate a McFish sandwich right before he kissed me, and I guess a chunk of it got into my mouth. My throat closed up. I itched all over, and if it hadn't been for a bystander with an epi-pen I would have died, seriously died."

Zak held back the laughter, a smart choice considering his mouth was packed full of spaghetti.

"It's not funny. I'm serious. And I have plenty of other examples. On the day of the state spelling bee, I fell down the steps going into the auditorium and broke my leg. The alternate had to take my place. The year Santa brought me the puppy, I had to give him away the next day because I broke out in hives. Oh, I almost forgot the time I missed my flight to study abroad because someone stole my passport—the night before."

Zak washed down the spaghetti with the rest of his beer. "It's all coincidence. Now, I know it's terrifying to trust, but I promise I won't let you or Jude down. If my parents have taught me anything, it's being realistic in love. Good days, bad days, they happen. Feelings, emotions, they roller coaster. But love, it's forever. And I love you." He gestured to her untouched pasta. "Now, eat because you promised me a celebration."

"I said, *maybe*." She took a mouthful of spaghetti and moaned. "This is superb."

He cleaned his plate. "I told you."

"My nerves are just all over the place. But I'm sure once he signs the papers, I will be back to normal. I'll call Finn tomorrow."

"Sounds like a good plan."

And she did, first thing in the morning—with no luck. So, she turned to the one person in the building who'd know where to find him, Hannah.

The pop of bubble-gum made Lacey shudder. The mousy voice was no better. "You didn't hear? Finn has flown off to Europe on a promotional tour for the company, trying to drum up business with his charming good looks."

A charming mask covering the hideous person underneath, Lacey thought. "But I thought he was coming back today?"

"Supposedly, it was a last-minute change of plans. Now they won't be back for a couple of months."

Lacey pressed her palm into her forehead. "I don't have a couple of months."

Hannah popped her gum again. "What is so important it can't wait?"

Regaining her composure, she remembered Hannah's tendencies for gossip. "Nothing major, I just found something of his I wanted to give back. Wait, who is they?"

"Oh, you don't know do you? Hold on, and I'll tell you all about it." Lacey heard the phone rustle, and then Hannah returned, whispering this time. "The girl he's been dating from Zak's office. I hear they're pretty serious. Someone said he plans to pop the question while he's over there."

At least now Lacey knew he would be more than willing to sign the papers. The only problem—it would be after the birth. She'd fly to Europe, but her better senses told her Dr. Hart would never approve such a trip. "Thanks Hannah, I'll talk to you later."

"Wait—I have more."

"About Finn?"

"No, about the coalition contract."

Lacey's heart pounded in her ears. Her jaws tightened. She was almost afraid to listen, even contemplated hanging up the phone, but couldn't. If there was anything to know, she needed to hear it. "What about it?"

Hannah's voice lowered. "Apparently, the reason there's been such a delay is because they trashed the old design and made a new set of blueprints.... or used Jocelyn's. I can't remember. I heard Margot has ulterior motives. Which is not unheard of because she has that look. The woman owns every pair of Louboutin's ever created. Isn't that a sign of something? Or maybe it's just a sign of her richness? She —"

"Hannah," Lacey said, forcing her back on track.

"Yes, sorry. Well, I'm not an architect, but I know enough to know the design is nothing like you planned it. And those counseling centers you incorporated—wiped off the map. Now it's personal assistants on every floor, helping guide couples to products they need to help with their marriage for a price. Infidelity packages, addiction packages, love language packages, religious packages, gift-giving packages—"

"Hannah."

"I'm sure you get the point, anything to make money."

Every drop of moisture left Lacey's mouth. She could barely speak. "But the designs Mr. Caldwell sent me are still mostly mine."

"Because he doesn't know either. And I shouldn't be saying any of this. Shoot, if they find out I told you, they might get me fired. So swear you didn't hear it from me. And I'm sorry they removed you from the project. I heard Margot tell Jocelyn not to let you know until after the ground-breaking ceremony."

"But why would she do that?"

"From what I hear, she never really cared for your design. Brent Walker and the rest of the board did. But when they gave her complete control, she took advantage of the circumstances, with you on bedrest and all, to make it what she wanted. That gave her the perfect set-up to conjure up a way to ax your design. Oh my god, it's almost like one of those thriller movies."

Fire burned in Lacey's blood and smoke clouded her eyes. "I have to go, Hannah." Lacey hung up the phone and instantly dialed Mr. Caldwell to inform him of the diabolical plan brewing between the two witches. But before she could summon the courage to press the green call button, she stopped herself.

Mr. Caldwell, would support whatever Margot wanted, she was the boss and what was the saying he used before? *If she says jump, we say how high.* Lacey needed to reach higher, consult with someone who could force Margot to respect them. And Lacey knew just the person.

She called Zak and cried out the details about Finn and the contract.

"Calm down, it'll be okay," Zak said, in his *I'll pretend the sky isn't falling* tone.

But it wasn't working for Lacey. "How? Did you hear anything I said? I will give birth before you can adopt Jude. And Margot and her side-kick Jocelyn tore apart my design—then lied about it."

"It sucks. I feel you. But if you don't take time to breathe, you'll end up in labor before it's time." Zak paused, taking a deep breath of his own that came through the receiver like the sound of rushing water. "Now, I have a plan. First, Jude is mine whether we sign those papers a week from now or a year from now. And second, I'll call Brent and set-up a dinner—with one exception."

Lacey pulled air into her lungs and asked, "What's that?"

"Be subtle when discussing the project because Brent hates mixing business and family."

Jude somersaulted in Lacey's belly as she regained her self-control. "I can handle that."

"Great, I'll call him. Now, stop worrying."

21

Lucky for Lacey, Brent had agreed to come over for dinner the following Sunday. And ten minutes before his scheduled arrival, Lacey stood by the door wringing her hands.

Zak gripped both of her shoulders and escorted her back to the table chair. "You promised not to bombard him with work issues, remember? I'm serious, be subtle."

The only thing she could promise was that she would try her best. She scrubbed her palms over her thighs. "And I'm not. I'm just eager to get to know him better and to meet his husband."

Zak cocked his head. "Lacey—"

A strong knock sent her springing to her feet. "He's here."

But Zak beat her to the door and blocked her, the space between his eyes forming a deep wrinkle. "Promise me."

Okay, she'd settle herself before Zak had a stroke. She laid her hand over his. "I promise."

His chest raised high and then lowered. "All right then..." He turned the knob and gestured them inside the apartment.

At once, Brent reached his arms out to Lacey and then to her huge belly. "Look at you, you're so much bigger than the last time I saw you —but still as beautiful as ever." He kissed her cheek.

She never understood why people regarded it as a good idea to point out a pregnant woman's size. There was nothing fun about carrying spare tires around the waistline. And in her case, it might not be such a sensitive topic if the extra weight had gathered in more desirable places, anywhere other than her midsection.

Brent let go to introduce his husband. "Lacey, this is Vance. Vance, Lacey."

Even though Brent's husband wore clothes, a pair of slim-fit trousers and a v-neck sweater, he looked as if he had stepped off the pages of a Calvin Klein underwear ad. His hair was a mid-fade on the sides and back leading into a sexy, dark, tousled, *I want to run my fingers through it at the peak of passion* kind of mane. But it would never happen because he married a man—married to her brother-in-law, or soon-to-be brother-in-law.

"Nice to meet you," Lacey said, sucking up the drool trickling from the corner of her mouth. His face looked like someone had hand-carved it and then implanted two light-brown marbles with specks of plum for his eyes. She couldn't resist staring, any normal person would stare. And when he took her hand and kissed it, she nearly fainted. No doubt she had passed models on the streets of New York, but never in her life had she had one in her apartment—ever.

His good looks were hypnotizing, drawing her in and holding her there with awkward stares. And she didn't care if anyone noticed because the likelihood of her having dinner with another man as pretty as he held the same odds as her getting struck by lightning. Wait—finding herself in her current position held the same odds, but it happened.

Zak gestured for Brent and Vance to sit and then leaned close to Lacey's ear. "You know he's gay—and married to my brother?"

"Don't judge me. What would you do if Meghan Markle walked through the door right now?"

He tapped Lacey's lips with his. "I'd keep my eyes on you... And then, when you weren't paying attention, I'd look." He chuckled.

"Whatever," she said, taking a seat at the table across from Brent, who sipped on red wine as Zak prepared the plates. Lacey drank sparkling grape juice.

Zak handed Lacey a plate first, and then Brent and Vance before grabbing his own.

"I'm looking forward to this," Brent said, inhaling the steam from the pasta. "And to not having to talk about anything work related. I swear if I hear another word about the coalition project, my head will explode—"

Lacey choked. She snatched up a napkin and kept it in front of her face to block the spray of juice. Zak ran over and beat her back. "Are you okay?"

Her eyes bulged from the strained coughs as she struggled to catch her breath.

"Stand her up," Brent said, joining Zak. Both of them lifted her to her feet, held her arms above her head.

She took one big gasp and coughed two more times before she returned to normal. "I'm good now," she said, her voice more raspy than normal.

"What happened?" Zak asked as he took a seat beside her without taking his gaze off of her.

"My juice went down the wrong pipe."

Brent returned to his chair and twirled the thin noodles into a perfect spindle around his fork before sliding it in his mouth. "Well, if it makes you feel better, the spaghetti is amazing. Where did you learn to cook like this, Lacey?"

"The Italian place on 44th Avenue, *Carmine's*," Zak said with a devilish grin.

"Oh, you interned there?" Vance asked.

"I've never worked at *Carmine's*." Lacey popped Zak on the shoulder. "He's being facetious. It's my mom's recipe."

Brent pointed his fork at Zak. "Still the same jokester, I see. Well, tell your mom it's delicious. We travel so much we barely get to eat a homemade meal."

Vance set his wineglass on the table and picked up a fork. "And I sure miss a good homemade meal. Every once in a while we run across a mom and pop diner that sells them, like the one in DC where you ordered the collards and sweet potatoes, remember?"

Brent's eyes stretched. "Yes, and you had the fried okra. I can't recall the name of the place, but it was delicious."

Vance agreed as he bit into a piece of toasted garlic bread. He swallowed it. "Lacey, if you and Zak ever have time to visit DC, you must check it out."

She nodded, uninterested in DC, at least in that moment. The only thing she wanted to talk about was the coalition project, but Brent had shut it down before she had a chance to even mention it. Lacey nibbled her food, too nervous for anything heavy. But regardless of how she felt, she had to keep the conversation moving forward—until she could interject her concerns about the project. "Are you in DC often?"

Brent wiped his mouth. "It's one of our favorite cities. We spend at least a quarter of the year there." Vance rested his perfectly formed hand on Brent's forearm. Sprigs of wiry arm hair pushed their way in between Vance's finger's.

"I've visited lots of places, but would you believe DC was never one of them?"

Zak turned to her. "Really, you've never been there?"

It was as if he thought she had made it up as part of some plan to get Brent to talk about the project. But it was the truth. She had traveled nowhere unless it benefited her career or had been the destination of a childhood vacation. "No, I've never seen DC."

Using his last bite of garlic bread, Brent soaked up the remaining marinara sauce from his plate. "Well, that's it. We're planning a trip there together when the baby's old enough. Or, if you guys want to go alone, I'm sure you won't have a problem finding a sitter with all the excited grandparents."

"That sounds fun. We should do that." Zak frowned at Lacey's half-eaten meal, then gave Jude a quick pat. "Eat," he whispered to her, then grinned as she bit a piece of toast.

Zak stood. "I hope you guys saved room for dessert."

"Ooh, what is it?" Vance asked, his hands clasped together. "It doesn't matter. I'll take whatever it is. I'm addicted to anything sweet."

I'm sweet, Lacey murmured under her breath. Shocked, she slapped her hand over mouth, pretended to belch. "Excuse me." She closed her eyes for a brief moment, then turned her gaze to Zak. Who was she kidding? He was the most handsome man in the room. The most handsome man she had ever met. And not even Vance's model looks could compete. Zak was the love of her life.

He caught her staring at him and winked before turning to Vance and Brent. "It's Tiramisu. Do you guys want coffee with it?"

"Is it Starbucks'?" Brent asked, giving Zak a cheerful smile.

"No. It's fresh brew—um," Zak said, searching for the bag, "Dunkin Donuts brand. Take it or leave it."

"I'll take it. Coffee is coffee whenever Starbucks isn't available." Brent chuckled.

"Mom brought this bag over. You know, between her and Kathleen, Lacey's mom, we haven't had to even think about buying groceries." Zak poured the filtered water into the top of the pot.

And there it was, her chance. "Which is wonderful considering I'm still working on designs from home. Of course, I'm not too busy, not since they removed me from the coalition project." She dropped the bait. *Please bite it Brent, please.*

Brent twisted his mouth to one side and for a minute she couldn't be sure if he was angry with her or with the coalition contract news. And he kept her on edge, taking his precious time answering as her underarms dripped sweat. She couldn't take the uneasiness another second. "I'm sorry, I shouldn't have mentioned it. You said not to talk about work."

He scratched the side of his head. "No, it's okay. I'm just wondering how the lead architect can be removed? Especially since it's your design we're using for the building."

"Were using—but not anymore. Since I've been on bedrest, one of my co-workers has taken over and is working with Margot on the project. The last thing I heard is that they changed everything, redesigned it all. They've replaced the counseling offices with personal assistants to help guide marriage package purchases and to aid with online shopping. It appears they're putting an emphasis on advertising and selling products."

Lacey dipped her spoon through the layers of espresso-soaked ladyfingers and mascarpone that Zak plopped on the table in front of her with a big thud. Did he think she had gone overboard?

"I didn't know Margot authorized any changes. She had mentioned hiring personal shopping assistants to guide couples with major purchases—to keep them from getting into debt too soon. Financial problems are one of the leading causes of failed marriages, so I was on board with it." Brent held the spoon filled with Tiramisu by his mouth and then laid it back on his plate. "And you're positive she's done this? I guess it would explain the hold up on breaking ground."

While gossip couldn't always be trusted, sometimes a person had to know the source, and Lacey knew Hannah. She never spread rumors, only verified information. "Yes, in fact, the blueprints that my co-worker has been sending me aren't even the ones they pushed through to engineering."

Brent turned towards Zak. "Did you see them when they came through finance?"

Zak swallowed a mouthful of dessert. "They chose someone else to run the numbers this time."

"Which would make no sense if they're sticking to the original, but perfect sense if they're making major changes. And being that Margot knows you're my brother, I assume they wanted to keep them away from you. I might have had the wool pulled over my eyes."

Vance rubbed Brent's shoulder until Zak delivered him his second piece of dessert. He dug into it at once.

Lacey might have taken it a step too far. "I shouldn't have mentioned it."

Brent reached across the table, cupped her hands in his. "I'm glad you mentioned it. Vance and I have fought hard to expand the coalition, to offer resources to those who couldn't afford them. We've invested a lot of energy and personal money into projects that promote marriages, promote the future of people who want to be together, but need help learning how to battle the external factors. And not just for couples like us, but for anyone who knows how hard it is to stay together in a world full of distractions designed to tear couples apart."

Lacey dropped her gaze. "I hope I haven't ruined the night."

"No, if anything, you saved it, saved the coalition." Brent released Lacey's hands and took his coffee. "Zak, why didn't you insist they show the designs to you?"

Zak's jaw tensed. "Because it's not my job. I do what I'm told. I'm not the boss and throwing around your name to get what I want isn't the answer."

"Sorry. You're right, and I wouldn't expect you to. Well, looks like I'll be meeting with Margot and your co-worker tomorrow. Seems we have a lot to discuss." Brent sipped the coffee and winced. "After a decent cup of coffee, no doubt."

With dinner and dessert finished, Brent and Vance gave their last embraces and said their goodbyes. Zak locked the door behind them and kept his back to Lacey longer than expected.

"You're probably angry, but I don't think I went overboard. By no means was I harassing. I hope you understand that even though he didn't want to talk about work, I had to tell him." Lacey shifted her weight from one foot to the other.

He whirled around to face her. "Did I tell you how much I love you?"

"Does that mean you're not upset?"

"No, you're standing up for what you believe in. I have to support that. Trying to influence his actions would have been a bad move, but getting him to pay attention, that's smart."

"Well, I need him to do more than pay attention, I need him to take a hard look." She tangled her fingers. "The waiting will drive me crazy."

Zak's phone dinged, and he read the message. "Maybe not, looks like we'll have something to keep us busy in the meantime. Ms. Ethel wants us all to meet next weekend to finalize the plans so the contractors can get started."

Lacey poked her finger into his pecs. "You'll be busy. My part is finished. Better get to work."

His lips parted as he wrapped his arms around her. "I don't mind putting in some work."

He took her mouth until she pushed him away and giggled. "Ms. Ethel will not be happy if you don't finish, so no distractions."

"Oh, don't think you're off the hook yet, *Mrs. Always Over Budget.*"

22

"I still don't understand how it doesn't add up," Lacey said, dropping the spreadsheet on the table. She squeezed her temples. "I can't scale back anymore."

"You have to, there's no other way to make it work."

Zak had no clue what he was asking her to do. Ms. Ethel had a vision, and Lacey wanted to deliver all of those desires to her in a perfectly planned blueprint. But the more he forced her to take away, the less likely it was she could produce anything other than the bare bone necessities. She shook her head. "I guess if I strip it down to a skeleton, then it'll fit the budget."

He rubbed the back of his neck. "Now you're being dramatic."

"I am not. Maybe it's best if we don't work together."

"Quit saying things you don't mean—just because you can't get your way. Ms. Ethel has a decent budget, but she's not a huge corporation that can funnel out an extra ten-thousand dollars on demand."

He was correct. Lacey had to look at this from a realistic point of view and a scaled back one. "I hate to say it, but you're right. I've been looking at this all wrong. I swear designing a small business is harder than designing a skyscraper."

He leaned forward, laid his hand across hers. "But it's more rewarding. Now if I can offer a few suggestions."

She rolled her eyes. "Why not? It sounds like I don't have a choice."

Over the next several hours, they mingled ideas over mixed nuts and Green Goddess juice until it all fit together. Lacey sat back and scanned the finished product. Satisfied, she cupped both sides of his face and kissed him. "You're a genius. I didn't believe it would work, but you made it happen."

He gave a dimpled grin. "Thanks."

She stood up and stretched out the aches and pains of sitting in the same position for so long. "You're way more talented than you give yourself credit for." She grimaced as a pain shot from her lower back into her thigh. "I'm regretting sitting too long."

"Why don't you let me give you a massage?" He met her and led her over to the sofa. There, he guided her to a sitting position between his legs as he kneaded her back.

She moaned with relief. It felt so good. If she had known he gave five-star massages, she would have requested one sooner. But then again, he had lots of hidden talents she was just now discovering; the design suggestions being one. "Can I ask you something?"

"Sure," he said, pressing his fingertips deep into her back muscles.

"You've been helping people for a while with their businesses. Why not start one of your own? You're so good at it."

He pushed his fist against her spine in a motion that made her whole body tingle. "That is Brent's department. I'm satisfied doing what I do."

She suspected there was more to it than that as she recalled the tension in Zak's face when Brent asked why he didn't insist on seeing the design. "Then why did what Brent said last night bother you so much? I caught the look on your face."

"I don't know. It shouldn't have."

"But it did, so…?" He playfully pinched her, and she jumped. "Are you trying to hurt me?"

"Never." He stopped massaging and shifted his hands, still under her shirt, to her protruding belly, gliding his palms in smooth circles across the huge bulge. Jude responded with his usual strong kicks as Zak leaned forward and kissed the back of Lacey's neck. "I get defensive sometimes with Brent. I know I shouldn't. None of it's his fault, but… he's so successful and for years that's all anyone has talked about. While all anybody ever had for me was pity."

"What do you mean?" Lacey lifted her shirt, placed her hands over Zak's.

He held still. "When I had cancer, everyone treated me like I was too fragile to move. And whenever they spoke, it was with that *I feel sorry for you* tone. And because of all the attention I got for being sick, Brent compensated by overachieving. He did everything. And won everything, every reward, certificate, you name it, he had it."

"And you could have it too. You have the talent to accomplish as much as he has," Lacey ran her fingers over Zak's knuckles.

"Maybe. I don't know. It just never seemed possible, especially under his giant shadow."

In an awkward set of motions, Lacey repositioned herself onto Zak's lap, facing him. Her baby bump pressed against his abs as the rest of her body remained almost out of reach. "I'm not making you uncomfortable am I?"

"No," he said giving her a lopsided grin. "He's getting so big."

"He is." She watched one of Jude's body parts stretch out and slide across her stomach.

Zak watched, too. "You realize you could start your own business, as well. Design what you want to design instead of following in your dad's footsteps. In fact, we could launch one together. I'm sure we'd accomplish great things."

It would be a dream come true for her, but she doubted her father would see it the same way. Who would take over the family business he had worked so hard to build from the ground up? He would be devastated to have to sign over his legacy to a stranger. No matter what she wanted, she couldn't do that to him. "I don't think my dad would be kosher with that decision."

"Are you living for yourself, or your dad? Because you can't do both. Besides, once we're married, it'd make perfect sense to give up the big city jobs and move to the country. Create our mark on the world together with this little man." Jude gave his strongest kick yet. "See, even he agrees."

Lacey giggled. "You're not the baby whisperer? It was a coincidence."

"Nothing about him, or us is a coincidence. It was meant to be. And I believe starting our own business might be in the cards for our little family—now that we have each other to help push past our fears." Zak anchored his eyes onto hers, stretched his arms out to trace her cheekbones and lips with his fingers. "You are so beautiful."

Who was he kidding? She was a bloated mess with stick legs. "Liar. With my skinny legs and my huge belly I'm a dead ringer for a chicken drumstick."

"Yum, chicken. I'll have a bite of that." Chuckling, he lifted her from his lap and laid her on the sofa, hovered over her. He gently nipped at her skin with his teeth. "You taste finger-lickin' good."

Lacey tried pushing him off but found herself weak with laughter.

"Stop, stop. If you don't stop I'll pee on myself."

He stopped, his mouth only inches above her, his eyes stretched wide. "Seriously?"

"Will it get you to stop?"

"I knew you were lying." He attacked her, but this time with a fierce passion. Forceful kisses trailed down the nape of her neck as his tongue savored her skin, igniting an uncontainable fire in her center.

A fire that burned for him as his hands ran under her shirt and lifted it over her head and onto the floor. And while in the past she would have been ashamed of her new disproportionate body, she wasn't anymore. Instead, she lingered in the trail of desire he left with his lips, trembled as his hands explored every inch of her skin.

And when his mouth attacked the most sensitive place on her body, she thrust both of her hands into his hair and squeezed and groaned and writhed until he released her, leaving her aching for more. She ripped at his shirt, tugged and pulled until it was off his torso. Then her hands pleasured themselves in the warmth of his toned chest as he unbuttoned and kicked off his jeans, followed by his boxers.

Naked, he kneeled in between her legs and lifted her hips, fighting with her yoga pants and panties until he conquered, tossing them onto the floor with the rest of the clothes. And with a gentle but firm grip, he guided her legs around his back. She locked them in place, held them there despite her quivering thighs.

She wanted him to take her, plunge in deep and hard. But he did no such thing. Instead, he took her hands and intertwined them with his as what she yearned for the most slowly glided its way inside her, welcomed by her arched spine and his gentle moans.

Rocking back and forth without hurry, he drove her mad. She needed him to loosen his hold so she could pull him in closer. So she could dig her fingers into his skin. But he kept her hostage, took pleasure in the pain it caused her. The pain it caused himself, shown in his clenched jaws and eyes that rolled in circles behind heavy lids.

She tried raising her bottom higher as an explosion built itself inside her. But she wasn't strong enough. "I need my hands, Zak."

His grip on her tightened. His chest curled forward. But his control over his lower half remained steady. "Not yet," he said, winded.

If he didn't let go of her soon, she'd lose her freaking mind. Lose what ounce of sanity he hadn't stripped from her. Her legs squeezed his waist, the yearning for him too much to bear. "Please," she moaned.

He leaned forward, as close to her as possible, and stared into her eyes. "Almost."

His sweat lathered her. His heart pulsed against her. And at the brink of what she thought was a most certain death, he released her, burying himself between her thighs, pillaging all she had. She pierced his back with her nails and cried out. His mouth covered hers, stifled the gratified squeals as he pounded into her. Harder and faster, deeper and longer until his body shook with the magnitude of an earthquake.

Limp, he collapsed on the sliver of sofa beside her, his muscles still shuddering from the aftershocks—as was hers.

"It gets better every time," she said in a breathless whisper.

His chest heaved up and down, his breathing labored. "Who are you telling?"

She leaned on her side to give him room and caught a sharp twinge in her stomach. "Ow," she said, holding her hand over her lower belly.

Zak jumped to a sitting position. "What's wrong?"

The pain continued, took her breath. She held up a finger so Zak wouldn't panic. And when it finally passed a minute later, she said, "I had a bad cramp."

"We're going to the hospital." Zak's foot caught in a cushion as he leaped off the sofa, sending him plummeting straight to the floor with a thud. "Shit."

Lacey giggled. "Now what good will you be when it's really time to go?"

He curled on the ground buck naked, holding his ribs. "So," he moaned, "it's not time?"

"No, not even close." Lacey slid to the edge of the sofa, then rolled herself off carefully. She'd already had the unpleasant experience of trying to sit up straight from laying down. The pubic bone pain that followed was enough to remind her never to do it again.

She crawled on all fours to Zak and then laid beside him. "Want me to kiss it for you?"

He let go of his ribs and pushed the strays curls matted against her face behind her ear. "I doubt you could bend that far. Besides, I don't want you to go into labor before we can deliver those blueprints to Ms. Ethel."

"Well, let's give her what she wants—after a good night's rest."

"I like that plan. If I can get us both safely to the bed."

23

"What an amazing job you guys did for Ms. Ethel. She's had that idea twirling inside her brain for years. And thanks to you two, it's officially on paper," Meredith said as she stood in between Lacey and Zak with an arm wrapped around each of them. "Now it's time to celebrate."

"Not only was it fun to design—minus the times when the number pusher popped my bubble—but it is exciting to see how happy it makes her." Lacey studied Ms. Ethel, sporting an ombre silver to rose wig and a dentured smile, as she signed papers with the head of the construction company who won the bid.

"You need someone to keep you on track," Zak said, winking.

"Well, I think you both work great together. And beware, Ms. Ethel has spread the word. I'm receiving phone calls around the clock requesting your services. It might be something to contemplate... just putting it out there." Meredith let go of Zak and Lacey to pat Jude's soon-to-expire home. "Especially with this little man only three weeks away from his arrival."

Lacey scrunched her face. "Starting a business with a new baby? Sounds way too risky."

"I know I've said it more than once, but it's a great idea," Zak said, facing Lacey. "Consider it. We'd get to make our own schedule, work around the baby. Then we could choose to either stay in the city or move out to the suburbs. And it would be a fulfilling career. You even said so yourself."

Lacey had thought about it, a satisfying career with much less pressure. And she would no longer have to battle the Jocelyn's and Margot's of the world. But she couldn't afford to take such a chance, roll the dice on something so uncertain at the risk of disappointing her father. "It's tempting, but…"

"Why not at least try? You'll be out soon on maternity leave, and if we can get the business plans together within that time—you wouldn't have to go back and neither would I. We'd be helping the other Ms. Ethel's of the world start their small businesses." He gestured to Ms. Ethel now twitching her arthritic hips after signing the last of the documents.

"Okay, we can run through ideas, see what happens. But don't quit your day job just yet." Lacey squinted her eyes at Zak. "There's a baby on the way."

Ms. Ethel promenaded over and laid a hand on both Lacey and Zak. "I can't thank you both enough. You do not understand what this means to me, or the people that will use my services."

Ms. Ethel's joy warmed Lacey's heart, and she smiled. "You're welcome. It's been our pleasure."

"I won't hold you for too long. I know what it feels like to stand on swollen ankles at nine months pregnant. So go feed that beautiful baby and then prop those up," Ms. Ethel said, reaching into her purse and pulling out a couple hundred-dollar bills. She passed the money to Meredith. "Now, you take these two out to eat somewhere nice, they deserve it."

Lacey's mouth dropped. "Ms. Ethel—"

"Stop. I'll be offended if you don't allow me to do this." She pulled out another hundred. "Hell, take the whole family out, celebrate. I would go with you, but I have supply shopping to do."

Meredith hugged Ms. Ethel. "I'm so happy for you. And thank you for your generosity. I'll take them to the new Japanese place downtown."

Zak escorted Ms. Ethel to her car as Meredith called Rebecca to have her family join them at the restaurant. Kyle arrived just before the drink order, and Rebecca and her husband Roy, a man with linebacker shoulders, a square head, and chronically sunburned skin joined them after the soup delivery. The twins, Monroe and Ulysses, were in tow and as adorable as ever—until the point they realized they had missed the soup. Then both of them bawled.

Kyle offered his. "Here, take Papa's soup."

Ulysses almost batted it from the table. "I not want oars, Papa."

"Okay, then." Kyle slid his bowl out of harm's way.

Meredith coddled at the same time Rebecca changed her tone to stern and commanding. Roy glossed over the outburst, opting to converse with Zak about baseball. But Ulysses was having none of it. With his fists balled at his side, he screamed something incomprehensible at the top of his lungs.

Overshadowed by his brother's tantrum, Monroe fell into a prone position and swung his arm and legs across the main path of a lanky blonde waitress who'd missed his meltdown. She tripped over him, flinging a nearby table's drink order into the air. The stream of soda, tea, and alcohol headed straight for Rebecca, and despite her well-intended efforts to bend and twist her body out of the way, she got soaked.

Kyle's and Meredith's eyes bulged as they assumed a statuesque posture. Summoned by Rebecca's cries for help, Roy rushed over and swooped Monroe off the floor and carried him to the bathroom. Zak jumped up to help his sister. Lacey followed behind him.

No one was watching Ulysses.

Not until the squeals of nearby customers snagged the Cooper Clan's attention. Ulysses had painted the chairs, tables, and the pre-heated grill with the squirt bottle of white sauce. It was a catastrophic mix. The sauce sizzled, smoked, and wreaked a sour, burnt odor before filling the restaurant with smoke. The cook rushed over with his finger aimed at the vent hood in a valiant effort to prevent the fire alarm from triggering. But he fell short when he slipped on the slab of butter Ulysses had smeared on the tile floor.

It was a disaster that couldn't be escaped fast enough—and per the manager's request. There would be no Japanese for the Cooper family, only drive-thru Big Mac's and chicken nuggets.

On the way back to the house, Lacey whispered in Zak's ear. "Please say Jude will never do anything that embarrassing."

"He will do that and much more."

Meredith overheard her. "It's just what kids do. At some point, they all throw tantrums, hit, kick, and even bite. They'll fail a test, skip class, and break someone's heart. Sometimes that will be your heart Lacey—and Zak's. But regardless, the love and joy he'll bring you guys will erase those mischievous moments—most of the time." She narrowed her eyes at the twins.

To everyone's relief, the rest of the night proved much less eventful than the start. They all enjoyed spending time together as they sipped hot cocoa in the heated outdoor gazebo while playing board games. And when fatigue set in, they settled into a family movie approved by the twins, who both fell asleep five minutes into it.

The next morning, Zak offered his limited DIY skills to help his dad repair the garage door. No doubt, they had to make several trips to the home improvement store, leaving Lacey suspicious of their self-declared handyman titles. But who was she to crush the dream?

And while they kept busy outdoors, Lacey helped bake cookies for Meredith's auxiliary group.

Lacey measured out flour per the recipe, leveled it, and dumped it into the porcelain bowl. As she added a half-teaspoon of salt, Jude somersaulted. Reflexively, she rested a hand on top of her belly. Tiny body parts pressed and poked at her, and sometimes it was almost as if she were holding his hand. She couldn't believe how far she had come, how close she was to the finish line. And it amazed her how much she had grown emotionally. The pregnancy no longer terrified her, instead it excited her to know soon enough she would have him cuddled in her arms.

In fact, the only regret was not getting Finn to sign off on the adoption papers before the birth.

Meredith stopped creaming the butter and sugar and placed a hand over her heart. "Isn't that the most amazing feeling? It's what I miss most about pregnancy, that essence of life growing and moving inside you."

Lacey studied the joy in Meredith's face and decided she had one other regret—lying to her about the baby being Zak's. Because although he was everything a dad should be, he was not the baby's real father. And while she and Zak had considered sharing the truth with his parents, they eventually opted against it, choosing not to break their hearts in a time of celebration.

"I see you're daydreaming. I used to do that a lot when I was pregnant," Meredith said, now cracking eggs into the mixture.

Lacey refocused, scooping up the baking soda and checking her measurements twice. "My mind is always moving. I'm not even sure it stops while I sleep."

"That's expected, getting married and having babies fires up the thinking train."

"It sure does." Confident she had the correct amount, Lacey dumped in the baking soda.

Meredith added a splash of vanilla extract into the wet ingredients as Lacey whisked the dry.

Lacey's phone dinged, and she ignored it, certain it was nothing important. But Meredith insisted, worried it might be the guys needing help. Wiping her hands, Lacey pulled up the message. It was Mr. Duke demanding an urgent return call. A bubble rose to Lacey's throat and nearly choked her.

"It is them isn't it? I knew it wouldn't be long before they needed help," Meredith said, stirring the dry ingredients into the wet.

Lacey shook her head in a slow motion. "No, it's... um... one of my co-workers. I should take this."

She penguin-raced down the hall to Zak's old bedroom and locked the door. She then wedged herself into the cramped closet. Lightheaded, she perched on the edge of a plastic storage container and dialed Mr. Duke.

"Miss Winters, I'm so glad you called me back. There's been a slight complication. And how do I say this other than just say it?... Finn is not the father."

Lacey's fingers wrapped around her throat. "What do you mean Finn's not the father? You told me you were certain he was." She worked hard to lower her panicked voice and control her runaway emotions. "I've drawn up legal papers based on the information you gave me. I don't understand how the list keeps getting changed. So what now? There's no father, no leads. I'm three weeks from delivery."

"Stay calm, please. As you might have guessed, I'm not always the most organized—"

"You think?"

"Okay, I deserve that," Mr. Duke said before coughing into the receiver. "But if you can give me a minute to explain. I ruled Finn out in the beginning but didn't scratch his name off the list. Instead, I wrote that he wasn't the father on another sheet of paper I found... under a stack of folders."

Lightheaded, she shifted her free hand from her throat to the edge of the plastic bin and braced herself. "How are you certain which list came first? Maybe you took him off but then added him later?"

His voice elevated with confidence. "I can say I'm one-hundred percent certain which came first because I always date the lists— always."

Lacey imagined the conceited smile painting his face, imagined how he leaned back in his recycled gaming chair, patting his food crusted t-shirt. She wanted to scream at him, call him a few inappropriate names, but instead, she steadied her breathing and asked, "So what do

I do now?"

"I'm glad you asked. When I realized my mistake, I returned to the beginning—"

She refused to listen to him toot his horn, give his *look how smart I am that I fixed my mistake* speech. "Do you have the father's name or not?" Not that it mattered because it wouldn't be Finn's, which meant she couldn't have him sign away his parental rights. And what would she tell Zak? That she had changed her mind?

Mr. Duke cleared his throat. "Yes, to the point. It's right here, Oliver Callum—from the original list might I add. Now there is a slight hiccup... He moved to North Carolina."

Lacey stood straight and locked her knees, pressed her palm against her forehead. "Of course, he did."

"I'll email you his contact information, and for your inconvenience, I'm refunding half of the money you paid."

Half? She should get it all back after what he put her through, but she didn't have the energy to even argue. Instead, she ended the call wishing he had never called.

"Lacey, is everything okay in there?" Meredith asked, knocking on the door.

Nothing was okay. Mr. Duke had single-handedly destroyed her world, created false hope, and worst of all made her believe that she could have a life with Zak—even get married for real. Blindsided, she fought her way out of the closet before Meredith could rush the door. "Be out in a minute."

"Okay, just checking. I'm almost ready to put the first batch of cookies in the oven."

"Great, I'll come sift flour for the next batch." Lacey hid her quivering voice, held back the swell of tears threatening to fall. And she regained her composure before joining Meredith in the kitchen.

"I hope everything's well at work," Meredith said, pointing to the phone still in Lacey's hand as she entered the room.

Lacey laid the phone on the countertop beside her, wishing she had thrown it on the floor instead. "Everything is fine." It was anything but fine, but she wouldn't share that news with Meredith. "One of my co-workers wanted to catch up and see how the baby's doing."

Meredith walked over to the stove and checked the temperature. "No surprise there. But get used to it because those calls will become more frequent before the big day. And God forbid if you go past your due date, they'll blow your phone up around the clock, force you into labor."

Lacey dumped the second batch of flour into a bowl, measured out the baking soda. "So I hear."

"Well, that's what happened when I was pregnant with Zak," Meredith said, reaching into a cabinet and pulling out a basket full of cookie cutters. "Or maybe they only cared so much because he was my rainbow baby."

"Your rainbow baby?"

"A rainbow baby is the baby you have after having a miscarriage, or miscarriages in my case. I had three before I had him. In fact, Kyle and I came close to giving up on having another baby... but then I guess God had other plans."

Lacey whisked the dry ingredients the same as before, tried to focus on the fluffy powders and Meredith rather than the terrible news she had received from Mr. Duke. "That had to be hard on you guys."

"Beyond hard, but nothing was harder than watching him battle cancer. That was my worst fears realized." Meredith found a leaf-shaped cookie cutter, held it up and grinned. "This will do. Oh, the diagnosis devastated us, and for a while, we feared he wouldn't make it. But now look at him, twenty-eight years old with a clean bill of health. And to see him having a child of his own—that alone is a miracle."

Lacey leveled the salt in a measuring spoon. "What do you mean?"

"Well, the doctors told us he might never have kids after all the chemotherapy. He said most aren't able to and then gave us the old spill about adoption and blah, blah, blah. At that time though, nothing mattered but saving our son." Meredith pressed the cutter into the thinly rolled dough. "His reproductive abilities weren't high on the priority list."

Meredith lifted one of the shaped cookies. "Perfect. But later on when he was better, I regretted not having explored all the options. I apologized to him, but he wouldn't accept it, said what's meant to be is meant to be."

Lacey dropped the salt and measuring spoon into the dry ingredients, sending up a cloud of white powder. She wiped her faced and brushed the remaining dust from her clothes. "Yeah, sounds like Zak's laissez-faire attitude."

"He truly is my most laid-back child. But I have to admit, knowing he can have a baby of his own is the most wonderful news a mother could ever receive. I always worried for him seeing how much he loves children and how much he wanted one of his own."

Great, not only had Lacey lied to Zak's family about him being the father, but she had unwittingly convinced them that his plumbing functioned. When not even he knew if it did or not. The newly discovered information Meredith shared, along with the devastating mistake by Mr. Duke, hampered any plan to marry Zak. Because what would they do when his parents expected more grandkids? Say Jude was the last sperm he had left?

Lacey's stomach rumbled as she watched Meredith place the cookie sheet filled with the maple leaf cookies into the oven, but not with delight. No, she was sick. "I didn't know that. I mean I knew about the cancer, but he never said anything about the possibility of not being able to have children."

Meredith giggled and pointed at Lacey's bulging belly. "Well, considering how fast you got pregnant, he probably didn't have time."

Lacey white-knuckled the island countertop. "Yeah, I guess you're right."

Kyle and Zak walked in from the garage with big smiles on their faces. "Guess who just saved us a bunch of money?" Kyle aimed both thumbs at his chest. "I did."

"You mean *we*, right dad?" Zak asked, making his way to Lacey.

"Yes, I'm man enough to admit it. I needed help," Kyle said, planting a quick kiss on Meredith's cheeks. "Hey, honey, Zak's going to help me change out the faucet in the bathroom. But we need to pick up the attachment piece."

Zak slipped his arms around Lacey. "Is everything okay? You look pale. You should probably lie down." He leaned back, took a hard study of her. "Better yet, I should stay and take care of you."

Laying down wouldn't fix a thing, only the truth would. But she couldn't tell them without a plan, couldn't face the pain in their faces, no matter how much she realized it was the right thing to do. And what would she tell them? She had no clue who Oliver was, or if he even remembered her. Or hell, with Mr. Duke's track record, if Oliver was even the real father. So instead of destroying their perfect day, she would summon the strength to keep herself together until she figured out the next step. "No, your mom and I have plenty more cookies to bake. Stop interrupting us. I'll be here when you get back."

Meredith held up a turkey-shaped cutter. "Yes, and we have a couple dozen of these still left to make. I won't work her too hard, promise."

"Only if you're sure," he said, seeking assurance from Lacey.

She delivered with a quivering kiss on his cheeks.

"We won't be long," he said, "and Mom, please make her rest if she needs to." Zak headed towards the door behind his dad, but Lacey snagged him by the arm, pulled him back. His eyes widened as he probed her face. "You want me to stay?"

It was more than that. She wanted never to let him go. But after he found out about Finn, she feared she might not have a choice. So she committed every line of his face to memory... his long lashes, auburn brows. With restrained tears, she hugged him tighter than ever before and hoped she would never forget his outdoorsy scent or the tiny fires his touch ignited. "I just needed one last hug goodbye."

He obliged her for another minute before his dad honked the horn outside. "Got to go," he said, pressing his lips against hers before jetting out the door.

"I think Kyle's been watching too many DIY shows." Meredith laughed as she greased the next cookie sheet to prepare for the next batch. "And Zak loves that stuff, though I'm not sure he has much use for it in the city."

Lacey swallowed the bile in her throat and returned to the mixing bowl. "I never imagined him with anything but a spreadsheet in his hand."

A smile warmed Meredith's face as she laid sugar cookie turkeys on parchment paper. "For Christmas one year we brought him the play tool-bench set, and he worked for hours, screwing and unscrewing those plastic pieces. Most kids would have lost interest fast. But he stuck with it, took his time to build it right. He was such a good kid, and now, he's an even better man."

He was the best man... but the more Lacey considered her new circumstances, maybe not the best man for her. Or more so, she was hands-down not the best woman for him. He deserved better. She scanned the kitchen walls, the copper backsplash and warm oak as she folded her arms across her chest.

She would miss this for sure.

Meredith slid another batch of cookies into the oven. "How about I show you Zak's old childhood pictures while those finish?"

Why not stab a knife in her gut and twist it? But she deserved it. "I'd love that."

Meredith walked into the living room and over to an antique chest. She pulled out a variety of aged photo albums as Lacey found a seat on the sofa. Meredith spread them out over the coffee table in front of Lacey, then picked up a photo of Zak on his first day of Kindergarten. "I was so happy they waited a few months into school before they took these because if they hadn't all I would have is a portrait of him bawling. I swear he cried so much the first several weeks I thought he would never adjust."

Lacey took Zak's first school picture from Meredith and studied it as she did the others, recorded images of his first lost tooth, first haircut, first broken arm, first time riding a bike, first wheelchair ride out the hospital, first prom, and many, many more firsts. Through the frozen pieces of time, she watched him transform from a boy into a man. And no matter what his age in any of the pictures, he still sported the boyish good looks that made her warm with pleasure.

Until the reality of losing him sucked the heat from her veins.

Meredith removed one of Zak's baby pictures from the album and passed it to Lacey. "I want you to have this for Jude's first baby album. You can stick your baby picture beside Zak's, and then put Jude's underneath, like a family tree. We did that with our children, and it gave them years of entertainment arguing over who had whose features."

Why, Lacey asked herself? To make it obvious that Jude had none of Zak's features? Lacey backhanded away the beads of sweat forming across her forehead. "Great idea." *Not!*

Meredith flipped through the album and laughed. "Poor Brent, the only thing he has of mine is his eyes. Rebecca and Zak teased him all the time, told him he was the mailman's son, even though he's the spitting image of Kyle. Still, he'd get so angry."

Lacey peeled her tongue from the roof of her mouth as she tightened her grip on Zak's baby picture. "I have a good feeling Jude will look more like me than Zak—strong genes."

"It doesn't matter either way because both of you are such lovely people, inside and out." Meredith laid her hands on Lacey's pregnant belly. "We're just blessed to have you—and this grandbaby in our lives. Between the miracle of Zak's birth after those miscarriages and those uncertain days after his diagnosis, I'm sure you can understand why Jude is so important to our family. And why you are too. I've never seen Zak so happy."

She couldn't do this to Meredith, couldn't smile and lie at the same time. It was a travesty. And Meredith deserved better, too. They all did, and Lacey would make sure they had better. She dropped her gaze to the floor as the truth crawled to the tip of her tongue, preparing to release.

The timer for the cookies beeped before Lacey opened her mouth.

Meredith jumped to her feet. "It looks like those batches are done," she said, beelining for the oven, leaving Lacey to her own mental demise.

What Lacey had done to Meredith and to Zak for her own selfish means was terrible. And it was unforgivable. Meredith removed the perfectly baked goodies from the oven. A sweet aroma escaped into the air that was soon overtaken by the only thing Lacey could smell, the bitter rot of her soul.

It was a sickness that wouldn't shake, a sickness that attacked her the rest of the day, on the way home, and even when she climbed into bed that night beside Zak at the apartment. But she said nothing, never exposed the raging war in her brain. No, she pretended all was well and dreamy, although she stood on the front-lines of her worst nightmare.

And when she kissed Zak goodnight, his warm body enveloped hers as it had every other night. But in that instant she felt the cold sting of lies, lies that held power enough to destroy innocent people.

And why did she believe it was okay to do this, to keep up a well-orchestrated sham? For the contract? Impossible, Margot and Jocelyn had taken it from her despite Lacey's most valiant efforts to not lose it. No, the current charade had nothing to do with her career and everything to do with her feelings, those things she didn't plan for or put on the list, like falling in love with Zak.

Yes, it happened. And she couldn't change it, couldn't go back in time. All she could do from this point was to push forward, make better decisions—no matter how hard those decisions were for her. Because it was no longer about her. Now it had to be about them, the people who mattered, to include Jude.

After the most heart-wrenching night of her life, she made a choice. A choice that stole her breath, stopped her heart, and required an entire box of Kleenexes. When Zak left for work in the wee hours of the chilly fall morning, she packed her bags and called Doby.

"I need a favor," Lacey said, tying a purple ribbon to her suitcase.

"Anything, name it. And by the way, how's the mom-to-be doing?"

"It doesn't matter how I'm doing because it's over. I'm ending the whole fake marriage with Zak. In fact, I'm on my way to find Oliver

Callum." Lacey stomped over to the printer and snatched her plane ticket from it.

"Wait—you're not making any sense. Why? And who is Oliver?"

Lacey folded the ticket, tucked it into her carry-on. "Supposedly, he's the real father. Mr. Duke made yet another mistake —surprise. He ruled Finn out—again. So now the papers are useless, and Zak can't adopt the baby unless Oliver signs off. But that means I'd have to confess. And I won't, not before I have something to confess. It's time for this to end. His family deserves more than what I've given them—as does Zak."

"Okay, you sound stressed, but try to calm down. Where is Zak?"

Lacey placed her ring beside the handwritten letter she had left for him on top of her tall dresser. He would find it quickly. She made sure with the perfect placement. "At work."

"Lacey, you know Zak loves you. You can't just walk out on him. Please, don't do anything crazy. I'm coming over so we can talk this through."

A loud rustling noise shot into Lacey's ear. "You won't stop me. And it doesn't matter if he loves me, everything—" Lacey broke into a sob so powerful her whole body shook, "—Everything we have is fake, a hormone-fueled delusion. And I won't keep hurting him or his family."

Lacey took a quick breath. "But more importantly, I won't have my child grow up believing in a fairy tale—no matter how beautiful that story might be." Lacey steadied her legs and marched to the front door.

"Zak won't care. He loves you." Doby's voice raised.

Lacey rolled her suitcase into the empty hallway, closing and locking the door behind her. "And I love him... That's why I'm leaving. Now, I'll be in North Carolina. I'll text you the details and trust that as my best friend you'll keep them secret. I'm serious."

"Just tell him. He'll understand. They all will," Doby pleaded with breathy desperation.

Lacey fought the flood of tears as she transported her baggage on and off the elevator and then into a waiting cab. The driver loaded it in the trunk as Lacey slid herself onto the back seat filled with the lingering stench of stale cigarettes and musk, closing the door behind her.

She leaned her heavy head on the frigid window. "I can't continue disappointing them."

"And leaving them like this? What do you think that'll do to them—to Zak?"

"It's better this way." Lacey drew in a long breath, walled off her emotions as best as she could for her own personal sanity.

The silence between them lasted forever.

"You're so wrong. Nothing about the way you're leaving is right." Lacey caught Doby's muffled tears and the raspy intake of air. "But since I can't stop you, at least be safe."

"I will. And Doby, thanks for everything."

24

As the plane wheels touched the runway in the forest-covered state of North Carolina, Lacey hid her eyes behind dark glasses and hesitated to power on her phone. The anticipation that Zak had probably called twenty times, or worse, had come home early and found the note disrupted any hope of peace. She realized she would have to talk to him—face her decision to walk out. But not before she settled into the hotel and made sure she had an accurate location for Oliver Callum.

And while every part of her wanted nothing more than to climb into Zak's comforting arms, she reminded herself Jude deserved the truth about his real father. And she deserved to have the truth about what happened that night.

After a smooth debarking, a quicker than usual trip through baggage claims, and a fast exit from the airport, Lacey climbed into a passenger-filled shuttle. Thankfully, the first stop was the Hilton where she would be staying. Inside, a stout woman with heavy makeup and a strong southern drawl passed her a pair of room keys and directed her to the closest elevator.

She rode the slow moving steel box to the fifth floor and at once collapsed onto the fluffy white comforter. Mustard walls, beige curtains, and a busy floral carpet in navy and cream surround her. She closed her eyes for a brief minute before opening them to a sunset sinking behind a canvas of crimson, spiced yellow, and burnt orange foliage covering the mountains. It was a stunning contrast to the concrete grays and brick reds of the bustling city streets and skyscrapers.

Her stomach growled. Unable to ignore the growing hunger, Lacey pulled out the menu for room service and dialed in an order for a club sandwich and a fruit bowl. In the meantime, she studied the details Mr. Duke had collected on Oliver Callum. He had moved for a job only a month before Lacey hired Mr. Duke to compile the list, which would have been shortly after getting her pregnant.

She considered her method of approach. She only had a contact number and an apartment address. Neither of those were sound methods for confronting him. If she called, it might scare him off and then what? And meeting him at his residence alone? Well, the last time she did that it ended with her in jail. No, they needed to meet somewhere neutral like his job. And if she wanted that information, it meant powering on her phone.

She drew in a long breath, held it, and then blew it out before pressing the power button and watching the screen light up. The dings that followed were never-ending, multiple messages and voicemails. It was safe to say Zak had read the note. She clicked on one message but stopped short of reading it. Oliver Callum's employer's address was the priority. She stayed on task and texted Mr. Duke.

Room service arrived while she waited. And although it was not the most delicious meal she'd ever had, it satisfied her enough. She tossed the last bite of sandwich in her mouth and downed it with a bottle of spring water. Full, she leaned back against the fluffy pillows and lifted her sweater, exposing her forever-growing, bare belly.

Jude always put on his best show after a meal, extending his arms and legs where he pleased, leaping from one side of the womb to the other. Boy, did she enjoy the tiny hands and feet beneath her stretched skin. Loved that no matter how the craziness ended, she would always have him.

Mr. Duke sent the address for Oliver's place of employment. She wrote it on the hotel notepad. So when Zak called again, right after she clicked the pen closed, she had no excuse not to answer. Even though the thought of hearing his voice left her core a fluttering mess. He deserved to know that she had arrived at her destination. Although, she had no intention of sharing the details of just where that was.

"Tell me where you are. I'll come get you." The desperation in his words made her heart ache.

"I'm safe and that's what matters." Lacey worked to keep her emotions hidden, her voice steady. "I explained everything in the note —"

"Everything in that note is bullshit. You didn't force me into any of this—I chose this. I chose to be your husband." Zak's words entered

Lacey's ears as a heartbroken wail. "I chose it because I love you and want to spend the rest of my life with you. Who cares how this started? What matters is what we decided for our future—for Jude's future. I don't care what anyone else thinks. Let's tell them the truth. I'm willing to do whatever it takes to get you back." Zak's voice faded into a cry, a cry so strong she could almost hear his tears fall.

She hugged her belly with her free arm, held Jude. "You don't understand. It's not just about us. My lies affect everybody, and I can't keep spreading them. I'm hurting real people. They all think you're able to have a baby because of Jude, but we don't know that. So what happens when they expect the next baby? Your mom—"

Zak interrupted her, louder. "My mom wouldn't care if Jude was the only one, but he wouldn't be. I'm sure of it."

"You can't be sure. And when your family finds out you can't and that Jude isn't yours, it will devastate them. I won't allow him to be the outcast stepchild." It was a low blow that disgusted her. Deep down she knew they'd never mistreat him.

"Nobody would treat him any different—or you. They love you, but more than that, they're aware of how much I love you. People make mistakes. We're human. Please Lacey, I need you." His voiced cracked.

And left a matching crack in her heart. Did he think she didn't need him? She did, but it didn't mean she could have him. Life dealt crappy hands with overinflated stakes. And this was one of those times, leaving her no choice but to fold.

"Talk to me, Lacey. Do you love me?"

Her eyes fixed on the bedside lamp switch with its only two options, on or off. She reminded herself the same was true for her relationship with Zak. It was stay or go. And while she longed to stay with him, yearned for one last kiss, one last brush of his hand against her face, to go caused the least destruction.

"Do you love me?" He repeated the question, his tone rich with suffering.

The growing anguish ate away at her soul like a black hole stealing every bit of warmth she had, leaving her frigid and lifeless. She curled into a ball and hugged the feather pillow that collapsed at the first squeeze. "You know I love you."

"Then come home or let me come get you."

"You are the greatest person I've ever had in my life...but I can't. The crushing guilt, the heavy weight I carry every time I see your family, see you, is too much. I only hope that one day you'll forgive me. I have to go—bye, Zak."

Unable to take another second of torture, she pressed the red button and then threw the phone across the room. Heartbroken, she squeezed the pillow against her face, smeared black mascara onto the stark white linens. If only she could rewind the track, start over with the truth. How stupid was she to risk everything for a contract, to let pride overtake sound judgment?

She always had believed Kate was the competitive one, the one who had to be a step above everyone else. But the truth was—it was her. She stomped on people, used them for her own selfish gains. Zak and his family were a prime example.

But those mistakes would not define her. She would fix them. And Oliver Callum would know he had a baby on the way. Heck, he might even turn out to be worthy of the Dad title. The odds were stacked in his favor, considering the other potentials had turned out to be total losers. Either way, she would find out tomorrow when she planned to visit him.

As for tonight, she'd pray for a peaceful mind and sleep.

The driver, a young guy with an auburn ponytail, dark glasses, and a six-month beard, stopped in front of an enormous, red-brick building with a welcoming steeple on top. Her gaze roamed to the other ornate construction; massive doorway arches and stained-glass windows. Confident she had arrived at the wrong place, she slipped the address from her pocket and showed it to the driver—again.

He slowly nodded and pointed out the matching street sign and number. "Yep, this is it."

Lacey took a double-take. "He works at a church?"

After tipping the driver, she waddled onto the sidewalk. A nippy breeze blew past, cutting through her pants. And so she picked up the pace, arriving at a set of overbearing, dark-stained doors. She stepped inside to an amazing interior filled with colossal wooden arches, stone floors, balconies, cathedral ceilings, large lantern-lights, and hallways for days—any of which could lead to Oliver. Or so she hoped.

She guessed her way into the left corridor and scanned for offices, although she wasn't even sure he had one. For all she knew, he could be part of the housekeeping team.

"May I help you?" asked a throaty voice. Lacey spun around to the elderly lady with make-up free skin holding a hymnal against her chest.

Lacey fiddled with her purse strap. "Yes, I'm looking for Oliver Callum. Someone told me he's employed here."

"Lucky you, you've caught him right before lunch. Come, I'll take you."

Lacey followed the flow of long silver hair and a floral skirt, stretched tight by widened hips, down another hallway and into an office full of the same dark-wood furniture as the rest of the church. In the center of the desk was a nameplate stamped *Oliver Callum*, but the office was empty.

"Stay right here, sweetie. I'll grab him. And what's your name again?"

Did she even give him a name? "Will you tell him an old friend is here?"

The woman grinned. "I certainly will."

Lacey shifted in place as her nerves vibrated, made her feel as if she'd tumble over at any second. So preventing a disaster, she seated herself in the leather chair.

Soon after, Oliver Callum made an appearance with his china-blue eyes, honey-blonde hair, and same boyish good looks as Zak. He smiled at her with a chipped front tooth and offered his hand. "I'm Oliver. Mrs. Finch said you were looking for me. She said you mentioned that we're old friends?"

Lacey braced her knocking knees. "*Friends* might not have been the most appropriate word, associates would be better."

He stared a hole through her, his expression blank. "Please forgive me, but I don't believe we've met. If we had, I'm sure I would have remembered. Are you from around here?"

Well, either his memory was less sharp than hers, or Mr. Duke had screwed up again? Because both of them couldn't possibly have sex amnesia. "I'm from New York. We ran into each other before you left."

"Oh..." His eyes locked onto her obvious pregnant belly and stretched. "... Oh... and just how long ago was this... encounter?"

"Thirty-five or thirty-six weeks ago. I'm thirty-seven and a half weeks pregnant. But apparently conception happens two weeks after the last—sorry, the technicalities don't matter."

He scrubbed the side of his face with his palms. "Well, I guess I'd have to be a fool to not put two-and-two together. Is this why you're here?" he asked, gesturing towards the basketball-sized belly.

Lacey twisted her hands. "In my mind I pictured the whole scene playing out different, but yes." She waited for the words *get out* to barrel from his mouth, but nothing. Not one word or response.

His hands shifted, and he raked his fingers through his hair with such force that his face stretched to surgical-lift tightness. "This is a shock, even more so because I don't remember you."

She narrowed her eyes and locked her gaze on him. "So we didn't have sex?"

"I'm not saying we didn't. We very well could have." He dropped his hands to his sides. "I was a big partier in New York. Sometimes I did wild and crazy things on impulse—like get blackout drunk and sleep with women—with their consent, no doubt. The problem was I didn't remember most of them by the next morning. But I changed."

He sat in the chair across from her, straightened his desk nameplate. "Somewhere, in a moment of sobriety, I found Jesus Christ. And he put a calling on my life to go into ministry. It's why I moved here, to attend Bible College. So to say this is a shock would be the biggest understatement of the year." He tapped his foot.

"Imagine my shock when I got a positive pregnancy test," Lacey added, not wanting her despair marginalized.

"How are you certain it's mine? I mean—just because we had sex doesn't make it mine, right?"

Lacey reminisced about her encounters with Mr. Duke's unreliability as she tucked a loose curl behind her ear. "No, it doesn't, but I paid plenty of money to find you. And I've ruled out any other potential, even slight ones. You are the last man standing."

"I hope you'll understand I'll want a DNA test."

"I assure you, we both want that." The urge to urinate struck. "Sorry, but I need to use your restroom."

He pointed across the hall.

Lacey found her way inside the small bathroom and sat on the toilet. A decorative cross hung above it, prompting her to think, *What would Jesus do?* Nothing came to her except flashes of Zak's tousled hair and one-sided dimple and whiffs of his scent, the one she recognized better than anyone. She pressed her fingers against her eyelids and scrunched her face until the strong urge to cry passed. And when it did, she finished her business and then stood by the tiny pedestal sink, staring into the ornately framed mirror.

In the million times she had run this scenario through her mind, she imagined Oliver remembering her and their night of passion. She had delighted in the relief she expected would come with closure about what happened. But for both of them to not have a single memory about any of it left her jittery to the bone. How could they have created another tiny human being with no idea how it happened?

She studied herself in the mirror, noted the long strands of curls that had escaped her messy bun. With the few extra bobby pins she had stored in her purse, she repined them as her mind stayed locked on Oliver. Sure, she would admit he favored the vague image of the dreamy guy she had made love to that night, in what she had mistaken for a dream. A dream Dr. Hart so bluntly informed her was reality.

But still, she had a ton of questions floating around in her brain that might never have answers. Like for starters, why did she bring him into her apartment?

A knock at the door startled her, and she gripped the sink for support. Thinking it might be Oliver, she steadied herself quickly and washed her hands before rushing out. She nearly bumped into a random red-head before waddling her way back to Oliver's office.

Once there, she found Oliver with his head buried in his arms on his desk. She cleared her throat.

He lifted his gaze only as high as her pregnant belly and held it there for an uncomfortable minute before looking away. "Look, I was headed to lunch, but given the circumstances, why don't I take the rest of the day off? That will give us some time to talk and... figure this out."

What other choice did she have? She forced a smile. "Sounds like a plan."

He drove them to a lunch spot called *Moe's Original BBQ*. It was a quaint place that resembled a shack, but the large crowd gathered by the door suggested it was anything but. Oliver guided Lacey inside to décor that included at least fifty license plates lining the walls and a mini tin-roof mounted above a full-service bar. A hostess in skin-tight pants and a revealing v-neck sweater seated them, just as Lacey's phone dinged.

Is he a psycho serial killer? If you don't answer this text, I'm calling the police. Doby.

Lacey responded.

He's not, but if he was, he could steal my phone and text back as me.

* * *

The phone rang at once after she hit the send button. "Are you *you*, Lacey?"

Lacey rolled her eyes. "Yes, Doby, it's me. We're grabbing lunch."

"So he's not crazy?"

"I don't think so. But the day is young. I'm hanging up, now." Lacey glanced over and noticed Oliver staring at her as she laid the phone in her lap. "It's my friend checking up on me."

"That's understandable. I hope this place is okay. I figured if you came to North Carolina, you probably should try the barbecue."

And she did, along with the collards, macaroni and cheese, cornbread, and apple pie, washing it down with a mason jar glass full of sweet tea.

Oliver squeezed hot sauce over his greens. "Is it a boy or a girl?"

The last bit of cornbread melted in her mouth. "A boy—Jude."

"Jude. I love it—a good Biblical name." He stacked a scoop of his barbecue onto a piece of Texas toast and took a bite.

Lacey sipped the syrupy sweet tea. "Thanks, I like it, too." Flashes of Zak telling her the story of his grandfather rushed her mind, made her heart skip beats. But she outed them, realizing if she didn't they would turn her into an emotional basket case. "I'm sorry about springing this on you without warning."

"Only if you forgive me for not knowing where to start. This is unprecedented. I don't even think I got your name." He wiped a drip of sauce from the corner of his mouth.

She stared at the black-and-white checkered paper lining her tray before glancing up at him. "I'm Lacey."

He grinned and shook her hand. "Nice to meet you, Lacey. Well, since we're having a baby together maybe we should start by trying to get to know each other. If that's okay with you?" His hand accidentally grazed hers as he reached for his drink.

She didn't feel a thing, not the tiniest spark. The same touch from Zak, even before the fake marriage, would have shaken her core, sent hot blood flooding her veins. "I really don't know where to start."

"Where are you staying?" he asked, his eyes soft and sincere.

They were like that now only because, like he said, he had changed his life for the better. When she had slept with him, he was the old Oliver, the blackout drunk one that would have never met her standards, which made little sense. Yet again, maybe it was why she had forgotten, lost her memory, because she was so ashamed of what she had done—no matter how good the sex was.

"I'm at the Hilton," she said before thinking through her answer. *Was it even safe to tell him?*

"Okay, so I'll take you to pick up your bags, and you can stay with me."

"I can't—" Lacey started, but Oliver interrupted.

"I insist. It's not fair to make you pay for a hotel. Plus, it gives us more time to get acquainted," he said, taking out his credit card and placing it on the table. The waitress jetted by and scooped it up.

What he suggested was crazy. She couldn't stay with a stranger. "No offense, but we don't know each other well enough. How can I be sure I can trust you? And you should be concerned about me, too."

"Should I? Are you secretly insane?"

"No, I promise I'm as sane as expected given my condition."

The waitress brought back the card, and he returned it to his wallet. Then he stood and reached out a hand to Lacey, helped her and her extra thirty pounds out of the cramped booth.

She followed him to his charcoal gray BMW sports car and realized, as her nine-month pregnant butt struggled to get into it, how impractical it would be for a newborn. He climbed into the driver's seat and fired up the purring engine but kept it in park. "We're having a baby... so obviously we slept together. And since we've slept together, I don't see the problem with staying in the same place, just different rooms."

She picked off a layer of cornbread crumbs from her sweater. "That's my point. You got me pregnant, and we didn't even know each other's name. And neither one of us even remembers having sex. So what if I'm ruining your life by showing up like this, and now you want to get rid of me? It happens more than you think. Watch *Dateline* or the local news." The more she thought of the possibilities, the more fear pumped through her body. She kept her thumb tight against her phone's side button.

"So I take you out to lunch in public for witnesses to place us together before I kill you? Does that make sense?" he asked, scratching his head.

"No, but what if that's part of your plan, to make it look like you're having a good time with me, throw them off?"

"Because that's what someone going into the ministry dreams about —killing pregnant women?"

"Two words—Jim Jones," Lacey said, confident she had proven her point.

"Okay, so you're a lawyer."

"Architect."

"Well, you missed your calling. I have an idea. I'll drive you to your hotel, and you call your private detective and have him run a background check. Other than a few drunken bar brawls and traffic tickets, my record is clean. You can also tell him where you're staying. That way if anything happens, he's able to lead the police straight to me."

Lacey thought about it. It would be helpful to get to know him better. And with all those people knowing the plan, she felt safe enough. "Okay, but I'm calling Mr. Duke right now—and my best friend next."

Mr. Duke cleared Oliver, declared him unlikely to cause her any physical harm. His exact words. And it was just the comfort Lacey needed to settle into the spare bedroom at Oliver's apartment.

"I just got off the phone with the church. I'm off for the week. It's not much, but it should give us some time to figure this out. You want something to drink?"

"A glass of water is fine, thanks," Lacey said, finding a seat on the gray microfiber sofa. His apartment was plain and just what she would expect for a bachelor pad. He had no paintings or portraits on the wall, only a huge television out of proportion to the space. The kitchen was tiny but updated with quartz countertops and new appliances.

Oliver sat in a chair across from Lacey, and sipped on a glass of lemonade. "So how has the pregnancy been so far?"

She shrugged her shoulders. "I have nothing to compare it to, but the doctor says everything is good."

He rubbed his forehead. "Wow, it just hit me. Doctor bills, newborn necessities. I'm sure the expenses are racking up. But don't worry, I'll help cover anything you need. I don't get paid while I'm in training, but I have money saved from when I worked on Wall Street. So there's plenty to help support the baby."

Lacey held both palms against her knees. "I'm not here for a handout. I can support Jude by myself."

"It's not a handout. He's my baby too. It's only fair I do my part." Oliver took another sip of lemonade.

She conceded, positive he'd keep insisting. "Do you have family in

North Carolina?"

He nodded. "Three brothers and one sister, each one born and raised right here. After I graduated with my MBA from Duke, I snagged a job in New York City. Everything started off great at first. I made tons of money, more than I knew what to do with, which turned into a big problem. I got bored and spent my nights partying, lived life in the fast lane. Women became a blur as I picked up a different one most nights of the week. I barely remembered anyone's name, didn't even ask."

No surprise there, Lacey thought. "So what made you want to change your life?"

He ran his finger around the rim of his glass. "One day, a co-worker invited me to church for his newborn's dedication service. I went because everyone else was going for support, and I thought it might help me meet a good girl. Not that I was ready to settle. But what I didn't expect was the conviction I felt, the calling on my life. At first, I brushed it off as a sentimental moment. I made excuses for the feelings until I couldn't anymore. Then I returned, time and time again. When I told my parents, they encouraged me to pursue my passion, even talked to the pastor here and landed me this position. Now, here I am."

"From Wall Street to the pulpit, a brave move."

"A true calling. The Bible says one must be willing to lay down everything to follow Jesus. And that's what I've done."

Lacey remembered Sunday school, those Bible verses she had learned as a small child, the ones that earned her Skittles and Sweet-Tarts. "It also says he won't put more on you than you can bear." She pointed at her belly and gave a dry laugh.

"It certainly is a test. So tell me something about you."

She shared with him stories about her job, her family, her sister's pregnancy, her goals and ambitions, and her desires for Jude. But not one word about Zak. And as the day fell into night, as the eyelids grew heavy, they both retreated to separate bedrooms, promising to talk more in the morning.

And they did, over breakfast at *Biscuit Head*. Another quaint building of white cinder blocks with a blue and gold sign. And yet again, another delicious meal. The biscuits melted in Lacey's mouth and tasted even better with a big scoop of sweet potato chai butter. Who would have guessed a biscuit could become a work of art?

Oliver broke the yolk on his over easy eggs. "Now that the

introductions are out of the way, we should talk about the baby and our future, seeing how it's so close to his arrival."

Lacey swallowed the bite of biscuit. "Okay... I guess we probably should."

"I'll cut right to the chase. Last night, I spoke to my parents and my pastor. I think we should get married," he announced, taking Lacey's hand in his.

She yanked away her hand and nearly choked on the food making a return trip into her mouth.

"It's quick. And I know we don't know much about each other, but it's the right thing for the baby."

No way was he serious. It was one thing to carry out a one-night stand but another to marry someone without getting to know them first. She clung to her glass of water and downed it. He waited patiently for her to finish, his gaze locked on her. From the looks of it, he meant what he suggested. "Oliver, people raise children together without getting married every day. We don't love each other, and we haven't spent enough time together to even know if we like each other."

"Couples get married all the time without knowing each other, and it works. Think about the arranged marriages. That's how monarchies did things back in the day."

Lacey held out both palms. "But we're not running a country. We're normal people. We can't just get married. I have a life in New York, a job, a family."

"Well, it's important that I raise my son in a Christian home with a mother and father present. And how does it look for me as a pastor to have a child out of wedlock?"

"I'm sure everyone would understand it happened before you had the calling." She poked a scrambled egg with her fork, but couldn't eat it. The bouncing nerves in her stomach refused to settle.

"My point is, I want us to raise our baby together. I don't want him to have to go back and forth between homes. If we can do this together, shouldn't we try for him? No, we don't love each other now, but it doesn't mean we won't one day. You're attractive, smart, and you're carrying my baby. I wasn't looking for a wife before I finished school, but what if this is a sign from God?"

More like a cruel joke, Lacey scoffed to herself.

"Look, it's a lot to take in. But why don't we start by meeting my family today? They can tell you all about me, and you can get to know them." He met Lacey's eyes. "For Jude, at least."

She couldn't fathom he would stoop low enough to use her son against her. But it worked. She had to start somewhere in deciding what would be best for Jude, because at the end of the day the only thing that mattered was giving him the best life possible. "I'll meet your parents, but just so we're straight, I have no plans of marrying you. So please don't convince them that will happen. Now, I need to use the bathroom before we go."

"Thanks, at least it's a step forward." He smiled and aimed her toward the restrooms.

She chose the cleanest stall and slid the lock closed at the same time her phone dinged. She thought she had silenced it but apparently not. Pulling it from her purse, she changed the settings, but not before glancing the long message from Zak.

Lacey, I understand you didn't get pregnant the way you imagined. I also realize I probably don't know everything, and I'm ok with that. What's not ok is losing you and Jude. Please believe me when I say I will do anything— FORGIVE anything—do whatever is necessary to get you back in my life. I'm lost without you. But if you don't respond, I'll take that as you not feeling the same and go for good, just as you asked. Love, Zak.

Lacey could barely see the end of the message through the waterfall of tears cascading down her face. Was he saying what she hoped he was saying? That even if there were a twist to her story she hadn't told him, he would still love and accept her? Maybe, but still, she couldn't bring him or his family into this mess, couldn't cause them anymore pain than she had. And certainly not before finding out more about Oliver Callum.

She didn't have the courage to respond. But if she had, she would have told him how much she loved him, how much she always would. Unfortunately, sometimes love leads to hard choices—and this was one of them. She reread his message one last time and then silenced her phone.

In front of the mirror, she dried her eyes and freshened her makeup. She gathered her strength for Jude and decided the next step was to meet Oliver's parents—with an open mind.

25

His family welcomed her the way one welcomes a new neighbor, painted smiles, an air of curiosity, and with way too much food. Oliver's mom, Gloria, a platinum blonde with a spray-tan, greeted Lacey first. As she spoke, Lacey couldn't help but stare at her paper-white teeth and collagen-injected lips. Or the countless other areas tweaked by plastic surgery.

Gloria draped an arm over Lacey's shoulder. "Lacey, I can't wait to give you a tour of the house, but first, introductions." She gestured with the hand holding her wineglass to a tall, slender man in a Patagonia sweater vest and dress shirt. He wore slacks, fancy shoes, and porcelain veneers. "This is Leo, Oliver's father. And the gorgeous young lady standing next to him is his sister, Chanel."

Chanel, justly named after her inherited and expensive tastes. The jewelry adorning her bronzed skin cost as much as a small vacation home. The diamond clip holding back her perfectly coiffed hair, a year's salary. And her attitude?—Priceless.

"Unfortunately, the other family members couldn't make it on such short notice, but they send their love. Now, for that tour," Gloria said, giggling as she fanned her fingers towards Lacey.

The house was immaculate and rested on at least fifty acres of perfectly groomed land, but that was about all Lacey paid attention to. Her mind wouldn't rest, constantly shifting to Zak, Doby, her parents, the people she loved. And to the warmth those people made her feel. Because the Callum's house lacked that same warmth. Instead, it stood as a cold, sterile, castle of ice.

The tour ended in the dining room. A room spread with a variety of country cooking: a sweet potato casserole, macaroni and cheese, mustard greens, turkey and dressing, fried cornbread, and gizzards, which Lacey refused to eat. Dessert was a homemade banana pudding made with sugar-rich condensed milk and egg yolks instead of boxed pudding. She ate until her stomach could hold nothing else, not because of extreme hunger. But because eating filled the silence.

When they finished, the housekeeper gathered the dishes as Oliver guided her to the den where they shared a sofa. Gloria sat across from them in a buttery, leather chair. "If you're still hungry, Oliver can fix you another plate."

Lacey patted her pregnant belly. "I've had too much."

"That's wonderful to hear considering what you've been through," Gloria said, raising her brows only as high as the Botox would allow. "All of this is sudden—for both of you. So how are you guys holding up?"

Oliver's dad, Leo, sat on the arm of the chair where Gloria sat and twirled her hair around his fingers.

It creeped Lacey out, and distracted her enough so that Oliver managed to slip his hand over hers. Not wanting to embarrass him, Lacey let him keep it there—even though she felt nothing.

Oliver answered first. "Initially, the news shocked me, but the more I've prayed about it, the more I believe God has a plan for us, a testimony waiting to be birthed. Get it? Birthed like a baby," he said, chuckling as he faced Lacey.

Lacey threw up in her mouth.

"And what about you Lacey? The decision to seek Oliver couldn't have been an easy one," Leo said in his best news anchor's voice.

Lacey sank into the chair and considered the thousands of dollars she had pay to find Oliver and the others on the list. "Yes, it was a rocky road getting to this point, but I'm glad to be here..." She swallowed hard. "Oliver seems like he'll make a great father."

"And a good husband, too," Gloria said, motioning for Chanel to pass her a pen and paper. "Now, I understand we're working with limited time, but we could pull off a decent wedding by next week. That would give us enough time to get some last-minute invitations sent. I was thinking about something small here at the house, or at the church if I can persuade the pastor to shift homecoming to the following weekend."

The Botox had gone to Gloria's brain. Under no circumstances would Lacey be marrying Oliver, and definitely not in a week's time—never. "Wait—"

Gloria facepalmed Lacey. "I know what you're going to say. People will think this is a shotgun wedding, but I beg to differ. I suggest we tell everyone you officially married in New York before the baby but wanted to keep it private so as not to distract Oliver's studies. And now, you guys are eager to have a real wedding. I think it'll work."

Leo nodded, his eyebrows touching.

Lacey stroked the side of her face. "Gloria, we're not getting married. I'm sorry if that's the impression I gave you, but it's not happening."

Gloria's mouth dropped. "What do you mean? You must get married. Oliver is on track to take over the First Presbyterian Church. And having a baby out of wedlock would ruin his career. No, not ruin —destroy." She took a deep breath, worked her voice into a lower, more sympathetic tone. "Think of it this way. It's what God would want." Gloria stretched out her hand, laid it over Lacey's as she batted her fake lashes.

Chanel twisted the diamond bracelet around her wrist and poked out her lips. "If you guys need me, I'll be upstairs."

Leo didn't shift his eyes from Lacey. "I don't think you understand. Scandals such as these take down pastors across the nation every day. I have to agree with Gloria. It's what God would want. He wouldn't bring Oliver through what he's been through just to have him lose his opportunity over past mistakes. God is a forgiving God."

Gloria raised her hand in the air. "Amen and thank you, Jesus."

Lacey understood what it meant to have the livelihood of a career at stake. And she could only imagine the stress Oliver suffered over the possibility of losing his. But she couldn't marry him, not even for pretend. He was a complete stranger, and his family—borderline cultish. But for Jude's sake, she had to rectify the situation, especially since there was a good chance a judge would order visitation.

Lacey weighed her words despite the pulsating throb on the right side of her head. "I don't claim to have a direct line with God, or to know what *He* wants. However, I recognize what *I* want, and it is not to be married. We're just getting familiar with each other."

"What do you mean you don't know what God wants? God speaks to his people. You are a Christian, aren't you?" Gloria locked her face and slapped her knees.

Lacey turned to Oliver, who evaded eye contact before loosening his grip on her hand. "I need the bathroom. Be right back." He bolted from the seat, leaving Lacey to fend for herself. *Wimp*, she mumbled. Still, she had to stand her ground. At the end of the day, she had to live her life for her and Jude, not for them.

Which meant it was time to call an Uber. Lacey dug into her purse for her phone. "To be honest, Mrs. Callum, I embrace a more spiritual stance on life. Organized religion has never been my thing."

Gloria took the now empty place next to Lacey. "See, that's the problem. I can easily replace spirituality with the word *confusion*, doubts about the true divine power in the universe, God, and his son Jesus Christ. As sinners, we run from those things that make us feel guilty. Such as sleeping with random men, getting pregnant—"

Lacey leaped to her feet, her aching and swollen feet. "Okay, that's enough." She was two clicks into the side button for emergency services when a call from Mr. Duke came through. And she answered without hesitation. At least he'd have her location, maybe even send help to rescue her from the crusading Callums.

"I need to take this," Lacey said, stepping into the adjacent room. "Mr. Duke, I'm at Oliver Callum's family home." She spouted off the address. "And these people are lunatics."

"Really? Well, that could be good news."

Lacey jerked her head. "What? How is that good?"

He coughed. "It might make you less angry at my mistake. And just to let you know right off the bat, I'm refunding one-hundred-percent of the money you paid me because I feel awful about everything."

Her heart ping-ponged in her chest. "You're scaring me."

"That's not my intent, promise. It's just that investigative work is not a perfect science, sometimes the data might be faulty, or get twisted, or sources unreliable—"

"Spit it out, please."

"Oliver Callum never visited your apartment building. He's part of a different investigation as are the other men on that list." His words sped out without a pause between them.

Lacey laid a hand over her caving chest. "Excuse me?"

"The first list I gave you was for another investigation," he said in a cowering tone.

She unclenched her jaw. "I heard that part. What I need to know then—at less than three weeks from giving birth—is who the hell is the father? And you better not say you don't have a name."

"Okay," he said, followed by silence.

"Well, who is it?" She paced, worked off the frustration.

"You told me not to say."

"No, I want you to tell me."

He cleared his throat. "So it's safe to say what you told me I better not say?"

A strong wave of dizziness struck, sending Lacey in search of a seat. And she found one in a white, velvet slipper chair as she braced herself for the predictable news. "Sure, avoiding the truth won't make it any less painful."

"Now, the good news is, there is a father. The bad news is... I haven't identified him yet. But I will. My assistant and I are running a movie marathon on the surveillance tapes from your apartment building, scratching off the ones who visited your neighbors and not you. We had to have missed something, but not for long. We will find it."

"Hopefully, you'll understand if I don't count on it." She ended the call depressed about the lack of answers. But simultaneously relieved that it was not Oliver. And she couldn't wait to tell him.

When she re-entered the room, she noted Gloria's clasped hands above a full page of notes. Oliver had returned, but still avoided eye contact with Lacey. "There you are. Any possibility you've changed your mind so we can move forward with the wedding plans? I've got a ton of ideas."

"There won't be a wedding. My private investigator called and informed me he made an error." And in the spirit of dramatic reality TV, Lacey announced, "Oliver is one hundred percent not the father. I'm sorry for putting you guys through this stress. I hope you'll forgive me. Apparently, my private investigator has proven himself unreliable."

Telling them was easy. Waiting for their reaction was harder. She suspected they might fake a few tears, pretend to grieve. But their response was far from expected. They didn't hold back, dancing, speaking in tongues, shouting hallelujah to the top of their lungs. Leo even handed her a blank check, asked her to fill in the cost of her last-minute flight back to New York City. She declined his money, but accepted the silent ride back to the hotel from Oliver.

As he dropped her off, he promised to collect her things and have them sent over immediately, as they both agreed it was best not to go back to his place. It would be too awkward for either of them. Instead, she fumbled her way out of the BMW and began the journey to her room, keeping her back to him.

"Hey, Lacey," he shouted before she went inside.

In an effort not to be rude, she turned to see what he wanted. "Did I leave something?"

"No, all clear. I wanted to pray for you and the baby before you leave, pray God leads you to the father."

"Thanks, but I'll be fine," she said, declining the offer for religious intervention, satisfied God wanted nothing to do with her shenanigans.

26

Lacey tucked her phone between her ear and shoulder, preparing to drag her luggage from the baggage carousel. "Can you believe they holy ghost danced in front of me? They didn't even wait for me to leave. I mean, how rude is that?"

"So rude," Doby said, muffling her laughter poorly.

Lacey was glad Doby found humor in it, because she couldn't. "And I don't know what to say about Mr. Duke other than he should find himself a new line of work. And because he can't do his job, I'll be delivering alone."

"You could always ask Zak. Seriously, you both love each other. Why keep making this harder than it has to be? He wants to be the baby's daddy, dammit—So, let him be."

"That train left the station... which only leaves you for my birthing coach." Lacey reached for her bags, but a buff college student wearing an NYU sweatshirt stopped her. With one swoop he hoisted her luggage from the carousel onto the ground. "Here you are, ma'am," he said, swinging a backpack over his shoulder before chest-bumping a nearby group of friends.

Ma'am? I've gone from a cute, young woman to a pregnant, old lady.

"Oh no, childbirth terrifies me. I would faint," Doby said, "but I'll wait happily outside until you and the baby are cleaned up."

Lacey didn't want to do this alone. And more than anything, she wanted to do this with Zak. But after the most recent fiasco and break-up, she was certain he'd never forgive her. His telephone silence after his last text spoke volumes.

She chewed her bottom lip as she glanced outside the glass

windows. No sign of Doby. "Please say you're close?"

"I should be."

"Thanks again for coming to the airport just to ride home with me. I'm not looking forward to being alone, especially since I haven't been in months. But I'll adjust... eventually. Besides, it won't be long before the baby will be here to keep me company." Lacey imagined holding Jude in her lap, watching him sleep peacefully as Zak rested his head on her shoulder and watched, too. She shook away the image. No, Zak was gone. And she needed to accept her chance with him had passed.

"I've been your friend for a long time. And I'll step in wherever I'm needed because your happiness matters to me. Hold on." Doby paused for a minute. "Okay, I've made it. Meet me outside."

Doby hung up the phone as Lacey waddled towards the motion-sensored doors. She wheeled her suitcase through them and onto the outside sidewalk crowded with tons of people awaiting transportation, some already finding their way into buses and cabs. To her left, a mother and daughter reunited with big hugs and smiles. To the right, a babbling toddler sat in an elderly man's lap. And in front of her, a large group of students wearing matching shirts crossed the street together.

Doby was nowhere to be found.

Where was she hiding? Lacey rolled her eyes and scanned the crowd across the street, hoping to find Doby mingled somewhere amongst them. Still, no sign of her. Lacey tightened the plaid scarf around her neck as a blast of chilly New York wind iced her skin. Behind her, a high-pitched squeal pierced her ears. She followed the noise to its source, a small, dark-skinned boy running across the path of a tall, handsome—Zak?

Doby had double-crossed her. She met his eyes, then turned away. Still, he inched towards her, taking her breath with each step. Lacey could run, but where and how in her condition? With no other reasonable options, she waited. Fully expecting something dramatic, a passionate kiss, a confession of his undying love, or for him to sweep her off her feet and into his arms—with the extra weight probably not that, but something along those lines. So when he stepped within arms' reach, she stiffened her body, prepared to resist.

Zak kept a good bit of distance between them and pointed towards a waiting ride. "The car is over there."

No *Hello... How are you doing?... Where have you been?...* Nothing. She gripped her luggage, confident he would try to yank it from her, insist on carrying it. But when he sped past her with empty hands and climbed into the waiting car, she transported her own luggage to the bearded man standing by the trunk. He loaded it for her. And only because she was cold and ready to go home, did she slide onto the backseat with Zak, keeping a safe distance from his stoic body.

As the driver sped into the line of traffic leaving the airport, she studied the blank stare on Zak's face from her peripheral, the way he kept his droopy eyes locked onto the blurring city streets. And as expected, she spotted the missing wedding ring. It was the least of her worries. Soon enough, he would propose questions about why her luggage had North Carolina labels and concerns over why she had left. But he proved her suspicions wrong by asking nothing. And it drove her insane.

She preferred him to scream at her, twist his face in anger, or do something other than give her stone-faced silence. The same look her father had given her when she was younger and had mentioned not continuing in his footsteps. The look that says, *you disappoint me*. She could take anything he dished out to her, but not that.

She closed her eyes, controlled her breathing, and hugged herself to stop the shaking. She couldn't fall apart. It was time to be strong, not slip into his reverse psychology plan, doing the opposite of what she expected in hopes of what?—Driving her crazy?

Well, what he didn't know was she could be just as stubborn when pushed. So when the driver stopped in front of her apartment building, she gathered the last scrap of pride she had remaining, forced her shoulders back, and marched forward—penguin style.

Her actions forced Zak to bring in the luggage.

Inside the apartment, she poured herself a glass of peach juice and then plundered through the cabinets, noting the restocked groceries. The next destination was the spare bedroom, to see if he had followed her instructions.

He pushed her luggage just inside the apartment door. "Here you go," he said, turning to leave.

The audacity! Not even a goodbye? So now it was okay to torture a highly vulnerable and emotional pregnant woman with the silent treatment? Well, she would not allow him to walk away from her without at least a word. She aborted the spare bedroom trip and faced him.

"*Excuse* me? So that's how it is now?" she asked, propping both hands on her spreading hips.

He turned and faced her, stepped closer. "I'm sorry. Maybe I'm confused. You're the one that left your ring beside a very detailed break-up plan instructing me to leave. How should I respond, Lacey? Do you have a plan for that, too? Please, let me see it." The space between his brows narrowed.

Annoyed, she gulped a mouthful of peach juice and worked to keep it contained behind quivering lips until she swallowed. "I thought we could end this on a good note, remain friends. But I guess you're out for revenge. So go ahead, play with my fragile emotions."

He pointed at himself, lifted his voice. "I'm playing with *your* emotions? What do you think you've done, from the moment you dragged me into Mr. Caldwell's office claiming I'm your *husband*?"

She gasped, shocked he would dig up the past to use against her. "Well, you could have been man enough to say no."

He leaned closer, locked his gaze on her eyes. "And leave you without a job? Ruin your credibility? Make you have to tell your family and friends the truth? I'd never do that to you. But sadly, that's exactly what you did to me. Left me broken with instructions to break everyone else. I'm beginning to think you and Finn are made for each other." He broke the trance, tousled his wild hair.

His assessment was correct about her. It was indeed what she did. In a moment of cowardice, she crumbled and left him to sweep up the mess. Because he didn't know the full story, didn't appreciate everything she had been though, she reminded herself. She blinked longer than necessary. "I had my reasons for what I did. And it's more complicated than you realize."

"You said you loved me, made me believe we were a real family. Then out of the blue, you throw it away—in a freaking letter. Yeah, some might call that complicated." He shot towards the fridge and yanked out a beer, popping the top with one quick motion. After taking a giant gulp, he wiped his arm across his mouth.

A rush of warm tears drowned Lacey's face. Her insides trembled. "I'm not purposely trying to hurt you."

"Well, it damn sure feels like it. You know what I don't get though?" He returned his glossy gaze to her. "You rant about the Finns and Jocelyns of the world, how self-centered they are, but what you fail to see is you're just like them. Our relationship has always been about your needs. Every action and decision has been based on how they affect your life—never mine." He jerked his head to the side as a single tear breached his bottom lid.

She curled her shoulders over her chest. "That's not fair, you have no idea what I've been through—"

"In North Carolina? No, I don't. In fact, I don't really know anything about what's going on."

Mentally exhausted and too tired to fight, she stopped responding. It took two to argue, and she refused to be a willing participant any longer. Besides, witnessing the hurt on his face was too much. And the hurt was there because he loved her so much, loved her as much as she loved him.

And that love meant enough for her not to spend the rest of the night spouting out hurtful words that couldn't be so easily retracted. "I'm tired so I should lie down." She wobbled towards the hall and stopped, facing him once again. "You're right, it's not fair to make you tell your family, so I'll do it. I'll call Meredith tomorrow and let her know."

He sprang in front of her path. "I don't think so. If you want to break-up with them, then you're doing it in person. They deserve that much."

They absolutely deserved that much, although the thought of facing them sent her body into involuntary convulsions. But she knew she had to do it—eventually. She folded her arms across her chest. "Fine, now I'm going to bed." She worked to hold herself together, just long enough to make it to her bedroom.

She didn't get far. Zak followed her, grabbed her arm, and spun her around to face him. She had expected something dramatic when she arrived, but he waited until she was angry and on fire to give it to her. He cupped both sides of her face and pressed his lips firmly against hers, parting them in a delicate balance of passion and exasperation that lasted long enough to inflame her insides, burning everything until she was nothing but a pile of ashes.

And when he'd finished sucking every bit of life from her, he pushed her out at arm's length. "I don't know what the hell is going on, or why you're doing all this crazy stuff, but I can't be a part of your plan another day. I deserve more." He grabbed both sides of her head, pulled her forehead to his lips, and left her with one last kiss. "I love you, Lacey. I always will..." His hands drifted down until he found her belly. "I love you too, little buddy."

Jude kicked.

Fearing collapse, she broke away and rushed into her bedroom, turned the lock behind her. She leaned her back against the door and slid down until her bottom landed on the crisp, hardwood.

Why did he make breaking up so hard?

She woke up in her own bed—alone—even if she didn't remember how she got there. Too bad her lack of memory hadn't spread to her conversation with Zak. Because she'd loved to forget about how defeated and lonely she felt.

Her phone rang, and she answered.

"How's my best friend in the whole wide world doing?" Doby asked.

Lacey pushed herself up in bed, stretched her free arm and legs. "How do you think I'm doing after being sabotaged?"

Doby giggled. "I was doing you guys a favor. So did you have make-up sex? Did he stay the night?"

Bump sex, ending on a good note would have been satisfaction enough. But instead, they had ended things with a nuclear blast. "Neither, he did tell me how he no longer wanted to be a part of my plan." Lacey patted down her wild curls and sighed. "I'm confident I ruined any possibility of us getting back together, ever."

"You guys love each too much to give up on each other forever. He's upset, that's all."

"Yeah, well, it's not something a simple *I'm sorry* will fix."

Doby paused. "Then you have to get more creative, tell him, confess. I'm sure he'll still be there when you're done—if you want him to be."

Lacey studied the four walls of her bedroom, listened to the silence, endured the cold draft of loneliness. This is temporary, she told herself. Jude would warm the space soon. She plucked lint balls from her black leggings. "And what about his family? It will be hard enough to tell my own parents."

"They will still love you. From what Zak has told me, it sounds like they're cool people."

Someone knocked. Lacey's heart skipped a beat, secretly hoping it was Zak. "Doby, I'll call you back."

Lacey climbed out of bed wearing yesterday's clothes and hobbled down the hallway. She reached the door and looked through the peephole. "Wonderful, Zak's parents," she mumbled under her breath.

Now, she would be forced to tell them sooner than planned. Lacey ran her hands across her sweater, smoothed the edges. Then she opened the door and waved them in, although they took a few minutes to get inside.

"I take it Zak's at work," Kyle said, sweating profusely as he heaved a large piece of covered furniture into the apartment. Only the wooden legs peeked out.

"Why didn't you tell me you were bringing this? I'd have gotten someone to help you guys," Lacey said.

Kyle pretended to flex a muscle. "We needed the exercise."

Meredith, still panting, said, "Not me. I just wanted to surprise you."

How many more surprises could Lacey's fragile mind take before it broke? Meredith headed straight for Lacey and gave her a big hug. "And how is little Jude this morning?" Meredith laid a hand on Lacey's belly.

Bile rushed into Lacey's throat, gagged her. She considered letting it out, just vomiting the deceptions and lies so she'd be free. But being the coward she was, she swallowed them. "He's good, kicking and punching all over the place."

"It's almost time." Meredith clasped her hands together and gave a smile too big for her face. "We're so excited. And to show you how much, go ahead, take off the sheet." Meredith gestured to the gift now sitting in the middle of the living room.

Taking a few quick breaths, Lacey steadied her quivering fingers and removed the cover. Underneath was a vintage cradle stained a dark gray. The bedding was a cream comforter accented with baby-blue pinstripes, and above the head of the cradle hung a mobile of moons and stars. It was breathtaking.

Lacey ran her palms over the smooth finish, even pictured Jude sleeping inside, right before reality struck. The reality that Jude would never sleep in that cradle. But she contained those thoughts. "Wow, you guys, this is amazing."

Kyle tapped the wooden edge. "It's a handmade family heirloom, one we've passed down throughout the years. The twins and Jude make the fourth-generation to have slept in this cradle. Zak probably remembers sleeping in here."

"We had to get it refinished. I hope you like the gray stain," Meredith said.

Like it? It was impossible not to love it. The cradle was stunning. The only part she didn't care for was the remorse she would suffer if she accepted, almost like stealing a family treasure.

Meredith took Lacey's hands into hers. "Well, it's customary in our family that all the Cooper babies sleep in that cradle. So it's only fitting that the newest member of our family join the long-honored tradition." She gave Lacey a warm grin. "And you know I could never dream of a better daughter-in-law to bring our grandson into the world. You have no idea how happy we are that you're a part of our family." Delighted tears rolled across Meredith's cheeks.

Self-condemnation drove the knife that stabbed Lacey in the heart. And the resulting unadulterated conviction oozed from her pores. What was she doing, allowing Zak's family to spend money on her and pass along the family heirloom? And worse, leading them to believe that it was their flesh and blood that would sleep in it? When it wasn't, never would be.

Today was the day. The lies, the deceit, had to end—if for nothing else, for Lacey's own sanity. "I'm sorry, but I can't accept this. Please forgive me."

"Forgive what? I insist. He's family. If you don't like it, we can have it refinished, or change the comforter." Meredith pointed at the heirloom cradle.

"It's more than that." Lacey squeezed Meredith's hands before letting go. "Sorry, but I have to go. Please, let yourselves out whenever you're ready," Lacey said, snatching her purse from the wall hook and racing as fast as her skinny legs would carry her out the door and onto the elevator. Zak had every right to hate her, but underneath, she knew he loved her. And she knew she couldn't live with herself if she didn't fight for him, for them. It was time to tell him that Jude was not Finn's son, that she had no clue whose son Jude was.

And if he could live with that, then she would marry him.

27

Lacey stepped off the elevator and bumped into her babbling secretary Hannah. She tried escaping, but to no avail. Hannah cornered her and wouldn't let go.

"Did you hear the latest news? Brent took over the project." Hannah heckled. "And he reverted the design back to your original blueprints."

"Great news, now where's Zak? It's very important that I speak with him." Lacey's gaze jumped from one side of the room to the other, her eyes searching for one man, who wasn't there.

"Oh, you must be here to help him pack. But then again, it's not like he has a lot of stuff. And he would be stupid to make you carry stuff when you're obviously hours away from delivery—"

"Hannah," Lacey interjected.

"Yes, he's in his office, well what used to be his office."

Lacey gasped. "They fired him?"

Hannah popped her gum, then gave her schoolgirl giggle. "No, silly. He quit. But you knew that, didn't you?"

"Of course, I did." Lacey faked a smile. "Nice seeing you, Hannah," she said, speeding off to the finance department.

Why would he quit? Was he moving? But more importantly, why didn't he tell her last night? Oh my god, yesterday was his final break-up, move-on, and *never want to see you again* kiss. She propelled herself as fast as she could with a swollen belly.

"Lacey, what are you doing here? Did you get my email about the coalition project? The design is back to your original. Aren't you thrilled?" Mr. Caldwell asked, his bald spot the shiniest it had ever been, distracting even.

"Absolutely. I hate to rush, but I really need to speak to Zak."

"I hope you didn't miss him." Mr. Caldwell pinched his chin. "Hey, you're not following in his footsteps are you?"

Air leaked from her lungs at the thought he might have left before she could tell him everything, before she could plead her case. "Talk to you later, Mr. Caldwell," Lacey said, rushing over to Zak's office. She barged through the door—to an empty office.

She was too late...

Weak, she plopped herself onto his work chair and lost it. Her body jerked and fell with each tear it forcefully pumped from her body. She moaned, groaned, and mumbled words that didn't even make sense. She had lost the chance to get him back. And it was all her fault. How long did she think he would follow her around like a puppy dog, surviving off of crumbs?

"Lacey? What are you doing here?" That voice... it was Zak's.

She lifted her head, certain her make-up had smeared everywhere. "Zak? They said you left—quit."

He stepped over to a small box packed with miscellaneous items and added a paper weight to it. "I did. This is the last box."

Lacey wiped her face, swiped her fingers firmly under her eyes. "Where are you going?"

He braced his arms on the box. "What are you doing here, Lacey? And what does it matter what I do?"

She stiffened her body, forced herself to stand on two feet. "It matters because I love you."

He scoffed. "Well, you sure have a funny way of showing it."

She eased closer. "That's why I'm here now. To show you that I love you."

"Okay, you've got my attention." He crossed his arms over his chest. "Show me."

Body language spoke louder than words, and she was pretty sure his was anything but open and accepting. In fact, it was borderline contemptuous. But he would not intimidate her. She closed the gap between them, wrapped her arms around him, though he kept his right where they were. "I can't hug you if you won't let me."

"It will take more than a hug to show me you love me."

Frustrated, she yanked her arms back to her sides. "Okay, what will it take? Me to say I'm sorry for everything I did to you? I am sorry. I regret it, and if I could do it over again, I would."

He shook his head. "Not enough."

The pressure got to her. "Are you trying to sabotage me? If you want me to give up, then let me know."

"Do you want to give up?" he asked, his crossed arms holding tight against his chest.

This was going nowhere fast. Taking a deep breath, she tried calming herself, but nothing seemed to work. Zaps of electricity, and not the sexy kind, coursed her veins. What did he demand from her? How could she tell him what happened—confess—when he was being such an ass?

"I'll take that as a yes," he said, uncrossing his arms and lifting the box. He stepped out of his office and into the walking path surrounded by occupied cubicles filled with nosey employees.

Lacey waddled out behind him. "Wait, Zak, please." Her face trembled. "I'm sorry for everything. I'm sorry I hurt you."

He glanced at the floor with the corners of his mouth turned downwards. "Apology accepted."

She drew closer within whispering distance, not wanting anyone to hear. "And I don't want us to break-up. I want us to stay together, get married, just like we planned."

He pressed his lips together, shook a finger. "Um… that word again… planned. I'm not following any more of your plans. I need more than a plan that changes based on whatever benefits you. You waltz around here and act like it's okay to keep me in the dark, hide stuff, and then dump me for no good reason. And on top of that, you make everything about your career, this place, pleasing your father. Well, what about me? What about our life?" He shifted the box to his other arm. "You want me to be your husband but only in the role you plan for me. That's not fair, and not the life I'm looking to live… no matter how much I love you."

Lacey's fingers and toes tingled. "Then tell me, what can I do to prove it to you? I can't lose you," she said, whispering.

He took a deep, contemplated breath. "If you don't know, then we're probably not meant to be." He turned away from her, walked at a slow and steady pace.

She knew what she had to do, the one thing she hadn't since they had been together. Show him he was more important to her than contracts and blueprints, show him he deserved the truth—the whole truth. And show him she wasn't afraid of who overheard. If ever there was a time to spill her guts, a time to own her truth, it was now. Enough hiding behind her mistakes. Otherwise, she would lose him forever.

He kept walking.

"Stop, Zak," she said, loud and commanding, no longer caring what anyone thought. Because it wasn't about them, it was about her and Zak. And what she craved more than anything was him—and freedom from the burden she had been carrying, the dark cloud hovering over her head. Zak was the love of her life. And she refused to live another day without him.

He turned around slowly, his brows raised.

"You want the truth? I'll give it to you, every ugly bit." Embracing the spirit of revelation, she tried climbing onto an unoccupied desk, but couldn't get her leg high enough. So, she grabbed a chair and put her foot in it for a boost. It slipped. And if it hadn't been for the woman in the desk next to her stopping it—Well, she'd rather not think about the disastrous end.

"Stop, you're going to kill yourself." Zak stepped closer, laid his hand on her shoulder.

But she shook it off. No, she was doing this. She spotted a step stool beside the desk in front of her and used it. And once she made it on top of the desk, she gained her balance and stood tall.

And he stood on the floor right beside her, holding her calf for support. "Whatever you need to tell me, you can do it on the ground."

"No, you want me to show you, and that's what I plan to do. I'm not climbing down until you know everything. First off, I'm quitting my job. You're right, this is my life, not my Dad's. And if he loves me, he'll be proud of me. And second," she said, swallowing hard, "Finn's not the father. It's just another one of my elaborate lies." Lacey pressed her palm to her chest as the salty streams free-flowed against her will.

"You could have told me you had a one-night stand. I never would have judged you for that. Now, get down before you get hurt." His face wrinkled.

Lacey dried her eyes with a tissue a young girl with thick glasses passed her. "It's more complicated than a one-night stand. I had the most toe-curling dream of my life with a guy whose face is only a blur. But the funny part is, it wasn't a dream, it was real. Apparently, having great sex caused me to lose my freaking memory." Lacey let out a nervous laugh. "So I hired a private investigator to help me find this mystery man. And that went absolutely nowhere. All the potentials he offered turned out to be false leads."

By now, the entire office had silently encircled them. Zak squeezed her leg. "Lacey—"

"Please, let me finish. Mr. Duke, who calls himself a private investigator, said he'll get back to me but until then... I have no idea who Jude's father is, have no leads, and don't know why I slept with a stranger. I never do shit like that." She threw both hands into the air.

He shook Lacey's leg, smiling. "Lacey—"

"Stop interrupting me, please." It was tough enough to get it out. Him interjecting made it harder. "Now, I'm sorry for dragging you and your family through this. I just hope one day you can truly forgive me."

The silence was deafening, despite the abundance of gaped mouths. She did it, laid her soul bare for all to see. And what a show she gave him. With the replay freshly reeling through her mind, and Zak's lips sealed, Lacey decided it was best to make her escape sooner than later. But first she had to get down. Zak stood at her feet with both arms stretched open. A slow-building, dimpled grin painted his face. Totally not what she expected.

He helped plant her feet on the floor. "Can I talk now?"

"It's too much. Just spare me the speech, please. I can go, let you live your life," she said, ready to escape through the nearest stairwell.

He tightened his grip. "You're not going anywhere."

Her heart couldn't take another beating. Sure, she wanted him to say it was okay, tell her he still wanted to be with her. But she couldn't risk hearing the opposite side of that speech. And she definitely didn't want sympathy, pity, or lectures. She just needed to get away quick, but the more she squirmed, the closer he drew to her.

"Please, let me go." She pleaded, seconds from a breakdown.

He gave her a toothy smile. "Are you crazy? I'm not letting you go —not when you're carrying my baby."

She found his eyes. "I know you want to adopt Jude, but—"

He glued his gaze to hers. "You're not listening. I don't have to adopt Jude—he's mine. Biologically mine."

Lacey paid attention to the spreading pink crawling up the side of his neck, the sparkle in his eyes. But none of it made sense. "That can't be." Her voice cracked. "Don't say things that aren't true. I've done enough of that for both of us."

He cupped Lacey's face, pressed his lips against hers with purpose, and reminded her of his love. She pushed him back by placing her hands on his chest and then locking her arms. She needed to clarify his claims.

Zak's eyes stretched wide. And with an unwavering voice, he fed Lacey a crumb of hope. "I guarantee you when Mr. Duke gets back to you he'll give you my name."

Lacey unlocked her arms and froze—speechless.

"I'm the real father." Zak stroked the sides of Lacey's arms, warmed them.

She yearned for his story to be true. But it was too far-fetched. "How's that possible? We never slept together before I got pregnant."

Zak's head rocked up and down like the bow of a ship in large swells. "Yes, we did. That's why when you first said you were pregnant, I asked you if you were sure it was Finn's. You said yes, so I let it go."

Lacey's heart skipped beats at what had to be the slimmest of possibilities. But if they'd had sex, why didn't it come up before now? Regaining her wits and facing reality, she confronted his story. "I'm just—I mean you mentioned nothing about us having sex. That would have been important to share, or talk about at some point, especially when we became closer. You let me think it was our first time."

He held her hand, circled her knuckles with his thumb. "I tried to talk to you about it. I dropped serious hints that you shut down, so I took it as something you wanted to avoid. I thought it made you feel awkward, or worse, that you wanted to forget that it ever happened."

She scrunched her face. "What hints?"

"It'll help if I tell you what happened," he said, brushing back the stray spirals from her face.

"We were working on the coalition project together on the sofa in your apartment because you insisted I come over to explain how you went over budget—again. It was also the same night we ordered cheap takeout that came with those flimsy cardboard cups. I asked you to pass me my drink from beside you, but you told me to grab it myself. I did so and knocked it on the carpet."

Her mouth dropped. "The red Fanta…"

He grinned. "Yes, the red Fanta that you told me if I mentioned one more time you'd run away kicking and screaming."

She winced. "I said that. But how did we go from a soda spill to having sex?"

He pulled her closer, well, as close as her growing belly allowed. "In my attempt to catch it before it spilled, I knocked you over and ended up laying right on top of you. When I looked down to apologize, your lips were right there. Without even thinking, I did what I had wanted to do for so long, I kissed them. And you kissed me back." His face reddened. "Then you yanked off my shirt and one thing led to another and—well, the rest is self-explanatory."

She shook her head, still finding it too good to be true. "So you're the blurry man that rocked my world. Why did you leave before I woke up? You could have at least left a note."

"I stayed the night. But I didn't want to wake you because you looked so peaceful."

"I might have remembered if you had."

He gave her a lopsided grin. "Okay, the truth is I didn't wake you because it scared me. I didn't want you to regret having sex with me. Sometimes that happens when friends sleep together. And our friendship was too important to lose. But as time passed, I knew I couldn't keep my feelings for you bottled up, so I tried to bring it up, pick your brain, see how you felt. You made it very clear we were nothing more than friends. Then you said Finn was the father... so... what could I do?"

Lacey slapped his chest. "You could have told me it was possibly yours. Saved me nine months of hell trying to find the real father."

"But you were so sure it was Finn's. How was I supposed to know you had lied?" He caressed both sides of Lacey's pregnant belly. "But none of that matters, now. Jude is mine—really mine—without a doubt." Lacey studied the sharp upward turn of Zak's lips that never wavered. They remained suspended from heaven.

And for once, the puzzle pieces fit together perfectly. In fact, they fit together so perfect she was afraid it was all an illusion, a story that would fall apart at any minute. "But what if there was someone else?"

"There's not—"

Her phone rang, partially muffled by her purse. She pulled it out, noted it was Mr. Duke. She pressed it to her forehead, afraid his news might shatter her glass bubble. But the truth mattered, she reminded herself. And she needed to hear it, good or bad.

She answered, bypassing the *froufrou* salutations. "Please say you have a name for me."

He gave a raspy cough, cleared his throat. "I do, but unfortunately the only man left is Zak Cooper, but you ruled him out. I'm sorry—"

The phone slipped from Lacey's hand. She didn't care if it broke into a thousand pieces. It was something that could be replaced. But not Zak. He was something she needed to hold on to forever, along with their baby Jude, the best part of their love, blended into a precious boy.

In that moment, the hopes, dreams, and aspirations she thought she had lost, were hers to hold onto forever. And those things she once believed lied beyond her reach, now rested in her hand.

She buried her face in the nape of Zak's neck and cried happy tears.

"He confirmed I'm the father?"

With a beaming grin stretched across her face, she nodded. "Jude is your son." The words echoed throughout the room for the listening ears to catch. And they responded with a heavy round of embarrassing applause. Everyone except Zak.

With perfect intention, he took her mouth, took his time exploring those tender places. There was no need to rush. They were two people in love, two people destined to spend the rest of their lives together, two people fate had brought together in the most unconventional way.

And for once, she found pleasure in admitting none of it was on her ten-year plan.

When he finally released her lips, he lifted her high in the air, twirled her around, and then placed her feet back on the floor. Warm fluid rushed down her legs, a never-ending flow that wouldn't stop. "Um... Zak... My water just broke."

28

"I don't want to let him go," Lacey said, staring down at Jude. She ran her fingers through his golden ringlets, planted kisses on his soft baby cheeks. He drifted off to sleep, giving her a crooked, sleepy smile as he went. A newborn reflex she was sure, but heartwarming nonetheless. "Mommy loves you," she whispered in his ear before leaning back, studying him, pleasuring in his long lashes inherited from his daddy.

Lacey's mom stole Jude, taking him into her arms. "He'll be okay. It's not like you're going far."

"You guys don't understand. I could hold him all day," Lacey said, rubbing her fingers across his tiny toes.

"She *holds* him all day," Zak added, planting a quick kiss on Lacey's cheek.

"There's my girl," Lacey's dad said, bear hugging her from behind. "Let me steal you away for a minute. I have something I want to tell you."

He wanted to discuss her leaving the firm. She was certain. Because they had not had a deep, heart-to-heart conversation about her decision since she had announced it. When she first mentioned it to him, he simply nodded. No frowns or negative expressions, but no smile or show of support either. She could tell it disheartened him. But today was not the day she wanted to hear about it.

Her skin prickled as she followed her father to the corner of the room, the only corner not overflowing with purple and pink peonies. She eased her bottom onto the parson chair.

"I want you to know I'm happy for you and Zak. And I'm sorry for not always showing it. After talking to Kate, I realize there are a few things I need to make clear."

A Not So Immaculate Conception

Kate had blabbed. Great, a few virgin daiquiris and a night of venting with her overdue and emotional sister had now turned into a sentimental conversation with her dad, the most unsentimental man on the earth. "It's okay, Dad. We're good. Let's enjoy the day."

"No, I have to say this. Ace, there's no wrong way to fall in love and have children. Nobody does it the same. And if I ever made you believe there's a perfect path in life you're not on, then I apologize."

She wished her eyes weren't welling up, but they were. And she hoped the waterproof mascara Doby bought her held up to its claims.

Her father stared down at her. "Do you see everything you've accomplished, Ace? You started a successful business before thirty, landed yourself a good man—and gave us the most handsome grandson ever." He gestured towards Jude resting on Lacey's mom's shoulder, sound asleep.

Her dad towered above her as she once remembered. Back then, he looked at her with hard eyes and a stoic face that had the power to take down a strong army. The face that screamed, *you disappoint me.* But today, it was softer, not nearly as scary as she recalled.

Not wanting to cry, she kept her words simple. "You're too kind."

"No, I haven't been kind enough." He did something he never had. He kneeled in front of her, met her eye to eye with a broken body, no longer hard and stiff. His stern eyes melted into puddles, the kind young girls danced in. He brushed the side of Lacey's face with his hand, spoke with a voice powerful enough to propel, but not strong enough to destroy. And she listened, her ears a sponge for all he poured into them.

"I'm so sorry for ever making you feel like you didn't deserve my love. That was never my intention for you. In fact, it's my love for you, Kate, and your mom that keeps me going—that gives me a reason to live. I'm nothing without you."

Lacey lost it, throwing her arms around her dad's neck as her body jerked with hard sobs. He stroked her back, kept telling her how sorry he was. She had spent her entire life thinking she would be nothing without her dad's approval. But here he sat telling her, of all things, that it was the other way around. He was nothing without her.

"Thank you, Dad. I love you so much."

"And I love you." He shifted away from her and pulled out his handkerchief. With a soft pat, he dried her face and assured her the mascara had stayed in place. "Now, help me off the floor so we can do

236

this." Using her hand as leverage, he hoisted himself back to his feet and gave her the biggest smile ever. "It's showtime."

"After I check on my baby one more time," Lacey said, heading straight for Jude.

Meredith stopped her. "No, no, you're required up front. Don't worry, we'll take good care of him, promise."

Doby slid into a velvet-cushioned seat behind Meredith. "And if they don't, Carson and I will take over. We're going to need the practice." Doby patted her flat stomach.

Lacey's mouth dropped. "I knew you were hiding something. We're having a chat after this is over."

"After this is over, I'm celebrating," Zak said, taking Lacey by the hand and leading her away from their plump baby. "Let's take advantage of the babysitters while we can."

She didn't know about that just yet. It had been hard enough to hand him over, even though he stayed in the same room. Such a sharp contrast from the early part of her pregnancy, when she wasn't even sure she wanted him. She cringed at those old thoughts, and thanked heaven she had returned to better senses. Funny how a spit-up shooting, diaper-flooding baby she thought she would never be able to take care of could bring her more joy than life itself.

She kept her gaze on Jude as Zak pushed her along the center aisle. "But what if he needs us, Zak? He's still so little."

"He's ten feet away, not ten miles." Zak squeezed her hand, guided her to the front and center of the room, underneath an archway of greenery.

She took a breath and turned her gaze to Zak, to his long auburn lashes and jewel-toned eyes. "You're right. It's our time."

He showed his one-sided dimple. "Thank you. Now, can I officially marry my *wife*?"

She nodded, as the priest, the one from her mother's church, led the ceremony.

Lacey couldn't help but think about her life before this moment. For so many years, she had spent every waking minute plotting every aspect of her being. But now, she realized life wasn't meant to be planned. Life was meant to be lived. And her new life was proof of that.

So if she had to give advice to the future planners of the world, what would she say? She would say, *buy a big steel barrel, a jug of gasoline, and a box of matches—then set those lists on fire. When the smoke clears, and the ash settles against the earth, take a good look around. Something or someone not part of the plan might be right there in front of you.*

That someone for Lacey was Zak Cooper, a man she now loves with all her heart, mind, body, and soul. He was the one thing she had never planned for—and the one person who gave her something she never knew she wanted, her handsome son, Jude. And she said those exact words as part of her vows, ending with—"I do."

For *real* this time.

Made in the USA
San Bernardino, CA
21 March 2020